Readers love the Alchemists and Elementals by CASSIE SWEET

Eye of Truth

"I found that the writing of the story was brilliant and dragged me into a world where change is happening and dark forces are working in the background."

—MM Good Book Reviews

"This book was fantastic; I loved every minute of it."

—The Romance Reviews

"…this story is too damn fine to miss. Highly recommended, and I personally can't wait to read the next one."

—Top 2 Bottom Reviews

Taste of Air

"A rich tapestry of intriguing characters living in a complex, well presented world intertwined with heaps of magick, political scheming, and supernatural elements."

—It's About The Book

"…it is easy to lose yourself in the magical fantasy world Ms. Sweet has invented."

—Crystal's Many Reviewers

By CASSIE SWEET

Hot Water

ALCHEMISTS AND ELEMENTALS
Eye of Truth
Taste of Air
Kiss of Death

Published By DREAMSPINNER PRESS
http://www.dreamspinnerpress.com

Kiss of Death

Cassie Sweet

Published by
DREAMSPINNER PRESS

5032 Capital Circle SW, Suite 2, PMB# 279, Tallahassee, FL 32305-7886 USA
http://www.dreamspinnerpress.com/

Kiss of Death
© 2015 Cassie Sweet.

Cover Art
© 2015 Brooke Albrecht.
http://brookealbrechtstudio.com
Cover content is for illustrative purposes only and any person depicted on the cover is a model.

ISBN: 978-1-63216-834-4
Digital ISBN: 978-1-63216-835-1
Library of Congress Control Number: 2015902189
First Edition May 2015

Printed in the United States of America
∞
This paper meets the requirements of
ANSI/NISO Z39.48-1992 (Permanence of Paper).

To all my faithful readers. *As Above So Below.* Thank you.

Chapter One

GOLD SCHOOL Headmaster Oberon Bertolini stood on the edge of the slaughter. Flames from the villa that once housed the Agia family belched upward into the night, singeing the decorative trees that stood as a protective barrier to prevent onlookers from seeing the spectacle from the street. Those not involved in the bloodbath of the night should not have to bear witness to the atrocity. And yet Oberon's feet were planted as firmly to the spot as the trees that smoldered and failed to catch.

The entire scene disgusted him. He knew it had to be done, that the *prolates* as a whole had decided to rid the world of one of their own—one who had upended the natural order of the world and brought the necromancers back into the Dominicál city-states. The Agia had to be made to pay. The *prolates* had decided that payment should be made in blood.

A nasty turn in politics and magic had brought Oberon here. One of revenge and retribution. In his heart he knew alchemists should be above such petty emotions. They had no place in the study of his beloved discipline, nor did they bring back the dead. The only beings able to do that were the Gods—and the necromancers. However, mortal men such as the *prolates* and their guards were no match for the wicked savagery of necromantic magic. To not lend the *prolates'* combined forces assistance was to send them to their death. Either way, blood—lots of it—would be spilled. Reservations or not, the alchemists were here to ensure the necromancers did not win the day.

The scent of charred flesh hit his nose. It coated the back of his throat, making him gag. He turned his head so the others wouldn't see his reaction. He had no stomach for death. No want for seeing an entire family destroyed for the crimes of a few.

But restitution had to be made, the balance restored, and necromancers pushed back from the Dominicál borders.

The necromancers were a vile threat who would not give up their quest to control the city-states until every last person residing within was under their skeletal thumbs. Friends of his had died because of their continued expanse into the peninsula. The elementals were threatened and for a very brief time held captive by the death dancers. Their entire way of life teetered on the brink of destruction, and strong, ruthless choices had to be made.

A guard wearing the crest of the House of DiCarni stalked out of the rolling smoke, his harsh face covered in soot and brass breastplate painted in blood smears. He held his short sword in one hand, his grip white-knuckled. He gave a curt nod to Oberon. "What do you wish us to do with the men held in the Agia's prisons?"

Oberon was rather taken aback. Why were they asking him? He was the Headmaster of the Gold School of Alchemy, not the ringleader of this butchery. "What are their crimes?"

The guard shook his head. "I can't rightly say. We haven't interviewed them yet."

"Have them taken to the cathedral. We will process and sort them out there. Have the records been burned in the conflagration?"

The guard had the good sense to read the disgust in Oberon's voice for what it was. He gave Oberon a pleading look. "Master Nico gave us specific orders to burn the premises immediately afterward. He said it was the only way to cleanse the land."

Oberon let out a breath. It was one way, but not as Nico stated, the only way. "That may be, but it doesn't answer my question. Have the records all burned?"

"Not the court records."

"Then have those removed and taken to the school. I'll have the journeymen students review the case files and see if the charges and petitions match the prisoners' stories. It might be the Agia prosecuted the individuals on false charges." Sadly, it wasn't the first time in the history of the city-states that corruption of that sort had been left to run rampant, and Oberon doubted it would be the last.

Theodyne Thespacian, adept-level alchemist and *terrathant*, folded from the smoke, a wraith of power and vengeance. He'd made no attempt to hide his disdain of Oberon for sheltering the necromancer, Hazrael, but then, Theodyne did not realize the reasons behind the decision. No one did, except Master Nico. Perhaps that needed to change.

Theodyne walked past Oberon with only a cutting glance before slipping into the darkness to perform some other task before this night of horrors ended.

So many men he'd once counted as friends had shut him out since Hazrael's arrival at the school. Even sweet, gentle Master Jolen had failed to keep in touch as often since removing to the court of the Medovin *prolate*. Jolen had been angry as well, and with good cause. Hazrael had murdered a child who had shown great potential in the same odd form of magic Hazrael had possessed long ago, before it was corrupted by the necromancers. And therein lay the crux of the matter.

Oberon and Nico saw Hazrael as the man he used to be—not the thing he had become after years confined in the keeping of the necromancers. Problems stemmed from the fact they had yet to find a way to purge the necromantic control from Hazrael's mind. Once that task was completed, Oberon knew the others would begin to see Hazrael as a man with something to contribute to the order, rather than a parasite to be smote.

He understood his brethren's reservations. As it stood, Hazrael posed more danger to the order than he offered information to topple the necromancers.

Oberon began the lonely trek from the Agia's burning palace to the cathedral. The fires of the deposed *prolate's* house were so bright he needed no torch or light sphere to see his way there. Bits of ash fell onto his robes and caught in his hair. He didn't bother to brush them away. What was the point? It fell across the city square like rancid snow.

A cacophony of chains dragging across cobbles echoed in the square. The prisoners shuffled their way down the road at the points of the guards' swords. Some of the prisoners had not seen the light of day in years. Others appeared fresh enough to have only been incarcerated for a few days. A cleric came down the steps of the cathedral and tried to shoo the guard away.

"What is the meaning of this? We'll not have them here."

The guard used his sword to point at Oberon. "He said to bring them here, and we're following *his* orders."

The cleric looked over at Master Oberon and frowned. "We will not have the church defiled by filthy criminals."

Oberon crossed his arms. "Then see they all have baths. And while you're at it, feed them. They look half-starved to death."

The cleric's mouth flapped a few times. "They have committed crimes against the state."

"How do you know?" Oberon challenged. "Because the Agia said so? You'd take the word of a necromantic collaborator over mine? I fear you may be on the wrong side of a very horrible conflict, Brother."

The cleric paled. "Well, since you put it so bluntly."

Oberon waited until the last of the freed prisoners were inside. He hailed the guard. "Make sure none of them leave here until we have them sorted. If we find any real criminals, they'll be transferred to one of the other facilities."

"Yes, Headmaster Oberon."

He turned on his heel and started back for the school. There was nothing here left to see. The night had been scored across his memory in an indelible stain. Let the others bury the remains in salted earth and nullify the pieces so the necromancers could not make use of them. He trudged through the town, bone weary and heartsick. If the portents were accurate, a lot more people would die before the necromancers were ousted from the city-states. History was set to repeat. Not since the Great Purge had the country been in such an uproar—or so the legends read. The only being he knew still alive from the time of the Purge was the fire elemental, Anjufer, who resided in the school.

Full elementals were odd creatures that more often than not had their own secret agendas apart from humans. Anjufer conversed with Master Nico, but did not do so with many of the other masters residing at the school. With Nico living across the country in Sadonia, it was impossible to get any information from the fire elemental. All the *aerothants, pyrothants, terrathants,* and *aquathants* living at the school had stopped speaking to Oberon unless it had to do with class studies. All eyes of both students and colleagues turned aside when he passed in the halls. Even Nico's communications had trickled to almost nil, until he'd shown up at the school leading a great army composed of guardsmen from the whole of Dominicál.

His compassion to Hazrael may have cost him friends, but it had not undermined his self-respect.

Not a day went by that he regretted his decision.

Lights rose in the sky, an eerie green glow coming from the direction of the school. The thunder of a horse's hooves at full gallop sounded in the distance.

"Headmaster! You're needed at the school!" The cry came from the dark.

Oberon angled toward the voice as a lone rider came into view. He hurried to intercept. It was one of the journeymen—Griegs. His young face was covered in soot. Hair singed in patches. There was a cut bleeding above his eye. It looked as if he too had been in a battle.

"What's happened?"

Griegs's breath sawed in and out. It was a few seconds before he could speak. "It's the necromancer. He's gone mad. Power is rampant all over the school, and we're having a hard time trying to contain it."

Fear bit at his soul. Hazrael.

Oh, by the Eye!

Oberon took off at a run to find his horse. There wasn't time to spare. Why in all the hells had he come down the mountain tonight to bear witness to the carnage when he should have stayed in the school? That was his place, not playing errand boy to bloodthirsty *prolates* and their armies.

His horse had wandered over to a clearing, far away from the fire and confusion. A touch to its flank and it startled. Poor thing was terrified. Oberon had to agree. There was something heavy and horrible in the air, even without the stench of burned flesh.

"Easy now. Easy." He ran his hand over the horse's side, gentling him. The horse stamped and danced away.

He took the reins and brought the fractious mount close, holding a hand up in front of its face. "Easy. You hear and see no threat, my friend. All is calm and quiet."

By degrees the horse settled.

He climbed into the saddle and gave it its head. They thundered through the countryside, climbing back up to the higher elevations. Even at full gallop, he'd not make the school for another hour.

They really needed to crack that portal spell they'd been working on. He urged the horse faster.

His palms were damp on the reins. Air failed to draw into his lungs properly. His heart thundered with each hoofbeat. *Was Hazrael hurt? Angry? Frightened?*

Would he return to find the school in ruins and his friends and colleagues all dead?

As he grew nearer, the lights from the magical explosion illuminated the darkness. The gates were open, and the alchemists standing as sentries waved him through.

Odd creaks and groans came from the structure, as if the elementals present in the stones and wood protested Hazrael's presence. Loudly. Oberon had not as yet reached the main courtyard, and he could hear the moans of immortal beings echoing through the trees.

Master Fenelli met him at the bottom of the steps. "You must do something! None of us can even get near his room to contain him. The most we've been able to do is channel the destruction through the flues. Anjufer is not pleased."

Oberon climbed off his mount and handed the reins over to the stable lad. He didn't take time to answer Master Fenelli. Action was needed more than excuses and apologies.

He ran up the steps to the room assigned to Hazrael since his arrival some six weeks before. The door was locked from the outside— a mandate from the Adepts' Council. It and the key were composed of a special material resistant to alteration by alchemical or necromantic manipulation. He pulled the chain he wore around his neck to hold the key and slid it over his head.

Unearthly howls of pain and grief came from inside.

"Hold on, Hazrael. I'll be inside in a moment."

Oberon's fingers shook as he shoved the key into the lock. The mechanism failed. A scent of hot metal seared his nose. He looked over his shoulder at the small crowd of masters and journeymen who now surrounded him. "For love of the Elementals! What happened?"

"We don't know." Master Fenelli crossed his arms. A militant glare filled his dark eyes. "All was quiet until our... visitor in there started wailing and trying to take the school down around our ears."

Theodyne pushed his way through the crowd and placed his hand on the door. "He's wailing because we killed a good number of necromancers we found hiding in the Agia's palace."

Theodyne flicked his wrist with his palm up and out. A shock wave resonated through the wood grains. The stream of power cut off, and all grew quiet. "Didn't any of you think to send him to sleep?"

They looked down as one, not meeting Theodyne's gaze.

Oberon bit his tongue. He wanted to ask if Hazrael was all right, but he doubted, in light of the destruction he'd seen coming through the school, that he'd make any friends among the other alchemists.

He turned to the lock and tried again. This time it gave without the energy jolts. With the lock released, the door swung open on its own accord. Oberon took a deep breath and stepped inside, then closed the rest of his colleagues out. He didn't need an audience for what he was about to do. They'd see, they'd know, and they'd condemn.

But what was he to do? So far Hazrael had not cooperated with them on any level. The only gentle words they'd exchanged had been on the day Oberon and the alchemist guards had ridden to meet Theodyne and Jolen's party. Once back at the school, Hazrael had grown more hostile, violent. His corruption ran so deep Oberon feared he'd never be able to expunge it all from Hazrael's soul. And truly, many of them had tried and all had failed.

"Hazrael?" Oberon reached out with his mind, touching that part of Hazrael where they'd connected so long ago—and felt nothing. It was a void. A desolate area of ice and wind. A cold so complete, even in the ether it sucked Oberon's breath away and froze the marrow in his bones. He shivered.

How was Oberon to get through to Hazrael when Theodyne put him into a trance? It might have saved the school, but it didn't do a damn thing for their plight. Theodyne was an adept like no other. When he placed a block or tranced a person, they tended to stay that way for a long time.

Angry, Oberon went to the door and opened it. The masters remained assembled outside. Theodyne wasn't among them.

"Someone fetch Master Theodyne."

Oberon ducked back inside and closed the door again. He set about erecting shields around both Hazrael and the room. The double protection ensured that once Hazrael was awakened, there was little chance of damaging energy leaving the room.

He sat on the edge of Hazrael's bed to wait for Theodyne. The walls were stained black, singed from flares of energy. Pink goo ran down one of the walls. Ectoplasm? Had Hazrael tried to pull something through to the material world from the astral? One of the dead necromancers? Was that an attempt to save them once they passed over?

Shattered glass littered the windowsill. The only thing that remained intact was the bed, and that was questionable.

Oberon took Hazrael's limp hand in his. "What did those bastards do to you?"

Hazrael's white hair hung in oily locks, covering his face. He smelled as if he hadn't bathed in months, when in fact it had only been yesterday. Did decay seep from his pores, a product of his complete corruption?

Theodyne entered the room without knocking. He stood in the center, not coming near the bed, and glared. "You summoned me?"

"Yes. I need you to wake him up. All I find when I reach in there is a barren landscape filled with ice."

Theodyne shrugged. "What did you expect? A welcoming valley with lush green grasses and a blanket of flowers? The man is a necromancer. He deals in death. By the very fabric of his connections to them he is devoid of emotions."

Oberon narrowed his eyes. "He used to be an *etherealthant*. One of the most promising and bright lights of this world. The music he heard in the sunbeams was nothing compared to the symphonies he heard coming from the human soul."

The confession came out raw, bitter. Words turned sour on his tongue. He'd not wanted to ever have to explain the depth of Hazrael's powers to those who wanted to harm him, but he'd heard one too many accusations to not give the critics a little something to believe in.

Theodyne placed his hands on his hips. His brow creased. Anger shot from his golden eyes. "Glad someone finally told me the truth, since Nico has failed to enlighten me for weeks why you both place Hazrael's comfort and care above that of a small boy who harmed no one."

"It isn't that at all, Theodyne."

"Isn't it?" Theodyne stalked closer. "You have both placed every inhabitant of this school in grave danger and act as if we should pity poor, dear Hazrael for the atrocities he's committed. Well, I for one would rather see him dead if he doesn't start talking and make all the turmoil he's caused worth it."

Oberon fought not to retaliate against Theodyne. If their roles were reversed, he'd probably feel the same. But they weren't—he'd known Hazrael for too long and too well to turn his back on him when he needed support the most.

Oberon stood. "There was a time when you were ill-favored in this school and a lot of us chose to give you a chance. To see the man you are, rather than the product of the crimes you'd committed."

"We are not speaking of thievery. We are talking about murder!" Theodyne stepped closer. "How dare you compare my crimes with those of a necromancer."

"I wasn't comparing them. I'm merely illustrating that he deserves to be healed and brought back into the fold."

"Excuse me for speaking bluntly, Oberon, but he doesn't appear to want to be healed." Theodyne threw out a hand to indicate Hazrael slumped over on the bed like a rejected rag doll. "We've been trying until we're all tired to the bone from it and get nowhere. When are you going to face the fact he is beyond our help?"

"Wake him and we'll see."

"He hasn't talked to you coherently in six weeks."

Oberon ran a hand through his hair. Gods and demons, he'd never been so weary. "I know. Please, just wake him slowly and let me try and gain some control of his powers as you do. If he lost control after the death of the necromancers stationed at the Agia's palace, then it's quite possible one or several were his master."

The explanation seemed to break through Theodyne's stubborn resolve as nothing else had. "All right, but be prepared for a war to wage in this room."

"I've already shielded him from pressing power outward."

Theodyne glanced up sharply. "Then be aware it might implode on him. If that happens, I won't be able to bring him out once he succumbs."

Oberon nodded. It was a risk they had to take. "I know."

"Very well." Theodyne sat on the edge of the bed in the spot Oberon had vacated. He lifted his hand, fingers slowly spreading, pulling his arm backward as he did, drawing out the inducement to sleep.

Nothing happened.

Theodyne shook his head. "He's in there very deep. I'm going to have to go in and pull him out."

Fear raced a serpentine trail down Oberon's spine. What if Hazrael didn't want to come out? Many lost souls chose the astral as a place of refuge from reality. Those too corrupt to feel guilt never sought such solitude. This alone made Oberon believe that Hazrael was not beyond redemption.

Oberon slid into the blanket of the ether. Lights formed on either side of him, speeding along in the current. He jumped in behind the barrier he created and stood on the outskirts of Hazrael's consciousness. The snow had given over to a battlefield. Thoughts littered the ground like fallen soldiers. Shame and guilt writhed in pain. An image of Hazrael stood over them all with sword in hand. Ribbons of fire scorched the landscape.

"Help me, Oberon."

"I'm trying." Oberon dared not move closer. *"Put down the sword and come to me."*

"No. They killed my masters, and now they want me dead." Hazrael clutched the sword tighter, his face a white mask of anguish. *"I don't know how to control my powers without them."*

"Can you remember nothing of your time with us?"

Hazrael cocked his head as if not understanding the use of the pronoun "us."

"When you were training in the rites of alchemy."

Hazrael's expression changed. Fell. The battlefield scene was gone, replaced by the barren cold of a glacier. Icy wind did not penetrate Oberon's bones this time. He was too far behind the shields to feel the effects.

"The alchemists are the enemies! They've taken our lands and our world, casting us into the nethersphere."

"You were an alchemist once." Oberon held out his hand. *"Come with me, and let us bring you back to where you were before, to remember all you've lost under the necromancers' influence."*

Oberon felt another presence near him. He turned to see the lights he knew as Theodyne's dancing in the astral. He had not as yet taken human form, a practice that took tremendous energy in the astral.

"He's not listening to you, Oberon."

"He's still too indoctrinated by their taint, lived with them too long. It will be hard to break him free of their influence, but I think we

can manage." Even in the ether, Oberon's voice held a note of skepticism.

"*We have to do something more to get him to budge, or he'll terrorize all who come here.*" Theodyne shifted, coming into a watery image of his corporeal self. "*Do you think he trusts you?*"

"*At one time he did. I don't know about now. Perhaps he wants to but is afraid.*"

"*It will have to be good enough.*"

Theodyne disappeared, then reappeared behind the shields and Hazrael. It was a damn fool move but necessary. Oberon only wished he'd thought of it. Here he'd been contemplating how to get Hazrael to cooperate without using force. Theodyne apparently had no such qualms.

Theodyne pushed Hazrael from behind. "*Go. Oberon is waiting for you. He's the only one in this entire school who is on your side, so I suggest you go where he leads.*"

Hazrael looked up. Hope shone in his gray eyes, then just as quickly it snuffed out. "*You killed my master!*"

"*He deserved to die and much more than that. If you want, take your anger out on me, but you'll get nothing but your own destruction.*" Theodyne circled Hazrael like a wolf taunting its prey.

"*Then that's what I shall have.*" Hazrael struck out at Theodyne.

The astral lit up in a rainbow of jagged lightning. No matter how hard Hazrael struck, none of the blows made an impact on Theodyne. Finally Hazrael lay on the ground, heaving and spent. He gazed up at his opponent with hatred.

"*You are no more than a puppet used to do the necromancers' bidding. Stand up for once in your life and be your own man.*"

"*You know nothing, Theodyne Thespacian. Oh, yes. I know your name.*" Hazrael raised his hand, but the action produced no results. There was only spent energy about him.

"*If you know my name, then you know my story. I was once a puppet like you, and I broke my chains and chose my own path. One I am proud of, one that makes me a better man than you.*"

Hazrael collapsed.

Theodyne swooped in. "*Now! Oberon!*"

They tugged and pulled the resistant form of Hazrael. He fought back, gaining a second wind from an unknown source. Black mist oozed in from all sides.

"Damn, Oberon, pull harder. It's the necromancers."

Hazrael flipped over and reached out for salvation from the host of darkness floating their way. If the darkness touched Hazrael, Oberon feared they might lose him forever. There would be no redemption, no remorse, no going back.

Theodyne turned and shot another beam of multicolored lights at the necromancers. A horrible screech shattered the icy plains. The illusion dissolved, glittering like crystals on the ether.

Oberon hefted Hazrael and carried him from the ether, then deposited him once again in his body.

Sounds outside the door greeted Oberon as he returned. Theodyne was bent over the bed, trying to wake Hazrael.

"It didn't work?"

"It did. I think he just expended more energy than he had to give." Theodyne started for the door. "Give him time, and he'll come around. But I'd keep the shields on him if I were you."

Chapter Two

HAZRAEL WOKE to sticky eyes and a pounding head. Every time he tried to open his eyes, he was met with the crack of lightning passing through his brain. That pain was nothing compared to the vast hollowness located in the direct center of his chest. He rubbed a hand over his heart. His knuckles were skinned, bruised.

What had happened to him? Had he fallen down a well? Was he set on by thieves and beaten?

Last he remembered he was with Oberon in Delaneux. There had been something odd and shimmery as they passed the Agia cemetery. He'd stopped to try and figure out what it could be—then nothing. Blackness.

Odd dreams and disturbing thoughts filled his head, the memories of which put a bad taste in his mouth. He tried to sit up, but the pain was too fierce to do much more than moan.

Someone moved near the bed.

"Here, drink this. It might help the pain." Gentle yet firm hands helped him to sit up a bit and held a cup to his mouth.

Unsure if anything he drank would stay down, Hazrael shook his head. "I can't."

"Yes, you can."

Why did that voice sound so familiar—and yet not?

Hazrael tried to open one eye to see who helped him. An older version of Oberon stared at him. A wide streak of white painted the center of his otherwise dark hair. The bright green eyes were the same, but there were lines beside them now, as well as grooves at the edges of his wide, sensuous mouth. He'd not known Oberon had an older brother. Not one who looked so like him as to be cut from the same cloth.

Or maybe his head hurt so bad he was seeing things that weren't really there.

Hazrael took a drink. The beverage was strong, but not terribly unpleasant. He swallowed it down, then wiped at his mouth with the back of his hand. "Where's Oberon?"

Those gem-green eyes widened, and the man sat back. "Where do you think he is?"

Hazrael lay against the pillows again, closing his eyes as another pulse of pain shot from the base of his skull to the front. He gritted his teeth to keep from vomiting the healing tea back at his caretaker.

The man leaned over and offered a gentle caress down Hazrael's hair. "I think it's best if you sleep. Conversation will come when you feel more up to it."

Hazrael braced himself and spoke through clenched teeth. "Have I been injured?"

"Most grievously, my love. Most grievously."

The words followed Hazrael down into the bowels of sleep. Dream demons and death spirits surrounded his bed, taunting him at every turn. They wanted something from him, but he couldn't quite make out what. Not that he'd listen to them. He was a good and true follower of the teachings of Mercurian Dante, founder of the Gold School. He was also an *etherealthant* of the highest order. His parents were so proud of him. His family, so dirt poor they'd had to sell their only cow to pay for his passage to the school, expected great things from him. This was their one chance to rise above their humble circumstances and make a better life.

They'd be so worried if they knew he'd been injured.

Please don't contact my parents. Don't tell them what's happened to me.

The weight of a hand on his forehead lifted him from slumber. Now there were two more men in the room. One was a golden god of a man with the badge of a thief branded into his cheek, but in the robes of an adept. The second—oh sweet merciful Gods—was Nico.

"Nico?"

All three—Nico, Oberon's double, and the golden god—stared at Hazrael.

Nico approached the bed and sat down on the edge. "Welcome home, Hazrael. You've been away a very long time."

Air refused to move in and out of his lungs. He was going to suffocate.

Nico placed a calm, restraining hand on Hazrael's arm. "Easy. Nice slow, deep breaths. You've had a bit of an ordeal, but we'll get through this, I promise you."

The golden god scoffed and rolled his eyes.

Nico glanced up sharply. "Theodyne."

Wait. That name. He knew that name, but it flitted through his mind like a hummingbird, never stopping to land for more than a moment.

"How long have I been gone?"

"We'll get to that in a bit."

"No." Hazrael braced his arms on the bed and tried to sit up straighter. "Tell me now. How long have I been gone?"

Nico took Hazrael's hand. "Seventeen years."

But he was only twenty-one. If he had been gone for seventeen years, that meant he'd have been taken at age four. And he distinctly remembered coming to the school and beginning his studies in his tenth summer.

"I need to see a mirror."

Nico turned to Theodyne and gave a slight nod. Hazrael's gaze traveled from Theodyne to—oh Gods, it *was* Oberon. A memory surfaced, something from one of those strange dreams. He was on a horse, wearing a scold's bridle. Oberon was there, ripping off the restraint and helping him to another mount.

Had that really happened?

"Oberon? It is you."

Oberon's eyes grew misty, and he gave a nod.

Seventeen years was a long time to be apart. For Hazrael it had only been yesterday when they were so in love and made promises to stay by each other's side for always.

Theodyne handed Hazrael a small mirror used for reflecting the glow of flames during experiments. The image that stared back at Hazrael was that of a stranger. Eyes that were once a medium blue had faded to a clear gray. His skin was stretched over his cheekbones in stark relief. Odd scars covered his neck and upper chest. When he started to pull out his shirt to discover how far down the marks went, Nico stayed his hand.

"There will be plenty of time to learn all you've forgotten."

He held his shirt against his skin, suddenly afraid to look. "But where have I been?"

Nico frowned. "Far from us and our protections. If we had known or understood for one moment your peril, we would have moved heaven and all the hells to find you."

"That explains nothing." Hazrael rubbed his forehead. The pain remained there as a constant jab. "I have a right to know where I've been and who I've been with."

Oberon came around to the other side of the bed and sat. "Yes, you do, but it's not that easy. By telling you, we run the risk of giving you the information to find your former masters. There is inherent danger in the act. Not just for you but for all of us at the Gold School. We have to make sure you are completely well."

Chills moved to lodge in his sacrum. There were not that many sects the alchemists feared. The only ones Hazrael ever remembered hearing about were the necromancers, but they'd been cast out from the city-states for centuries. He felt for the thread that connected him to the elementals.

Silence!

A sensation like being submerged into an icy river enveloped him, stealing his breath and freezing his mind. He grabbed at his throat, trying to draw air.

"He's turning blue!"

"He's stopped breathing!"

Theodyne stepped into view. He took Hazrael's arms and pulled them up over his head. Air shuddered in, and Hazrael gulped it greedily.

"Where are they? I can't hear them!"

"Who?" Theodyne kept Hazrael's arms thrust upward.

"The elementals. I can't hear or feel them at all." Tears blurred his vision until Theodyne faded into a watercolor of his former image. "There's no music."

Theodyne leaned close so they were almost nose to nose. "Take a deep breath and relax. You need to regain control of yourself, or the elementals will stay away."

"What do you mean?" Hazrael tried to do as told. "Why would they desert me when I need them the most?"

"Because you tried to enslave them to your masters' whims. It will take time and proof of your healing before they trust you again."

Incredulous, Hazrael leaned deeper into the pillows. Theodyne released his arms, and they fell to his side.

Nico stood. "That is all I'll allow anyone to mention for now. I believe the information will be easier taken in small doses."

"And allow me to suffer more as I imagine all the horrible things I might have done." Sick with dread, Hazrael rolled onto his side and pulled the covers up to his chin. "I don't think I'll sleep at all now."

"Perhaps not, but you must try."

They left him alone. A sound of a bell tinkling slightly out of tune came from the door handle—a spell to lock him in, proving they didn't trust him.

OBERON STARED out the window at the untamed peaks of the mountains behind the school. How small and insignificant he was when compared to such majesty. Often when he considered the view, his problems dissolved as if they'd never been. How he wished things were as easy to resolve this time.

Theodyne stood behind Oberon with his arms folded. His reflection in the glass showed a man who was just as weary over the situation as all the others in the school. "I believe he will heal faster if the elementals help. Without them, he's on his own. Speaking from experience, it's a bad place to be without hearing their constant voices in your head."

"We can't force them to assist," Oberon pointed out.

"No. But we can ask at least a few of them to connect with him. It might ease the transition back to the order."

Oberon stared at Theodyne for a moment. He detected no trickery or malice coming from Theodyne. What had been there had slowly morphed into genuine concern.

"You've had a change of heart concerning Hazrael?"

Theodyne lifted a shoulder. "All I wanted was a reason to believe in him. You gave me that. The rest is up to Hazrael, and I reserve the right to change my judgment should I detect anything about him that suggests he's working under the necromancers' direction."

"Fair enough, I suppose." Oberon leaned against the windowsill. "I'd like to consult with Nico on the matter of the elementals before we proceed." Nico had gone to the workroom to draw up some plans for a device he'd envisioned, murmuring something about much needed distractions.

"I think you should consult with Anjufer over Nico."

Oberon scoffed. "Anjufer would as soon see Hazrael burned at the stake or beheaded in the courtyard than help."

"You can't blame him for his feelings. Good Gods, Anjufer more than any being at this school knows the horror of living in a world run rampant by necromancers." Theodyne rearranged a scrying bowl and candles. He made a face at the configuration, then moved them around again.

Oberon turned away from the window. "What are you doing?"

"Setting up a network. The communication between the various *prolatial* estates and here is slow and inefficient. Add to that the fact we're placing a great burden on the students by asking them to man the larger bowls in the scrying chamber around the clock when we've got our numbers so spread out, and we've got to come up with a better system."

Theodyne set more candles around the bowl, then stood back and evaluated his handiwork. "Also the water needs to be replenished too often due to evaporation. We need to find a substance that won't evaporate but will conduct sound and images as well as water."

Oberon held his hands out in entreaty. "I will pay you to let me work on this project. I need something to do besides worry about Hazrael. At this rate I'll be out of my head inside a month."

Though the office of headmaster kept him somewhat busy, he'd been so efficient in his duties up until now, the school practically ran itself.

Theodyne gave him a sly smile. "Glad to be of service to my fellow masters."

Oberon looked around the room. "Why aren't you doing this in one of the workrooms?"

"Because this is the western-most point in the castle. All signals will fan outward from here and carry at a greater distance from this location." Theodyne demonstrated by using grandiose gestures with his arms, Oberon supposed in order to imitate the signals moving over the air.

Oberon lifted a brow. "You work where you want, and I'll work where I want."

There was a little-used workroom up in the great tower. There were implements and substances in the various jars and bottles forgotten by time and progress. It might be a good idea to check the shelves and see if there was anything he could use. The trick was to find conduction liquid with an imperceptible rate of evaporation. Logic and physics implied there was no liquid that didn't enjoy some loss to the air. It was just the nature of the elementals. They were a thirsty lot.

Oberon bid Theodyne good-bye and started the climb to the top turret of the great tower. This tower room was the place where Mercurian Dante had performed some of his most awesome experiments, breaking down the barriers of salt, sulfur, mercury, and other substances. Oberon was surprised Nico hadn't taken over the workroom for his own space, but Dante's descendant preferred to use one of the workrooms ensconced among the classrooms.

The room was closed up tight, door stuck fast. He gave it a quick shove with a shoulder. It came loose with a squeal of protest. Dust fell on him like snow. He sneezed.

Gods, the room was a shambles. Cobwebs made lacy curtains around the room. Dirt and grime covered the surfaces, hiding the tables, bottles, and equipment underneath. It was going to take him weeks to get the place cleaned enough to where he could work with any clarity. The chore would also keep his mind engaged in the mundane. For that alone he was thankful.

Oberon left the room and gathered what he'd need for a cleaning job of such monumental proportions. When he returned, Anjufer burned brightly in the fireplace. Eyes of golden flames pierced through the glow that made up the fire elemental's face. Anjufer watched as Oberon set to clearing away the cobwebs with a broom.

After the second hour of being watched by a silent fire elemental, Oberon finally broke. "Are you here to act the foreman, or are you here for another specific reason?"

Anjufer let out a hiss, a wet log on a flame.

"Is that commentary, or do you have something constructive to share?"

There was another hiss and pop. "Your necromancer is awake and trying to get out of his room."

Oberon started to clear the shelves of the curio cabinet so he could clean and inventory the stores. "He is no longer a necromancer. He is an injured member of our brotherhood."

"He will always be a necromancer to the elementals. His crimes have convicted him until his last breath."

"Hazrael was not laboring under his own faculties. He was being used, a tool as surely as any crucible or mirror." Oberon took down the first bottle and made a face. The label was faded and the writing illegible.

"He allowed himself to be used by our greatest enemies."

"Allowed? Allowed!" Oberon turned from his task and stalked to the fireplace. "Do you think the necromancers sit idly by and wait for permission to infect a soul? I can tell you in no uncertain terms they do not. If you don't believe me, feel free to ask Masters Theodyne or Jolen."

Anjufer backed up in the grate as if afraid Oberon might do him harm. Oberon stared into the flames of Anjufer's body for a long silent moment before turning back to his work.

"Now, you and the other elementals can either decide to be obstructionists and continue to block your influence from Hazrael, or you can help see to his healing. The choice is yours."

Anjufer flew up the chimney, leaving Oberon alone.

Where Anjufer led the other elementals in the school would follow. He might be the most vocal, but he wasn't the only one who could communicate with those of the blood. Oberon had never shared so intimate a relationship with the elementals. None of his ancestors had been one. He'd had to use his other skills in order to rise in the ranks of the brotherhood. It hadn't harmed him or set him back. If anything, he felt it gave him an advantage. He had his heart and mind all to himself and could keep his council without the interference of beings with their own agenda.

Some days they were worse than any doting mama or strict master.

Oberon dusted the shelves, slow and methodical. He wasn't going to rush to Hazrael's aid. That's what was expected of him. He'd become both caretaker for the ill and focus for ire. He wanted to be neither. At least not every waking hour of the day. He cared for Hazrael in memory of the love they'd shared and the young man he'd been, because the art of alchemy had taught him compassion for all living creatures. While Hazrael might have been used by the necromancers, he was still of living flesh.

If Hazrael's care was divided up among the other masters, then they would come to see he was not a product of what his necromancer masters had made him, and more an individual deserving of pity. When he finished the majority of the cleaning, he'd come up with a schedule for the other masters to take their turns in caring for Hazrael's needs. It was about time they used their energy constructively rather than huddle outside the door like a band of frightened old men, hiding behind another's bravery.

Oberon continued cleaning until the sun moved to the other side of the school and left the chamber in darkness. He wasn't going to work longer or use the energy required to light the room using alchemy. He'd come across no candles in his cleaning and felt it pointless to leave and come back with the necessary illumination.

After giving the room a once-over and cataloging his tasks for the next day, he left, closing the door behind him. The halls were empty of students and faculty. It was near the evening meal, so most of the school's inhabitants were gathered in the dining hall. It gave him the chance to return to his room and clean up before making an appearance.

Truthfully, he'd been taking most of his meals in his room or in Hazrael's. No more. He was going to get back to the business of running the school. That was his prime duty, and for the past few weeks, he'd grossly neglected it. Now that Hazrael was on the mend, he had to reintegrate with his fellow practitioners. Much as Hazrael had to do, and for the life of him, Oberon didn't know which of them had it worse in that respect.

At least Oberon remembered the passage of time. He hadn't cared for it much, knowing the singular existence separated him from one who meant so much to him. Some moments he had to reassure himself that he'd not dreamed Hazrael's miraculous return—that it had actually occurred and death had not claimed Hazrael on that day so long ago.

Not much could be done to erase the past, and that worried him in no small measure, but what kept him awake at night was a fear of the future.

Chapter Three

HAZRAEL SAT on the edge of the bed. Days had passed since he'd come back to a world turned upside down by the years he'd lost. So far, his jailers hadn't allowed him books or writing implements. Either one would have gone a long way to stave off boredom.

Alchemical keys jangled in the lock a moment before the door swung open. Nico entered with a tray and a hesitant smile. "I thought you might be hungry."

"You wouldn't happen to have a book on there, would you? I'd like food for my brain more than my stomach."

Nico set the tray on the table and gave Hazrael a pitying glance. "I'm sorry for that, but words are power, and we—the Adepts' Council—feel that giving you anything by which to create a spell at this juncture might be detrimental."

Despair opened as a pit beneath him. "I fear I'm going to throw myself from the window."

Master Nico raised a brow. "As dire as that?"

"You stay locked in here without even the basic companionship of a book and see if you don't go out of your mind." Hazrael pushed off from the bed and went to the tiny window to look out at the mountain below. "I sit here and worry and wonder what I've done and why people I have known and lived with, trained beside for over ten summers, believe I mean them harm."

Master Nico stayed on the opposite side of the room, seemingly unworried if Hazrael might make good on his threat to jump. "Do you not remember what we told you when you woke?"

"Yes. It's all I think about. I want to know why I was chosen and not some other student. What was it about me that captured their attention, and how did I not know they were following me?" He rubbed his head. A pain started between his eyes whenever he thought of certain topics—the necromancers in particular.

"Are you in pain?"

"It comes and goes." Hazrael didn't want to make too fine a point of it. No telling how his former friends would feel if they knew thoughts of his time with the necromancers caused him pain. They'd believe the influence was still within him, when he felt nothing inside but an empty forever.

"There might be a way to fill your hours in a constructive manner while you recuperate."

Hope moved through Hazrael. He clutched at the opportunity. "What would that be?"

"I need a catapult built."

Hazrael frowned. "A rather ancient manner of warfare, isn't it?"

"True, but the most effective in this instance." Nico sat on the edge of the bed. "Also slated shelves for a wagon that will hold globes about so big." He put up his hands to show the dimensions he was after.

Hazrael could see them in his mind, though what Nico wanted them for, he had no idea. He wasn't about to ask. He was thankful enough to have a task at hand to keep him occupied. "Will I be allowed to leave the room?"

"Yes." Nico raised his hand in a cautionary manner. "However, be warned. You will be watched by two master-level practitioners and have a journeyman as your assistant. If you attempt to flee or raise your powers against them, they are instructed to put you down like a rabid dog. This is your only chance to prove you wish to rejoin the order. Do not make me sorry for this." Nico stood. "We were good friends once, you and I, Hazrael. It hurts me to take these measures with you, but I am responsible for this order and the institution at large, though Oberon is the headmaster."

Hazrael felt his jaw drop at the news. "Oberon? Headmaster?"

It was as unlikely as teaching a fish to ride a horse. Oberon might have been a dedicated student, but he was clumsy, awkward, and kept to himself most of the time. It had taken Hazrael months to get Oberon to speak to him. They'd arrived at the school around the same time, both of them foreign to the ways of alchemy, and yet Hazrael had heard the voices of the elementals and souls since he first learned speech. Oberon had been bigger than most of the other children, and still his eyes had seemed too large for his head. Add to that the fact Oberon had looked so damned frightened, and Hazrael had felt sorry for him and had rather attached himself to Oberon.

In the end, they'd complemented each other perfectly. Where Hazrael had performed experiments and spells naturally, he had never been a very good book learner. Oberon, on the other hand, was a natural student. Classroom study had come very easily for the quiet boy.

Nico gave a small smile. "He was the only candidate I'd have wanted in the post."

Hazrael gave a nod. He supposed Oberon had changed over the years, had been drawn out of his studious shell.

He wasn't sure he liked the thought. As long as Oberon had only a few select friends, Hazrael had his exclusive attention. That's the way it had been. They were inseparable.

What would it be like now, after so many years and such distances in both experiences and memories?

An image flashed in Hazrael's mind. Oberon as a young man, dark-haired, muscular, and beautiful. Summer sun glinted off his hair in a reddish glow. He was smiling, green eyes blazing with love. They had gone to Delaneux the night before and found a room at the inn and made love until the early hours of the morning.

They were walking back by way of the Agia cemetery when everything went black. The last thing he saw before his eyes closed was Oberon's horrified expression.

Hazrael bent over as searing pain flooded his frontal lobe. He held the sides of his head as if he could squeeze the pain out of it.

Nico gripped Hazrael's shoulders. "Are you all right? What's the matter?"

Hazrael grabbed Nico's hand, afraid he'd be left alone. "Headache. Feels like someone is stabbing me."

"I'm going to move you to the bed so you can lie down and relax. Try taking a few deep breaths. Slowly. Slowly. That's the way."

They moved in a shuffling walk to the bed. Hazrael squatted onto the small cot. Wood creaked under his weight as the ropes pulled taut.

He swung his legs up and lay against the pillow. He kept his eyes covered with his hands, as even the barest hint of light sent angry fingers lancing through his brain. "Could you close the shutters?"

"Of course."

Hazrael heard the scrape of Nico's boots as he crossed the room to the window. There was a slight squeak and click as the wooden pieces came together.

He tried to open his eyes, but they closed in reflex. "Is there any more of that tincture on the table? The one for pain?"

Bottles rattled and clinked together as Nico looked through the supplies. "Yes. Here it is. Open your mouth and lift your tongue."

Hazrael did as told and felt the liquid drip onto the sublingual space. One. Two. Three. It usually worked on the third heartbeat. Four. Five. Six.

Panic started. What if the pain never went away?

Seven. Eight. Nine.

"Nico. Oh Gods. I think I'm going to die."

"No, you aren't. I'm not going to let you."

Hazrael felt Nico move away from the bed. "I'm going to get Theodyne. He's an experienced healer. He'll know what to do. I promise I'll return."

Hazrael didn't want to be alone. Dark thoughts bombarded him from every corner of his mind. A vile sickness spread through his limbs, making them feel twice their normal weight.

Memories stirred like ghosts in a room that had been closed for centuries.

He lay on a slab, naked and cold. Gods, he'd never been so cold. His teeth chattered, and his scrotum ached. His breath made little white puffs as it came from his parted lips. He was alone.

He searched his surroundings from his recumbent position. Leather cords kept him secured to the stone with arms and legs spread.

"Oberon?"

No answer came.

Where was he? Was he somewhere hurt or dead?

Oh Gods, if Oberon were dead.... He cut off the thought too horrible to imagine. He had to get out of here and find Oberon.

A door opened, and the scent of rotting flesh wafted over to him. It was the scent of the grave.

AWARENESS CAME back a bit at a time.

A cool, wet cloth pressed to his forehead. The gentle touch of a hand in his hair. Murmurings of those who cared standing around his sickbed.

"He's waking" came a deep rumble from above him.

Oberon?

Hazrael's eyes flew open and to his lover, who leaned over the bed, brushing the hair at his temple with thick fingers. "Oh, thank the First Ones you're all right." He reached up for Oberon's hand and brought it to his mouth. Fresh tears slid from his eyes and down the sides of his face.

Oberon frowned. "Yes, I'm fine. What did you think was the matter?"

Hazrael shook his head, not wanting to relive the hell of his vision. "Nothing. Only a bad dream."

Oberon, Nico, and Theodyne exchanged glances.

Oberon sat on the side of the bed. "Perhaps you'd feel better if you talked about it?"

Hazrael shook his head. "No. You're all right. That's all that matters." He started to sit up. Oberon helped him, putting the pillows up for him to rest against. "Can I have some water?"

"Of course you can."

Theodyne poured a glass and handed it to him. Hazrael took it and started to drink. Down in the depths of the glass, a figure gazed up at him. A horrible visage of death.

Hazrael started and threw the cup. Water spilled over the blankets, and the cup hit the stone with a clatter.

Oberon stared at him as if he'd lost what remained of his mind. "What's the matter now?"

"N-nothing."

Theodyne retrieved the cup and poured more water. This time he held it for Hazrael to drink. When he'd gotten his fill, he backed away from the offering and gave a nod of thanks.

Hazrael looked at each of the assembled masters in turn. "I'm sorry to be such a burden. I want to operate under my own power again.

I just don't know how anymore. It's like I've forgotten that along with everything else."

Nico crossed the room and stopped at a small writing desk that hadn't been there before. "I've brought you a few things to help you pass the time. If you are sincere about my offer to help me with the catapult and the wagon, then you'll need implements to draw up your plans. I have provided all you'll need."

Hazrael shifted uncomfortably under the scrutiny he read in Nico's eyes. They'd been such close friends once. Now Nico was his master and jailer. "I thought you said you'd give me nothing to use against you and the others?"

"I did, and I haven't gone back on my word. I have provided you no reference materials. You'll have to make crude drawings to the best of your ability."

At least it was a concession of sorts.

"I'll get to work on it as soon as I'm up."

Theodyne stood by the bed, looking down at him with narrowed eyes. Of all the masters he'd met so far—and there were only a few he remembered from being a student—Theodyne was the one he feared the most. He wasn't certain why the golden god of a man with the thief's badge made him nervous. Scrutiny poured from Theodyne, a hole in a water bucket. He made no attempt to hide his inspection from Hazrael, though he never openly said anything that could be taken amiss. It was there in those deep, amber eyes. Hazrael looked away from the secret accusation there.

"Is it still light out?"

"No. Night has fallen." Oberon lifted the wet blanket and folded it. "I'll get you fresh linen. Are you hungry?"

The very thought of food made his belly turn a somersault. "I don't think I could eat."

"How about something small. Soup and bread, perhaps?" Concern radiated from Oberon. At least his compassion remained sincere. "I fear you haven't eaten much since coming to us. A proper diet will help you to heal faster."

Hazrael smiled. "I'll try the soup and bread. Thank you."

Oberon left with Nico hot on his heels, asking him to wait up. Alone with Theodyne, Hazrael swallowed down fear like a piece of rancid meat stuck in his throat.

Theodyne placed a chair by the bed and sat, holding out his hand. "Give me your hand."

"Why?"

"I want contact to look inside your head, and this is the easiest way."

Hazrael curled his fingers inward, hiding them against his chest. "No."

"You're acting like a child." Theodyne reached over and grabbed at Hazrael's hand.

"Don't."

"Why? Are you hiding something from us? Something you don't want us finding out?"

Heat rose to Hazrael's cheeks, damning him for a liar.

Instead of fighting for Hazrael's hand, Theodyne pushed up and placed his palm on the center of Hazrael's forehead.

"Stop blocking me, Hazrael."

He had to. If Theodyne saw all the evil visions cluttering his mind, he'd be sent away. He had no place to go. "No, please. Don't make me show you."

Hazrael felt Theodyne slipping into his mind, going through the layers of debris, dragging him down. They came out, standing near the vision of a younger Hazrael strapped to the slab, naked and shivering.

Theodyne looked up. "Is this how it began?"

Hazrael shook his head. "I don't know. It's out of time and place. I can feel and see and taste this memory now, but I don't know where I was or what came before or after."

Theodyne moved his arm in an arc, and the scene faded. They were back in Hazrael's room, seated as they had been before, only the chill of the crypt remained as a specter of the vision.

"I think it's safe to assume that your memories are coming back."

Hazrael shook his head in denial. "If they are as horrible as that first one, I don't want them back. I want to forget and start fresh." Even as he said it, he knew that wasn't true. He wanted to remember, to know why it was they hated him so. What had he done on behest of the necromancers?

"I think there is a great deal we can learn from your inside view of the necromancers. You're holding on to a key to defeating them, and you don't even realize it." For the first time, Theodyne's expression softened, and he looked at Hazrael more as a confidant and friend than as a person to be treated with suspicion and fear. "Help us help the city-states. The information you possess will be invaluable in our defense."

Hazrael nodded, however reluctantly. "If I do this favor for you, will you do one for me?"

Suspicion returned to Theodyne's eyes. "What kind?"

"Don't tell the others. Not yet. I'm afraid if they know my memory is returning, they'll try and kill me again."

Theodyne gave an uneasy chuckle. "No one has tried to kill you."

"Yes, they have. In the cave with the sarcophagus."

Theodyne paled and stood. "That did not happen here, but in Gusan."

Hazrael frowned. "The holy city? I've never been to Gusan."

He watched Theodyne as he went to the door. "I suspect you've been a lot of places you don't or can't remember, but you will."

Theodyne opened the door and exited the room without giving Hazrael the promise he'd asked for. But then what had he expected? Theodyne was no more than a hostile stranger with some remarkable powers.

Scents from the *terrathant* clung to his master's robes as rich soil and green foliage. They surrounded Theodyne as if he sprang from their earthy depths in full form. However much he feared Theodyne, there was another master he feared more. It was one he hadn't seen since waking in this room.

Hazrael forced himself to get up and put his meager artistic skills to work. Why not? He'd promised Nico he'd at least make the attempt. But what did Nico need such strange contraptions for? A catapult?

Even if the exercise was purely to keep an eye on him and ensure he wanted to participate in the defense of the school, Hazrael was going to excel at the projects. It was important he make a good impression—to prove he wanted to make amends for whatever it was he'd done.

Hazrael pulled out the chair and sat. The writing implements were not of any great quality, but they would serve the function for which they were made. He picked up the charcoal as an odd frisson of familiarity tingled up his arm. This wasn't the first time he'd held a color to draw. It was a very long time ago, though—another lifetime almost.

A bittersweet memory drifted through his mind. He and Oberon were sitting in the grass near the stone wall that bordered the school property. Hazrael held a book in his hand, making sketches of nearby scenery and surreptitious ones of Oberon. They had not yet become lovers, but Hazrael's feelings for the quiet Oberon had begun to change, grow into something much more. There was strength there in his face as much as in his character. Courage he had in abundance. Humor and humility. He was an ideal student, friend, and had become Hazrael's entire heart.

The thoughts faded, and Hazrael looked down at the page before him. A perfect replica of the original drawing stared up at him, rendered in black charcoal. Dust smudged his fingers and left prints along the edge of the page. Unsettled that he'd drawn a picture without consciously doing so, he set it aside.

Now to work on the shelf design. Nico had only given him approximate dimensions, not what materials were used to construct the spheres. Were they alchemists' spheres?

That created an entirely different set of problems.

He thought on it a moment and the possibilities and began to draw.

Chapter Four

OBERON HAD just finished pushing the cabinet back into place after cleaning the floor when a knock sounded on the door.

"Enter."

Nico stuck his head inside and glanced around. "You've done wonders. It actually resembles a workable laboratory again."

"It's a shame it was allowed to run to ruin. Suppose part of that was my fault. I should have taken stock of all our unused spaces and supplies when I took over stewardship." Oberon brushed his hands together a few times, then offered Nico a stool to sit on. "What brings you here? Looking for me I assume."

"You assume correctly." Nico sat and squared his shoulders, facing Oberon with an open and candid expression. "I saw the look you made when I mentioned the task I've set on Hazrael. I promise you, it is only going to exercise his engineering creativity and his physical body. No harm will come to him or the others."

"If that's why you came here, you've wasted a trip." Oberon moved to the curio cabinet and began to return all the little vials and bottles he'd taken from the shelves days before in order to clean. "I was more interested in the items you needed. Are you going to war?"

"Yes. Or at least I want to be prepared when war comes to us." Nico glanced down for a moment before looking up again. "I've had word from Jolen. The *demigoge* refuses to reside in the basilica. He's taken refuge in the Medovin villa in Gusan and asked for an alchemist to attend him. The entire order of clerics is up in arms, and he fears for his life."

Oberon made a scoff of sound. "As well he should. He's in bed with vipers and pulling their tails."

Nico raised a brow. "I know there is no love lost between our orders, but we must agree they have been very good to us lately. The *demigoge* is not without friends inside the sacred orders. It seems the church is on the verge of a catastrophic split."

"Only a few weeks ago, the *demigoge* told the Medovin there would be no official support of the alchemists. I find it odd he'd take one into his confidence now." Oberon brushed the dirt off a jar of dried lilies. "Doesn't he run the risk of alienating more than just a segment of the clerics?"

"Perhaps, but it comes down to this: the basilica is overrun by those who have cast their lot with the necromancers. The purge performed by Theodyne and Jolen was a temporary measure at best. Death dancers have reinfected the wound, and they mean to keep that foothold until they cleave the church asunder." Nico gazed out the window to a distant point. "The time has come to make our stand and gather our forces."

"So you've chosen sides?"

"I have. I've chosen the side of the city-states."

"By your own admission, at least the religious order is set to crumble. Can the city-states be far behind?"

Nico shook his head. "I don't believe so. The *prolates* are united on ousting the necromancers. I think the governmental bodies will hold together."

"And you plan to use Hazrael to build instruments to destroy his former masters?"

"I call it poetic irony."

"But not justice." Oberon had to agree it was devious, but what would happen if Hazrael regained his memory of living with the necromancers? Would he then decide to use the tools of war against the alchemists?

Nico held up his hand as if to stop Oberon from making any protests. "I've asked him to make shelves for a wagon."

"And a catapult!"

"Of course. How else am I going to get the spheres onto a battlefield? I will not risk our brothers to place them physically. And the spheres won't hold up under cannon blast."

Oberon's eyes felt as if they bugged from their sockets for a moment. "You really mean to take the fight to the necromancers?"

"Why does this shock you? You've known all along I mean to cut them off at the knees and ensure they are gone from the city-states once and for all."

"Because we've never really found a reliable way to do away with the bastards, that's why." Oberon motioned to the glass vials and equipment. "Even though I don't want to believe their magic is stronger than ours, I fear that might be the case."

"Fear is what they have, and they've used it against us time and again. I will not allow it going forward." Nico's expression darkened. "And now they've started in on the clerics."

"Who we feared were in league with them all along." Oberon didn't know why he felt the need to point out these shortcomings to Nico's defense, but gave them voice all the same.

"And we weren't wrong necessarily. We just need to separate those who are loyal from those who are not."

Oberon let out a weary sigh and sat at the table. "That is a major undertaking. Are you suggesting we send forces to the basilica?"

"No. I've suggested no such thing. I'm charging those assigned to the *prolates'* palaces the duty of scanning local clerics. They can then make the *demigoge* aware, and he can purge his ranks as he sees fit."

Oberon found the first genuine smile he'd had since beginning this most painful conversation. "You sneaky demon. Your diplomacy does you proud. Give him the information, but don't get involved until he asks—and he *will* ask. Just as he did Jolen and Theodyne when they were in the holy city."

"Oh, I'm counting on it. When he makes an official request, he will get his alchemists. Until then we stay on the periphery and pass information only."

"And in the meantime…?"

Nico flipped his hand in a nonchalant manner. "We prepare for war."

HAZRAEL WORKED into the night. The candle burned down until it was nothing more than a nubbin. He'd come up with a design he felt was flexible yet workable for the wagons. He'd yet to even begin working on the catapult. That had several considerations to employ first.

Weight of objects, distance thrown, materials used. He needed a book on engineering or warfare in order to feel at least a little confident in his schematics.

The key turned in the lock, and the door came open.

Oberon had a food tray in his hands. He set it on the desk and glanced down at the plans. "It's coming along, then?"

"As well as it can without knowing the particulars of what Nico has in mind. He only gave me a vague idea of the dimensions." Hazrael picked up one of the drawings and studied it.

"What can I do to help?"

Hazrael glanced over at his former lover. The chasm of lost memories was a breach between them that seemed too wide to cross. It ached and burned in places Hazrael had never even imagined. He cleared his throat. "I could use a book on warfare and weaponry. I know Nico is hesitant to let me have any books, but if he wants to build a catapult that will do as he wishes, then it needs to be made in accordance with the laws of physics."

"I know about as much as you do of his plans." Oberon poured a drink and set it in front of Hazrael. "Come, eat and drink something. You're already skinny enough without starving yourself here."

Hazrael looked down at his body. Gods and elementals, he'd never been so lean—so gaunt—in his life. Whatever had happened to him must have included ritual starvation. "You find me repulsive now, don't you?"

Oberon opened his mouth, but Hazrael held up a hand to stop him. "No. Forget I asked. I don't think I want to know your feelings. I couldn't bear it if you decided you no longer have feelings for me. Not yet anyways."

Oberon hung his head. "Hazrael. This is not going to get us anywhere. I'll grant you the time you need before we discuss our situation, but it will not alter the fact you've been gone so long."

For the first time since waking and realizing how much time had passed since his abduction, Hazrael felt a stirring pit of betrayal low in his gut. Evil and venom poured from the spot.

He shot up from his seat, upending the cup. Wine splashed across the pages of his diagrams.

The feelings of anger and violence spiraled upward. A desperate need to release the pressure and explode outward rode him hard.

Oberon rose slowly, his hands stretched outward in entreaty. "Hazrael? What's happening?"

Hazrael latched on to Oberon's calm, even voice. "Anger. Despair. Hate. Oh Gods! I want to die and kill and leave the walls awash in my blood." He turned away, unable to look at Oberon's beloved face, afraid he'd see horror there.

Hazrael tucked himself into the corner of the wall and slid down until his butt hit the floor. The stones were cool and soothing. He rested his forehead against the walls and took a long, shuddery breath in. The stormy sea inside began to quiet.

He let out the last of the anger on a slow exhale.

Oberon ran his hand over Hazrael's hair. "Are you unwell?"

Hazrael shook his head, not trusting his voice. He didn't know what had happened, only that a rent in the fabric of his being, right down in his very soul, had put him in a murderous rage. *This* was why they didn't trust him. Why he could not even trust himself.

Sobs wracked his being. He crawled deeper into the corner, trying to fold his body to become one with the stone. At one time in his life that might have been possible, but he'd forgotten all the tricks and devices used by the alchemists. He was now other—not one of them, but not quite anything else.

"Can you tell me what happened? Did I say something to upset you? If I did, I most humbly beg your pardon."

Tears ran down Hazrael's face. He licked their salty trail from his lips. "You are begging my pardon? You, who has every reason to fear me and what I've become?"

"If you'd have meant me harm, you would have done so." Oberon reached out a hand and stroked Hazrael's hair. "I saw the wild anger in your eyes, and I know the power you hold in your body, though you may not feel it at present. The thing you need to think about is that you fought back the urge to strike out at me. You fought it and won. Now consider that very carefully as you sit there and condemn yourself."

Hazrael frowned, not understanding how Oberon afforded such generosity when the rest of the alchemists wanted only his destruction.

No. That was untrue. He'd accepted the olive branch from Nico and shared a secret with Theodyne. They might not all be ready to elevate him to sainthood, but they weren't ready to see him burn on a pyre either.

"What if the next time I can't control myself? What if I hurt someone without meaning to?"

Deep emotional pain cut brackets around Oberon's mouth. He flicked his gaze to the side, then bowed his head before meeting Hazrael's eyes once again. There was something he wasn't telling, and it was bad enough to show on his face.

"You must remain in control. No matter what happens to you, you cannot allow your emotions to take precedence over reason." Oberon rested his hand on top of Hazrael's. "Not until we know for sure all the vestiges of the necromancers are gone."

"Do you think I don't know that?" Hazrael ran a shaking hand through his hair. "Nico has already stated quite plainly that if I strike out, he'll have me put down. I believe he'll keep his word."

Oberon stood and helped Hazrael to his feet. "Come, sit on the bed for a while. The floor is too cold to stay on for long."

Hazrael allowed Oberon to guide him to the bed. "You don't seem surprised by Nico's threat."

"Nico has been much more obliging and understanding than a lot of the other masters. He is also the descendant of our founder. If he feels our order is threatened, he'll do what he believes is necessary to protect it, including having that threat extinguished." Oberon grabbed the chair from the desk and brought it over and sat facing Hazrael.

Suspicions rose. "What are you doing now?"

"I'm waiting for you to tell me what agitated you."

It was Hazrael's turn to look away. Oberon was as handsome and intimidating in his quietness as he'd always been.

"It's been a very long time for you—since I was taken. So much time to be alone. To be lonely." Hazrael traced the fine lacy scars that wound up his arms in pictographs. "I wondered if you had a lover."

Flags of red stretched across Oberon's cheeks. "I've had them over the years. There is no one at the moment."

The knot of tension seated right under Hazrael's heart unwound a bit. "I'm sorry. I didn't mean to pry."

Oberon's mouth curled into a sly smile. "Yes, you did."

Relief washed his sins away, if only for a moment. It was as if they were as before. Hazrael felt his mouth curl into the ghost of a smile. The action so unfamiliar it almost hurt. "Yes. I did."

Oberon's smile fell away, and he rubbed his hands down his legs. "It can't be easy to wake to a world so altered from the one you remember. To believe you've only been gone a day or so."

"No. It isn't."

Oberon glanced to the desk. "Your drawings were ruined."

"I'll put them on the floor to dry. They might be stained, but the pictures will still be visible."

"Do you want me to take them to the library to dry? I'm sure Anjufer will oblige."

Hazrael shook his head in denial. "I'm sure he won't. None of the elementals are willing to help me. They've yet to even acknowledge my presence within the school."

"Let me take the pictures to the library and get them involved."

"Very well, but those are my only ones. Nico gave me limited supplies, and I hesitate to ask him for more."

"Don't worry about the supplies. I'll get you more should you need them. Being headmaster, I do have some privileges."

Hazrael leaned back against the pillows. Suddenly he was as tired as he'd ever remembered being. So much conflicting emotion and energy spent on needless things. "I find I don't have the stamina I had before."

Oberon made a face. "You need to eat more and get some exercise. Hell, you need a large dose of sunshine and blue sky."

Hazrael perked up at the thought of being allowed outside. "Can you take me to the lawns? To the glade by the stone wall?"

"Hazrael." Oberon drew the name out, giving it an extra syllable. "We can't relive the past. We can only go forward."

"But we were happy there."

"We were happy just being together."

"And now?" Hazrael steeled himself against the possibility that Oberon only cared for him with a sense of nostalgia.

"Now things are extremely complicated. My main concern is for your continued health and well-being. To bring you back into the fold and make you a productive member of the brotherhood."

Hazrael brought his knees up and circled his arms around his legs. "That's a tall order for someone who you aren't even sure you can trust."

Truth shone in the depths of Oberon's vibrant green eyes. "I trust *you*. I just don't trust the thing that was inside you for so long."

A shudder ran along the length of Hazrael's spine. Thinking of the possibility of another consciousness living within his own, having control of him for so long, made his skin crawl. Bile rose to the back of his throat. "If I've hurt you and the others, I'm sorry. I never meant—"

Oberon raised his hand to cut off the apology. "You haven't hurt us. Your masters have. It is them who will pay."

Hazrael glanced to the desk and the wine-soaked drawings there. "Then there is to be retaliation?"

Oberon folded his arms in front of him. His brow lowered in a frown, as if considering how much he should say. Finally, when he'd stared at Hazrael enough to unnerve him with the silent scrutiny, he said, "The necromancers have infiltrated every aspect of Dominicál life. They have now thought to take over the very bastion of religion. And while I do not believe in the same dogma as the clerics, I cannot stand by and watch as they are overtaken by evil."

"The *demigoge*?"

"Is still of his own mind and resides away from the holy palace. It is as much for his protection as it is to preserve ecumenical structure." Oberon leaned back with a sigh. "I suspect he was loath to make such a stand, and I don't agree with the choice, but his safety must come first."

Hazrael nodded. "If the *demigoge* came to harm within the walls of the basilica, it would mean panic among the people. If the Gods' own agent isn't safe within holy space, then no one is."

Chapter Five

OBERON WATCHED as Nico scrutinized the drawings. The adept tapped his lips as he studied one before passing it on to Theodyne. Tension hung in the air, painting it in a thick umber patina. Oberon had no control over the manifestation of his concern, but at least the color was only visible to him. The other two need never know of its existence.

"These are good. A bit crude in the execution of scale, but the concept is clear."

Theodyne pointed to the wine stains. "Was he drunk when he drew them?"

Oberon raised a brow in offense. "He doesn't get enough drink to become tipsy, let alone drunk."

"Then what's all this?" Theodyne fanned his hand over the stains.

"He knocked his cup over and spilled his drink."

"Seems to be a habit with him." Theodyne took the picture over to the window and studied it with a frown. "What's this up in the corner?"

"What?" both Nico and Oberon responded and hurried to where Theodyne held the picture to the light.

In the corner of the pages, with soft strokes of the charcoal, was the faintest picture of an ivy leaf.

Oberon's chest tightened. What had possessed Hazrael to draw that of all things? When they had first fallen in love, Hazrael had written a poem in which he compared Oberon's gaze to ivy, shading the world from what was inside. As a present commemorating their elevation to masters, Hazrael had commissioned a cloak pin in the shape of an ivy leaf for Oberon. The gift remained in his coffer.

Nico glanced over at him with a look hovering between horror and nostalgia, mixed with poignant sadness.

"It looks like an ivy leaf." Theodyne twisted the paper to get a better angle. "What is the significance of that?"

"It's nothing to worry about. I assure you, it's not a message to or from the necromancers." Oberon shot a glance to Nico, hoping he'd keep his mouth shut for once and not decide to spill a secret to his lover.

"But it's so out of place. Did he sign it? Is that what this is? Not much of a work of art, but not bad. I dare say it doesn't deserve a signature for posterity." Theodyne finally handed the drawing back to Oberon. "When do we start to build?"

Nico frowned at Theodyne. "We? You want to help?"

"Of course I do. When I'm not working on my own projects that is. Speaking of which, how is your end coming along, Oberon?"

Oberon scratched his chest. "I've managed to find a work area I think sufficient for the experiment. It should actually conduct the frequencies quite nicely."

"Good." Nico placed his hands on his hips. "We need those relays up and running more efficiently. They'll prove invaluable in the coming weeks and months."

Oberon didn't like where this was all headed. Didn't like it one bit. He'd always been a peaceable fellow, preferring study and reflection to all-out conflict. However, the scourge of the necromancers would make even the gentlest of hearts give a passing nod to violence.

"Has Hazrael mentioned anything about the catapults? Has he begun working on the schematics for those?" Nico passed the last paper back to Oberon.

"No. He says he needs more information on their construction. He has questions."

"Take a few books from the library on weaponry and let him browse through."

Theodyne made a face.

Nico turned a surprised glance in Theodyne's direction. "You don't like that idea?"

"It isn't that," Theodyne began. "I think it would be more beneficial to him to be able to select the books he needs himself. I'll go with him, or Oberon can. You have to start letting him move around the school on a limited basis, if for no other reason than for the others to get used to seeing him. Ease him back into the order."

Oberon held his breath, waiting for Nico's answer. Theodyne had just given the first real show of support for Hazrael that Oberon had seen yet, and it was unsolicited.

Nico lifted a shoulder. "I'm not sure that's a good idea yet."

"You have to take a chance sometime. Bringing him down here on the first day of the build and allowing him to integrate that way is going to cause a lot of wasted time while the others do nothing more than stare at him and feel him out. It's more productive this way. Trust me."

Theodyne's unexpected support warmed Oberon.

Nico gave a decisive nod. "All right. But I want you both with him when he goes, and I don't want even one book touched that might cause us injury."

Theodyne raised a brow. "He can hurt us just as easily with a hammer as he can with a word."

Oberon nodded. No truer words were ever spoken.

THE DOOR opened. Light and sound flooded the room from the hallway. There was something going on out there that intrigued. Hazrael slid off the bed and crept to the open doorway. As he neared he heard the low rumbling whisper of Oberon's voice.

He peeked out the door and saw a man he remembered from before—Master Rhone. This was not going to bode well if Master Rhone was involved in any way. They'd never seen eye-to-eye on any matter, whether it dealt with alchemy, politics, or life. To Master Rhone they were all one and the same.

Hazrael frowned. Odd how he no longer remembered how he felt about any of those subjects. Oh, he knew alchemy, but without the voice of the elementals in his head, without hearing the song of a living soul, he had no use for the rest—it just seemed empty somehow.

"I want his hands bound while he's outside his room." Master Rhone pointed at the door for emphasis.

"Who are you to order me about, Rhone? I am the headmaster, lest you're forgetting. I do not think he needs to be bound and neither did Nico when he cleared the visit to the library. He will be attended by myself and Theodyne. Unless you want to oppose all three of us, I suggest you back away from the door and let me collect Hazrael."

Hazrael took a step away, not wishing Oberon to know he'd heard the heated exchange. His heart wanted to burst with love and gratitude. His breath came faster, shallower.

"I will rally the rest of the Adepts' Council to my aid, and then we'll see how you feel about parading such a vile creature through our sacred halls."

"You're forgetting. He was once one of us. He was trained here as an alchemist. An *etherealthant* of the highest order, his place should be on the Adepts' Council, not locked away like some horrific mistake we made." Oberon's voice rose. His tone harsh as the lash of a whip. "It wasn't his fault he was taken. It was *ours* he was never found."

"How can you stand there and throw out blame when you know we searched for him until we were weak from exhaustion." There was a sound as if Master Rhone thumped his chest. "How do you think I felt? I gave both of you leave to go to Delaneux that day."

"This isn't about you. It isn't even about me." Oberon lowered his voice again. "It's about righting a wrong and cleaning away the taint of the necromancers from the city-states. If you've failed to see the connection before now, please let me enlighten you. If Hazrael was taken seventeen years ago, it means the necromancers have had a foothold and alliances here long, long before we ever suspected."

There was a bit of a strangled sound. Hazrael looked between the crack in the door and jamb. Master Rhone did not look all that well with the realization.

"Hazrael. Come. We're needed in the library."

Hazrael came back into the doorway. From this angle he could see it wasn't only Master Rhone but a host of others gathered there. Hazrael linked his hands in front of his body so they could see he hid nothing and did not have them raised. Whispers erupted as he was led from the room by Oberon. Neither of them spoke.

Tension painted the air, changed the texture.

Something brushed against his cheek. Elusive. Soft. An elemental.

Hazrael turned his head but only caught the faint tracing of it as it passed beneath the windows. The skin where it had touched him felt cool, tingled. He sucked in a breath.

Oberon glanced down at him. "Are you all right?"

"Yes."

They walked down the wide staircase to the lower level and to the library. Theodyne met them at the doors. He opened them with a nod and allowed Hazrael to pass.

Memories sharp as tacks assailed him from every corner. Scents of musty paper and old ink and leather fed his body and nourished his heart. So much knowledge held right here in the heart of the school.

Hazrael walked slowly across the floor at the base of the library. Flames licked the inside of the fireplace. Eyes stared at him from deep in the heart of the burning embers.

"Anjufer." Hazrael whispered the name under his breath in something close to benediction. First the unknown elemental in the hall and now the greatest friend to the alchemists. It was truly a momentous occasion. Perhaps they weren't as angry with him as he'd believed.

The fire elemental reared up, growing bigger. "Come closer, Hazrael."

"Anjufer," Oberon warned.

"I mean him no harm." The fire elemental sent one of his flaming arms outward, pointing to the second level. "The books you need are in that section. You'll find everything you need there."

"Thank you."

"Now come closer."

It was phrased as an order, one Hazrael had no intention of disobeying. If he wanted to reunite with the elementals, he had to go through a trial by fire. It seemed fitting after all he'd done—or forgotten he'd done.

He took a couple of shaky steps forward, unsure if Anjufer meant to sear him with flame. It wouldn't be the worst scars he'd endured.

"Lift up your shirt."

"You don't have to do that, Hazrael. Anjufer was just leaving."

Hazrael lifted his hand. "It's all right. I don't mind." He pulled the shirt up to show his belly and chest. Anjufer reared back in revulsion. Flames crackled and hissed.

Hazrael stood resolute, trying not to let the reaction hurt. "Do you know what they mean?"

"No. But I will find out." Just like that he was up the flue and gone.

The sudden move made Hazrael stagger back. "I don't believe whatever he discovers is going to be good news."

"Nothing branded or carved into your body like that ever is."

Hazrael let Oberon lead him in the direction Anjufer had indicated the books on war machines were located. Feelings of unworthiness and self-loathing slithered through his mind. They wormed their way past his defenses and lodged in his brain.

Keep walking. No matter what, just keep walking.

It took all of Hazrael's concentration to place one foot in front of the other and complete the circle up the ramp to the war and weaponry section. Horrible images threatened to drown him once more.

He batted them away like a pesky bug buzzing his head. No telling what he might do or say if he fell into an abyss of memories he couldn't control.

Oberon touched Hazrael's sleeve. "I'm sorry Anjufer upset you."

Hazrael waved the apology away. "It's fine. He didn't upset me. I know he'll make good on his search. It will be up to me to decide if I want to know the meanings behind the carvings or not."

Oberon frowned. "I know I may not show it most of the time, but you've been extremely brave. I don't know if I could have done as well under the circumstances."

"I think you'd have probably done a lot better." Hazrael turned from the book stacks and gave Oberon an unsure smile. "You were always the stronger of us."

Oberon shook his head. "I've never heard the elements, except when they want me to."

"What does that have to do with anything? It's emotional and physical strength I mean, not the source of your knowledge." Disgusted he had to explain such a thing to Oberon of all people, Hazrael turned to the books and began to scan the notations on the spines.

Tools of War.

Oh, that looked promising. He pulled the book off the shelf, went to the nearest table, and sat to leaf through the pages. It was old and bound by thick leather cord stitched through the vellum. All the drawings and details of weapons were handwritten, not made on one of the newer printing presses.

Hazrael frowned. How did he know that? Where had he seen one?

"Did you find something?"

"Not yet."

Theodyne came around the bend in the stacks from one of the upper levels. "I've found some other books that might be useful."

Hazrael glanced up expectantly. "For me?"

"No. For Oberon." Theodyne showed the books to Oberon. "Give these a read in your spare time."

"What's spare time?"

Hazrael watched the exchange, the animations and affection on their faces, and seethed. Were they lovers? But no, Oberon had said there was no one at the moment. Did that mean he had an unrequited love for the handsome master with the scarred face? It was not outside the realm of possibility.

Hazrael continued to thumb through the book but watched them surreptitiously. Symbols started to dance off the pages in front of his eyes. A crossbow rose and circled to show him a three-hundred-and-sixty-degree view. An arrow notched and shot off into the stacks, disappearing in a shower of golden light particles. Words scrolled by, giving specifics of the design and engineering.

Theodyne took a place across from Hazrael. "I never get tired of reading books written by the old masters. Until a few years ago, I never knew such volumes existed. Can you believe a thief as renowned as myself not knowing about spelled books?"

Hazrael's gaze slid to the thief's badge on Theodyne's cheek. "Does it bother you that it's there?"

Theodyne rubbed a finger down the mark. "Not anymore. I earned it in my previous life. It has to stand for something, or it was pointless. That hasn't stopped Nico from offering to remove it for me. Not that he loves me any less for having it, but between you and me, I think it bothers him knowing I had to go through it."

Hazrael stopped as he turned another page. "You and Nico?"

"Does that surprise you?"

"No. Not the two of you together. I thought... never mind." The next page showed the schematics for what looked like a spear but was notched at the end like an arrow. However, the bow used to propel the spear was as tall as a man and took two archers to pull back the string.

"This is a very odd device. I've never seen one of these before." Hazrael touched the image as it spun and showed the archers notching the spear.

"It's used for much bigger targets than a man." Oberon turned away from the display. "However, I do have an idea on how we can bring those back into play and exactly what they'd be useful for."

Theodyne turned. "I think I know what you mean. It's brilliant. We'll need those."

Oberon gave a nod to Hazrael. "Keep going. We might find other useful tools in the book."

Theodyne waved his finger around as if trying to call back one of the dancing images. "I think we could do with some of those crossbows."

Hazrael moved on, turning page after page of weapons used to maim, kill, and suppress an enemy. Most were of average design, nothing in their manufacture suggesting they were anything but what they appeared: weapons used by men of war. Why, then, was this book held in the library of the Gold School? Indeed, it was written by a practitioner of the Gold School. No one who lived outside the confines of alchemy could create a book that taught through live example.

Finally a catapult vaulted into the air. If he read the dimensions correctly, this was a big one, used for throwing stones at castle walls to break open a siege. They wouldn't need anything that big. Would they?

"Nico never discussed the weight of the spheres. Something this big might not suffice. It's made for durable missiles." Hazrael looked at the base and the arm. Images from the crossbow and compound bow superimposed themselves over the swirling picture of the catapult. "Unless we use the principle of the bows to fit the catapult with adjustable tension. Then it could be adjusted no matter the mass."

Oberon straightened from where he'd leaned against the railing. "Say that again?"

Hazrael pointed to the bottom of the catapult where the lever met base. "Feed a cable up under the neck and attach it here."

Oberon stepped closer. "Go on."

"We use a key to tighten or loosen the tension according to weight of object and distance needed to reach the target." Hazrael had no idea if the modifications would work, but they were worth a try.

"All right. We'll build a model and see if it works before trying it on a full-scale catapult." Oberon pointed at the book. "Take those, and we'll call this session a success."

Tightness wound in a band around Hazrael's chest. "You're taking me back to my cell?"

Oberon's face showed shock. "It isn't a cell."

"What would you call it? I'm being kept as a prisoner. It's a cell as surely as if it had bars." Hazrael rose and returned to the stacks. He no longer wished to stay in a room where very little daylight could be seen through the window, a place where loneliness haunted him like an unrepentant ghost.

Theodyne rose and came to him. "How would you like to accompany us to the dining hall?"

"Theodyne." Oberon drew the name out in warning, much as he'd done to Anjufer.

Theodyne held up his hand. "I'll take responsibility for him. If Nico wants to say anything, he can say it to me. But I doubt it will come to that—and even if it does, I'm the one who's been placed in charge of his healing, and I believe this is a good idea."

Hazrael studied Theodyne's face, concentrating on his eyes. No malice or trickery stirred in the amber depths. "I'll not make you regret this. I promise."

Theodyne gave a nod. "Are you ready, or do you need to look at a few more of the books?"

If given the choice, Hazrael would stay in the library all night and drown in the sea of learning. However, being allowed to spend so much time alone among the stacks did not seem feasible or possible.

Hazrael turned in a circle. "It doesn't look the same as I remember. It's smaller. Not as cavernous."

Oberon and Theodyne exchanged glances, the meaning of which was lost on Hazrael. He didn't ask them about it either. What was the point? They were keeping their secrets, and he'd allow it. He had some of his own he had no intention of sharing.

The horrible visage returned, screaming out at him from a dark corner of his memory. He shuddered and shook his head, trying to clear it.

"Is something wrong?" Oberon placed his hand on Hazrael's upper arm and started to move him away from the shelves.

"No. And would you please quit asking me that every time I have a thought of my own. It's disconcerting."

Oberon rolled his eyes heavenward. "I am only showing concern for you."

"I know, and I'm sorry for it. Sorry I am such a burden, but you don't have to fret so. I may have been through a horrific experience, but I'm stronger than I appear."

Oberon's expression was neutral. "Oh, I have no doubt about that, my friend. No doubt at all."

THE DINING hall was filled to capacity when they entered. Oberon walked as close to Hazrael as possible, protector and advocate. On Hazrael's other side, Theodyne strode, his expression resolute. No one within the dining hall had forgotten how Theodyne had shocked the entire faculty and student body when, as an apprentice, three years before, he'd turned Master Rhone's hands to stone for issuing a slight.

Oberon was glad to have the *terrathant* on his side. There was no way he'd be able to repay this kindness.

As they had done in the hallway to the library, people stared as they walked by. Oberon watched Hazrael from the corner of his eye. He stood tall and proud, as if he owned the world. At this juncture there really was no other way to be. The former alchemist turned necromancer was being scrutinized by every living soul within the walls of the school. Oberon only wished he knew what was going on inside Hazrael's head.

They came to the very end of a row, where a table sat empty. It was set for six diners, but Oberon doubted anyone would dare sit with them.

"You sit here with Theodyne, and I'll get us each a tray."

"If you think that's best?"

Theodyne pulled out a chair and sat next to Hazrael. "I think it's sound advice. Go ahead. I'll stay here, then get my meal after you return."

Hazrael cut a steely gaze to Theodyne. "Sitting with me like I'm an errant child."

"No. He's sitting with you to keep the curious at bay." With that Oberon crossed the dining hall to the serving table. He tried not to pay attention to those who turned to stare at him as if he were the worst sort of traitor. Hells, they'd been doing that since he'd brought Hazrael to the school.

He took a plate and heaped it with food, then took a second plate and placed it underneath. He'd divide the portions once he got back to the table.

Master Gervaise approached him, carefully selecting his meal. "How is he doing?"

"Better. Still no memory of the past seventeen years."

Master Gervaise made a face. "Theodyne might have been a bit heavy-handed in the attempted extrication, eh?"

"It was a chance we had to take at the time."

The wizened old master scratched his face and studied the back of Hazrael's head across the room. "We might have lost valuable information."

"The necromancers needed to be driven out if we were to save Hazrael." He'd been down this road with the entire Adepts' Council in the days following the extrication. He surely didn't want to go into it now.

"And did you save him? Is he the same man he was before his abduction? It will be interesting to see." Master Gervaise moved away, leaving that thought dying on the air.

Oberon carried the food back to the table and set the empty plate in front of Hazrael. "I've never made a decent servant. Have a hard time juggling plates."

A smile lit Hazrael's face, transforming him briefly to the young man Oberon once loved. "I remember." He turned to Theodyne. "There was this one time during elevations week that we'd been studying all day and long into the night. We'd missed at least two meals before we decided to take a break. Oberon offered to come down here and get some food, steal it out of the kitchen. He loaded several plates down with meat pies, cheeses, potatoes with gravy, fruit tarts, a bounty of everything Cook had made for the following day."

Theodyne glanced at Oberon, a sly smile curving his mouth. "Tell me you didn't drop it?"

Hazrael laughed with all the levity of his former self. "Not only dropped it, but tripped and threw it right on the robes of Headmaster Donando."

Theodyne bent his head back, laughing harder than Oberon had ever seen him.

"You think that's funny. Well I'd like to see you juggle enough food for a banquet."

Diners turned to study the commotion at the back table. Their gazes said what their whispering did not reveal: they thought the three of them mad.

Nico entered the dining hall, followed closely by the skulking figure of Master Rhone.

Nico made straight for their table, glaring down at them. "I believe my instructions were implicit."

Theodyne lounged back in his chair. "Hazrael was hungry. As you see, the poor man cannot spare missing a meal. It was more expedient to bring him here where he could dine on whatever he—or in this case Oberon—chose for him."

Nico's eyes flashed in anger. "We will discuss this later, Theodyne."

"No, we will not."

Hazrael tried to stop Theodyne from opposing Nico, but Theodyne ignored him.

"Hazrael is my patient and under my care. He needs to be healed completely, and to do so he needs not only food, drink, medicine, sunshine, and occupation, he also needs fellowship. This is just the prescription for him."

Nico stood there for a moment before giving a stiff nod. "Very well. I bow to your superior skills in the healing arts." He came around the table and took a seat next to Theodyne. "Is all that food for you, Oberon?"

In all the confusion and storytelling he'd not separated the meal. "Ah, no. I'm sharing it."

Theodyne smiled mischievously. "It seems Oberon has a problem holding on to plates when he carries them loaded with food."

Now Nico cracked a smile. "I remember. How long did it take you to get the stains out of Donando's robes?"

Oberon let the tension ease out of him. The focus, it seemed, had shifted to him, and that was perfectly all right.

Chapter Six

TWO WAGONS had been wheeled into the back yards, west of the stables. Planks of wood were set out on the grass and stacked nearby. The schematics Hazrael had drawn a few nights before were now on heavier paper and redrawn by one of the students with an amazing eye for detail.

Hazrael stood with his hands on his hips and let the fresh air and sunshine soak into his skin. It felt like a gift from the elementals, and yet he failed to hear their voices singing as he once had.

He clapped his hands together to get everyone's attention. "I think it would be better if we split up into teams. Each team will serve a particular function. One will cut the pieces for the shelves, the other the runners. Another for the slotted grooves. And then we'll have those who nail it all into place. If we work this way, we might get at least half a wagon completed by sundown."

So far he'd only experienced a faint hint of resentment. He hoped it stayed that way. "Journeyman Lorelli has your assignments since he knows you and can better fit your expertise to a task. Remember you are doing this for Master Nico and the defense of the alchemists as a whole. Not for me."

"Yes, because you aren't an alchemist," someone muttered. The people closest to the heckler blanched and shifted guiltily.

Hazrael had no rebuttal for them. None that could defend any of those behaviors he no longer remembered. "I was a first-level master when I was taken, which puts me on a higher rank than most of you."

He stepped down from the wagon bed he'd climbed on to speak. Oberon and Theodyne stood at the back of the crowd, looking none too pleased with him. At the moment he didn't have enough gumption to care.

While the workers were divided up, Hazrael made a circuit of the work area. The plans were laid across a table, held firm by large rocks in the four corners.

Oberon sidled up beside him. "I'd caution you to not stir the pot with quite so heavy a hand."

"What did I say that wasn't true? You were there when I tested and received my masters' robes. I think they ought to remember that fact as well."

"Some of these lads weren't even born yet when you were taken."

"Then the only things they have to judge me on are rumors and acts the necromancers forced me to do. How am I expected to reintegrate into the fold if I don't take a stand for myself?" Hazrael glanced down at the plans and ran his hand over the drawing. Charcoal from the drawing tingled across his palm like a life force.

He lifted his hand and spread his fingers. Motions that were once second nature returned, though stiff at first. The black lines rose off the pages and lifted into the air to hover about chest high.

He twirled his finger, and the wagon drawing began to spin in a slow circle. "Now that's much better. Easier to see when it's a living schematic."

Hazrael moved the empty paper over and repeated the process with the next drawing, which illustrated how the slats were to fit into the shelves. Over and over the pieces fit into place so the workers knew how to assemble the parts once they were cut.

Pressure from a multitude of curious gazes scored Hazrael's back. He turned to see the students staring at him from the workstations. "Is there not enough work to do that you have to stand and stare at me all day?"

Journeyman Lorelli made a face conducive to a plea for tolerance. Outside of Theodyne, Oberon, and Nico, Lorelli seemed to be one of the most sympathetic to Hazrael's plight. They had only met that morning as the materials were brought to the yard. He did not seem the type to be easily intimidated by a man who once knew the taint of the necromancers.

He was a big man. A full head taller than Oberon and wide through the shoulders. His physique seemed more suited for a blacksmith or swordsmith than an alchemist. Not that there was a particular physical type that was a hallmark of alchemists, but Journeyman Lorelli was rather more beefy than his fellows.

Journeyman Lorelli spoke to the other students, but Hazrael didn't hear the words. They were whipped away by a gust of wind that sheered across the mountaintop.

The papers rippled and tried to blow away, but the three-dimensional model that hovered in the air remained firmly planted.

Oberon looked to the sky. "I hope this doesn't mean we're in for a storm."

Thunderheads rolled into the area, fierce with fury.

Hazrael shook his head. "It's not promising. Maybe we can break for a while and regroup once the storm passes. I'll not risk the lives of students for this build. Even for Nico."

Oberon patted Hazrael on the back. "Nico wouldn't either."

"Call it, then. Let them know we will begin again later." Hazrael started for the tarpaulins used to protect the cut boards. "We need to cover the wood before the rain hits. If not, we'll have to wait until it dries out again to build."

Oberon cupped his hands around his mouth. "Let's get this covered before the storm hits and head for the school."

The students were quick to comply.

Another gust, cold and unforgiving, swept through the clearing. The wagons rocked back and forth.

"Someone pull those to the shed and secure them." Hazrael pointed at Journeyman Lorelli, who ran to the hitch and began to pull it forward.

The storm hit before they could finish putting away the equipment. They picked up what they could carry and made for the stables. There was no getting to the school in the downpour. Sheets of rain battered the land without mercy. Between the unrelenting deluge and the wind, visibility was poor. Hazrael had a hard time seeing in front of his face, let alone as far up as the school.

The students crowded into the stables, upsetting the horses and making them shift nervously in their stalls.

Journeyman Lorelli walked between the lines of stalls, with his arms out in entreaty. "Quiet down."

Hazrael wasn't sure if that was meant for the students or the horses, but whoever was the intended, both started to relax. So

Journeyman Lorelli had some of the *etherealthant* talents. No wonder they had sent him to help and watch over Hazrael. If he should turn and become an agent of the necromancers again, Lorelli could help Theodyne suppress the rage.

Had Oberon told what happened in Hazrael's cell? Was that why the extra precautions, or was it something Theodyne had said?

A gentle brush against his clothing and Hazrael turned around to face the person trying to gain his attention. No one was there. He peered into the darkness of a horse's stall and noticed the face of an elemental watching him from the darkness. He'd much rather have an elemental watching him than that horrible visage he'd seen in his drink.

A shiver ran through his blood, chilling him to the marrow of his bones. Awareness prickled his skin. This wasn't an ordinary storm. He'd been through one like this recently. But where? When? The patterns in the rain and clouds were familiar.

He stepped up to the door of the stable and opened it a crack to gaze out. Rain pelted his face. Wind blew his hair back. Debris from the yard battered the side of the building. It was hard to see, but that wasn't as necessary as it was to *feel* the storm.

From head to foot his senses tingled. The storm was alive with energy, intent, and anger. The necromancers had made their move, and he did not wish to alarm the others, nor did he want to....

Oh, by Mercurian Dante! He'd left the drawing out in the yard to spin. His energy was tied to that spell. If the necromancers absorbed it, they would have a piece of him again.

He rushed out through the crack in the door and ran blindly into the clearing. Over the lash of the rain and howl of wind, he thought he heard someone yell his name.

The memory struck him halfway to his goal. Like a ribbon of hellish lightning cutting across his consciousness, images out of time and place reached up and took hold.

He was falling, down into the abyss.

No! They would not win. He had to keep moving, even if he had to crawl on his hands and knees to get there. He clawed at the ground, pulling his body along, keeping his head down. Dizziness turned the world upside down, keeping the sensation of falling alive, though he was already on the ground.

He curled his fingers into the cool mud. Rocks bit into his palms.

If there was pain, there was life.

He lifted his arm and struck out, grabbing for the next patch of ground ahead of him. Then again, repeating the cycle until he reached the area where the table had been. It was gone now, blown over by the wind.

The drawing still turned in the midst of the tempest. A black charcoal wagon, spinning in a whirlpool of destruction. Just as he reached for the spelled schematic, he was pulled back into two strong arms.

"Hazrael, what are you doing?"

"Need the drawing. It can't stay out in this storm." He wriggled out of Oberon's grasp, unbalancing them both. They landed in the mud.

Oberon stared down into his face in confusion. "All this to gain control over a few animated drawings?"

"Necromancers." It was the only thing he could get out as his throat closed and breathing became a struggle.

They were trying to kill him before he talked. Before his memories returned and he spilled their secrets to the alchemists.

"Hazrael!"

No. He wasn't going to let them end his life like this. He'd not play into their plans or follow their rules. His mind was once again his own to command.

Invisible fingers squeezed his throat. He clawed at the sensation, feeling the cold, hard grip of bone closing around his neck. He planted his heels into the ground and bowed his back upward, hoping to dislodge the unholy attacker.

Spots formed in front of his eyes. The world bled down to only a pinprick of awareness.

He was going under.

Not without the picture. He reached out with his senses—what was left of them—and grabbed hold of the drawing suspended in air. Lifting a free hand, he pulled it to him, absorbing the charcoal into his palm.

He let the darkness come.

OBERON'S HANDS shook. His mind reeled. He'd felt the necromancers push past him in their bid to attack Hazrael.

He laid his fingers along Hazrael's throat, feeling for a pulse. It was there. He released the breath he'd been holding and gathered the fallen man into his arms.

The need to run from the storm was overridden by his concern for Hazrael's life. Oberon needed to get Hazrael to Theodyne. They had no time to spare. He slung Hazrael over his shoulder like a child's toy and ran for the shelter of the stable.

Theodyne ran out of the stable and met them halfway. "What in the hells was that all about?"

"He felt the necromancers. He ran out to get the drawing he'd animated." Once inside the stable, he found an empty stall and laid Hazrael on the straw. "He looks so pale."

"Stand aside. Let me see what I can do." Theodyne went down on his knees and leaned over Hazrael's unconscious form.

A strange glow lit Hazrael's skin through his clothing. Oberon sat in the straw opposite Theodyne. They looked at each other. Oberon gave a small shake of his head, hoping Theodyne understood the command. He did not want the others to see what he feared illuminated Hazrael.

Theodyne placed his hand over Hazrael's heart. Closing his eyes, he began to recite a chant. Wisps of bright green and gold light swirled around Hazrael's head, circled his body, and moved down to his feet. Once the energy reached the end, it turned and started back up to where it began.

Healing energies raised by the earth elementals, called forth by Theodyne's *terrathant* blood. A being made of gossamer wisps no greater than smoke from a candle flame moved through the wall from the next stall. The spirit elemental stretched an ethereal hand over Hazrael, gazing down at him with serene love and compassion.

Hazrael's eyelids fluttered, and he woke. His gaze fixed on the being, and he reached up with a hand stained by charcoal. The being stepped back and bowed, then faded from sight.

Students shuffled. Whispers grew to murmurs.

Oberon faced the worried apprentices and journeymen. "Make yourselves useful, for Dante's sake."

There was more movement and a bit of grumbling.

"Go!"

The movement turned to a fast walk, with the students heading to the doors of the stable.

Oberon helped Hazrael to sit. "How do you feel?"

"My throat is sore, but otherwise I'm all right." Purple bruises in the shapes of fingers colored Hazrael's neck. His voice was hoarse, scratchy. "Did I get it?"

Oberon gave a laugh. "Check your palm."

Hazrael gazed down into his hand. A look of relief washed over his pale features. "I felt them. Energy from the storm didn't feel natural. I knew if they gained possession of the energy I used to animate the illustration, they would be able to trap me." He rubbed his throat. "They tried."

"You fought them off," Oberon pointed out. "Quite valiantly I might add."

"There wasn't a choice. I'm not going to let them take control of me again. I was a young man when I was taken before—I am no longer that young." He took a deep breath. "I want to remember so I can know how to fight them off should they attempt another attack."

Theodyne cupped Hazrael's shoulder. "Do not push to remember. Let it happen as it will."

"Masters, the rain has stopped." Journeyman Lorelli came to the end of the stall but did not step inside. "Maybe you should move Master Hazrael to the school."

Hearing the title in front of Hazrael's name gave Oberon a jolt. It had been many years since he'd heard those spoken together. No one had addressed him so since he'd returned to the fold—sadly, not even Oberon had bestowed the honor on his former lover.

Hazrael sat there in mute surprise, blinking.

"I agree." Theodyne pushed to his feet. "Dismiss the other students to their studies. We will reconvene the build tomorrow."

"Can you stand?" Oberon rose and reached down to help Hazrael.

"I believe so."

Oberon took hold of Hazrael's arm. The man might be on his feet, but he wasn't steady. Vibrations rang through Hazrael's body, transferring to Oberon. The light that penetrated his clothing had dimmed.

"I want to go to my cell."

"It's not a cell." Oberon didn't even think about the rebuttal; denial was automatic. It also earned him a dark look from Theodyne. "Do you not want something to eat or drink?"

"Some water. Soup maybe. Nothing heavy." Hazrael walked between Oberon and Theodyne, his stride becoming more confident, his gaze further away.

They walked Hazrael through the school and to his room, then left him alone as requested. Oberon ordered Journeyman Lorelli to guard the door and serve Hazrael in case he needed anything.

For Oberon's part, he climbed the staircase to Mercurian Dante's laboratory. The books Theodyne had selected for him sat on one of the worktables.

He'd barely had a chance to look through them; he'd been so busy with one thing or another. The cover of the book on top was old but well maintained. Pages were yellowed, and the ink faded into the vellum, as if it not only absorbed the magic but the words as well.

The script was an older version of the alchemical dialect. Some of the symbols had passed out of favor in usage for more updated and streamlined sigils used to convey entire concepts. He glanced at the signature at the bottom of the title page. He should have guessed it was penned by Master Silvanus Gregori.

Entire shelves of the library were devoted to the numerous volumes of his works or scholarly treaties deconstructing his experiments. Pure genius was too small a title for one so creative in every avenue of alchemy as he. It also meant that the writings within were going to be precise on one level with the occasional flight of fancy thrown in. It was often hard to decipher Master Silvanus's work, because if he thought of a tangent while writing, he would explore it before it had a chance to fade from his mind. At the end, he'd draw a grid with the experiment sans deviations. Following Master Silvanus's advice was always better negotiated after having read the entire section several times first.

Oberon skimmed the sections until he found one he thought might be helpful for the task at hand. Though it didn't quite do the job he wanted, it was an interesting starting point.

Unlike Master Krutarch's books, Silvanus did not believe in animating his works, so there were no hidden fireworks or moving machines to navigate around while turning a page.

The table of contents for the section on communication had at least four different subheadings. None of them were even close to what

Theodyne proposed to do. He thumbed through the rest of the book. A section on conductivity caught his eye.

Lists of all the best conductors of life force, energy, and to harness lightning were listed from best to poorest. Topping the list was gold.

Oberon started laughing.

Oh, sweet irony.

The one substance sought by all who dabbled in the art of alchemy. It was simple and brilliant. Now if it would work the way Oberon envisioned it.

First he'd have to fashion a bowl to the dimensions he wished it. A big one, infused with metal he could turn to gold. It was much easier to work with bronze or copper at the foundry and then use his knowledge to turn the base metal into any substance he wanted.

Better yet.

He hurried from the room and down the long winding staircase to the kitchens below the school. Some of the apprentices were in there helping to prepare the food for the evening meal. All students had to take turns doing chores, including working in the kitchens. The school not only taught the principles of alchemy, but also humility.

"Headmaster?" Cook stood with a large cleaver in one hand. "Can I help you with something?"

"I need a large metal serving bowl, about yea big." Oberon held out his arms wide to show the size he wanted. "Rather shallow."

Cook frowned and scratched his beard. "Hmm. Let me think."

"Cook?" one of the apprentices called. "We have one over here for scraps."

"Headmaster Oberon does not want to use one that has been used for garbage for all these years." Cook waved the cleaver as he spoke.

Oberon gently pushed the cook's hand down so the cleaver did not endanger anyone within an unsafe distance. "I don't care if the pigs have eaten out of it. I'll need to cleanse it before I work with it anyhow."

"Suit yourself." Cook pointed with the cleaver to a large copper bowl heaped with various vegetable parts.

The apprentice slopped the garbage into another bowl and then wiped out the copper one with his apron. "Here, Headmaster."

Oberon took the bowl with a nod of thanks, then carried it over to the sink and cleaned it out better. It didn't have to sparkle, only be free of the surface dirt.

Excitement pulsed through him. He was definitely on the right path. It was there in the air that surrounded him. This was the solution they'd been searching for all along. Conduction properties of gold were well documented through the ages. Even the ancients had used gold to power some of their machines—technology that was lost to time and war.

Not wishing to waste more time, he climbed back up to the laboratory and started working.

He gathered all the equipment and sat at the table. This was going to take all his concentration. Generally, turning a base into gold didn't require much more than intent—when it was only a small amount. Any alchemist who passed into his adepts' robes, the highest level of master, could perform such a feat with merely a touch. Lesser masters had to use other means to transmute metals into gold. For larger pieces such as the bowl in front of him, however, it would take chemicals, time, pressure, and heat. The base metal the practitioner wished to turn determined what chemicals were used to effect the change.

Normally the size of a project didn't matter—it was all in the mind, but gold was a different animal. It was the prime substance—not to be confused with the Prime Matter. It was regulated by the Gods and protected by the elementals.

Oberon chanted as he worked the chemicals into the copper, scoring them across both inside and outside surfaces. He walked over to the flue and banged on it in quick syncopation.

Anjufer rumbled through the ducts and fell into the fireplace. "Yes, Oberon?"

"I need your help."

Anjufer blinked. "You are transmuting copper to gold."

"Yes. To use in the base of a new communication bowl. Theodyne hopes we can speed the transmissions between the school and our brothers at the various *prolates'* palaces." Oberon held up the bowl. "We need one with a better conductor than the current system."

Anjufer nodded. "Yes. I see." In the line of flames that passed for Anjufer's mouth, a smile appeared. "You've certainly chosen the right laboratory for your experiment."

Oberon frowned. "What do you mean?"

Anjufer shot up the flue but hovered there so he no longer touched the fireplace floor. "Lift up the slab, and I will show you."

Oberon knelt down and looked at the placement of the stones. There was one not locked into place as the others were. He lifted it up to reveal a hidden handle that attached to the slab. *What in all the elements?*

Oberon pulled the handle and lifted. Under the fireplace floor was an area used to pressure treat and heat objects for transmutation.

"Do you have anything pressing, Anjufer?"

"No. I don't."

"Care to help me create gold?"

"I would be honored, Headmaster."

Oberon placed the bowl into the space.

"Add a drop of mercury," Anjufer instructed.

Oberon hurried to grab the bottle from one of the shelves. He used the stopper and measured out a mere drop, letting it fall into the bottom of the bowl. It splashed, sending tinier droplets outward.

"Now take the stones over there in the corner, the ones that appear paint-splattered, and set those into the bowl. Put the slab back in place and close the grate."

Oberon performed the tasks, glad he'd not thrown the stones away when he'd first come across them. He closed the fireplace door and secured it. A flash shone around the seams. The entire school shook.

"You can open the door now."

Smoke smoldered out of the sides. Oberon retrieved a glove to use. He wasn't taking a chance. Fire elementals had the propensity to burn hotter and brighter than any flame. It was a wonder he didn't flash-melt the metal.

"All right in here?"

"Yes. Leave the bowl in the space overnight. I will heat it several more times. It is not an easy process to change matter this way."

No, it wasn't.

That was the price that alchemists without the blood of elementals paid for practicing the craft.

Some paid more than others.

Hazrael would wear the remembrance of their failures for the rest of his life.

Oberon should have tried harder to find Hazrael. Should have searched the cemetery again and again or looked for traces of him in unlikely places. The astral had shown them nothing but darkness, as if Hazrael's life had been extinguished. Once Oberon believed that lie, he'd stopped searching and honed his grief as a sword smith does a blade. To honor Hazrael's memory, he had started over—relearning those skills he'd believed imperfect, until he had risen to the excellence Hazrael had assured he'd be capable.

Oberon contemplated the manner in which he would transform the bowl.

If not for Hazrael, he might not have been appointed headmaster.

The weight of his office had never felt so heavy.

Chapter Seven

MORNING DAWNED with gritty eyes and a need for more sleep. Blasts had continued throughout the school for most of the night, waking Hazrael each time he dared fall asleep. At first he'd feared the necromancers were attacking, but no one else roused from their beds. He found that strange. It was as if the entire population of the school had decided that the percussion of minor explosions somewhere within the fireplace systems was a normal occurrence.

It never had been when he'd resided here before.

Headmaster Donando would never have allowed it.

Hazrael wiped at his eyes and rolled off the bed. The charcoal drawing remained on the wall where he'd placed it the night before. He hurried through his ablutions, then made his way down to the dining hall, escorted by Journeyman Lorelli.

"What were those sounds shaking the school last night?"

"No one knows. Headmaster Oberon was locked in his new laboratory working on a project for Master Theodyne."

Panic shot through Hazrael's body. "Has anyone checked on him this morning? Is he all right?"

"I believe so. I saw him with Masters Nico and Theodyne before I came back to walk you to breakfast."

Hazrael took a deep, shuddery breath and continued on to the dining hall.

Breakfast was a quiet affair. Most of the students had already gone to class. Those who would help with the build were already on the field. Hazrael didn't linger over his meal but finished quickly to get to the yard.

He found the materials already set and students working under Nico's directorship.

Hazrael took his place in the thick of things and lifted his palm, sending the picture to once again spin in the air.

"Is that wise after what happened yesterday?" Nico lifted a board and laid it over the sawhorses. "I don't want the necromancers back here."

"Neither do I." Hazrael looked out over the school grounds. Images out of time and place superimposed over the present. Every place he looked held a special memory of friends he'd lost or who had since turned against him.

He'd been so happy here once. Why did that feeling elude him now? It was as if deep down he knew he didn't deserve joy, his soul as black and rotted as a corpse.

A vision out of time rushed to him.

He was back in the cave where he'd awoken after his abduction. This time he wasn't alone.

Breath fanned out around his face in a steamy veil. The room so cold the tiny hairs in his nose began to grow frost. Why so cold? His body exposed to the frigid air. Above him, a man in the ragged gray robes of a burial shroud chanted words both haunting and strange. The language sounded not of this world, but backward. In his skeletal hands was a blade, fine and thin. It gleamed with deadly intent in the flames from the candles stuck sparsely throughout the chamber.

Hazrael lay nude. His arms out to the sides and secured to the altar with leather restraints. He tried to move, but each tug and pull only tightened his bonds. His tormentor leaned over, holding an icy hand to Hazrael's torso, and began to cut. The blood sent up swirls of steam from the incision, yet the blood did not run down his sides. It froze in the cold air.

Screams built in his throat, but he choked them down, knowing instinctively his pain would excite and entice his tormentor to continue. Silence didn't stop the cutting, though—nothing did.

"Hazrael?"

He came back into the present. Sweat dripped down his face. No—not sweat. Tears.

"I'm all right."

"I don't think you are." Nico pointed to Hazrael's belly. Spots of blood dotted his shirt in crimson stains.

He lifted up the tail to look underneath. The old scars had ripped open to bleed afresh. Air lodged in his throat. "I don't understand. How...?"

Nico hurried Hazrael from the yard, pulling him by the shirt collar. "Theodyne needs to see this immediately."

"I didn't do anything wrong, Nico."

"Did you scratch it in your sleep? Have you taken a knife to it?"

Horrified his old friend would think such a thing, Hazrael merely shook his head. "You know I don't like blood."

He was tired of being dragged around from this place to that and treated as if he had no more will than a piece of straw. He dug his heels into the ground. "No!"

Nico stopped and stared at him as if he hadn't heard him correctly or was shocked to have his authority challenged. "What?"

"I said no." Hazrael wrenched his shirt from Nico's grasp. "I can walk under my own power. You don't have to forcibly move me or treat me like a rag doll."

Nico backed up a few steps with his hands in the air. "Of course not. But you must realize your very presence here places this school in danger. There are things going on with you that we don't understand. Can you give me that much at least?"

Hazrael hung his head. His shoulders slumped in defeat. "You know I'll give you anything you ask for. Just please don't keep treating me as if I am the enemy. I have no idea what I did when I was with the necromancers, but believe me, if I could have fought against them, I would have. Even as a first-level master I wasn't strong enough."

A light came into Nico's eyes. An idea of great import, if the set to his jaw and clench of his fists were any indication. He was ready for battle. "You are—were—an *etherealthant* of great talent. Do not mistake your destruction on the fact you weren't strong enough. It was because the necromancers knew how and where to hurt you the most. To use your own power against you to ensure cooperation."

Hazrael gazed off into the distance. The blood dried on his clothes, stiff and sticky. A feeling of dread skimmed across the back of his neck. A memory from before his abduction swirled into place. "I remember... though I hadn't until this very moment. The weeks before my abduction, I remember feeling as if my every movement was being tracked and weighed. I thought it was the elementals testing me in some way. I remember believing it strange, because they'd never made me feel afraid before. Why should they do so for a test?"

Nico started to put his hand on Hazrael's arm but stopped just short of touching him. "Come. Let us have you looked at, and then we will discuss what you might have felt back then."

Hazrael fell into step beside Nico. "I'm tired of talking and analyzing. Action is what I need. Action and answers."

"We'll get both of those things, I promise you."

Hazrael ground his back teeth together to keep from speaking out. Nico and the others were trying to help him, and he acted like the spoiled prince who didn't get his way. The time had come to be a man and throw such childish behavior away.

They found Theodyne holed up with Oberon in one of the labs way at the top of the school. A large gold bowl sat on a table under the window.

Oberon poured a pitcher full of water into it. "I think perhaps we'll leave the ink out of this one, see how well it works with the reflection of the gold shining through the water."

Theodyne nodded. "If we don't get the results we need, we can add the ink later."

They turned as Nico and Hazrael approached.

Theodyne frowned. "I thought you would both be out at the build site?"

"We were." Nico pointed to Hazrael's stomach. "Show him."

The thought of lifting his shirt in front of both Oberon and Theodyne unnerved him. It was bad enough Nico had seen the evidence of the necromancers' influence long after the event that caused the scars occurred—but Oberon.

"Can we step over there, Theodyne?"

Theodyne glanced to the other men before agreeing. "Yes, of course."

Hazrael moved off with Theodyne into one of the corners near the door and lifted his shirt. Theodyne grew very still, his expression neutral.

"When did this happen?"

"Out in the yard. Nico said something, and it brought back a memory—the one of me being cut. When I came back to the present, the scars were bleeding."

"I've seen this before, though on a much fresher wound, but one that had started to heal nonetheless. They are able to cause you injury because they are still tied to you in some way. Not through memory alone." Theodyne ran his hand over the marks. "But through your scars."

"Wait here." Theodyne walked to the flue and banged a tune against the metal.

The sound rumbled through the school, as did that of something moving through the ducts. Anjufer plopped down into the fireplace. "Yes, Theodyne."

"Have you gotten very far on discovering the significance behind the marks on Hazrael's skin?"

"Yes, but it is difficult. I am in communication with one who can explain it best. Also, we need the testimony of our friends of the dirt and rocks. The ones who witnessed the ritual, to be precise. My hope is to also discover the location in which it was performed."

Cold ran through Hazrael's blood. "Who said it was performed in a place of rocks and dirt?"

Four pairs of eyes stared at him as if waiting for him to refute the claim.

Anjufer wavered a bit. "It was, though, wasn't it?"

Hazrael turned away, unable to stand the accusation in his flaming gaze.

Oberon left his place by the scrying bowl. "Is your memory returning?"

Reticent, Hazrael turned farther away, not wanting to admit the truth. He'd rather fix the problem or learn to control when the flashes of memory hit him before he divulged his secret.

Oberon tugged on Hazrael's sleeve. "Hazrael?"

Theodyne gave a subtle nod that the others didn't see, permission and advice to tell the others.

"A few flashes here and there. Nothing helpful as yet." No, only the most painful experiences of his life. All of them charred into his brain in such a way he had no means to resurrect them on his own. Instead he had to wait for them to climb from the ashes like a phoenix rising.

Stark horror filled Nico's eyes. "Why didn't you tell us?"

Hazrael forced himself not to glance at Theodyne again, to give away Nico's lover and cause strife between them. Luckily Theodyne cleared his throat and stepped to intercept Nico as he crossed the room to Hazrael.

"I knew."

"And you didn't tell me? Theodyne, why?" Confusion crossed Nico's face.

"Because he asked me not to say anything yet, and as the one in charge of his health, I chose to honor that request." Theodyne placed his hand on Nico's cheek. "If we are to make him whole again, we should try to work within a framework that allows these memories to return naturally. I fear the rebound should we attempt to force them to surface."

"I understand that, but not the need to keep me in the dark." Nico glanced at Oberon. "Or the headmaster. We have an obligation to protect those within these walls, and to do that we need all the information about Hazrael laid bare."

Panic threatened to squeeze Hazrael's throat closed, but he resisted it, swallowed it down. "As I...." The croak of sound was nearly unintelligible. He cleared his throat and tried again. "As I understand the matter, it was *you* who insisted I be brought here and sequestered. If you no longer wish for me to reside here, I shall leave, though I cannot think of one place in the city-states I can go to for either shelter or help."

Pride lifted his shoulders and set his chest out a bit more than usual. Tears threatened to burn his eyes, but he held those in check by some force he'd never known he possessed. "I've been abandoned by the elementals and tortured by the necromancers. Having the alchemists turn their backs on me is not insurmountable."

"Stop it!" Oberon turned wet, sorrowful eyes to Nico. "How can you insist he stay here and make him feel unwelcome all in the same breath? You, who have lived as a moral and just man? You were the best of friends once. You even still carry his copy of *The Codex* with you."

Shock registered across Nico's face before he slammed a neutral mask into place.

Oberon advanced on him. "Thought I didn't know about that or how you took it out of the library?"

Hazrael raised his hand to silence the escalating argument. "Please, don't fight on my account. Having you at each other's throats biting and sniping is what the necromancers want. They would rejoice in the fracture and see it as a victory."

Nico took a deep breath and stepped away. "We aren't fighting. We're enjoying a difference of opinion."

"The name doesn't matter, only the outcome." Hazrael held out his hand to Nico. "We *were* good friends once. I'm sorry if what has happened to me makes that impossible now. There are no words of comfort I can give or reassurances to ease your mind. I only know that I will continue to work toward the common goal of helping to rid the city-states of the necromancers. If only for the reason of vengeance."

Nico took his hand. "It's I who owe you an apology. I did not mean to make you feel unwelcome. I only wanted you to know where we stood should your former masters take control of you again."

Hazrael gave a nod of understanding. What else could he do to convince his former friend he meant no harm? The real threat came from outside him, apart from him. He knew no words in any language to secure his position.

"Let me see the injuries again." Theodyne tugged at Hazrael's shirt. "Can you lift it, please?"

Hazrael did as told. Theodyne poked around at the affected areas. They didn't hurt or feel tender, only numb, as if all feeling in that area had been removed.

"It isn't hot or angry looking. It just seems to have bled. Actually it's rather cold to the touch, like you've been plunged into an ice bath." Theodyne straightened again. "You can lower your shirt."

"What do you think?"

Theodyne rubbed his chin. "I want another look around in your mind to see if the necromancers are still in there. To see if I missed something the last time."

It seemed a reasonable request, but that didn't stop terror from pooling in Hazrael's gut.

OBERON DIDN'T like the idea of going back into Hazrael's mind so soon after a manifestation occurred. It was bad policy to try. His protests had fallen on deaf ears. Even Hazrael seemed all for the idea, though one look at his haunted expression told Oberon he did not go into the rite with enthusiasm.

They used the upper laboratory for the examination. The scrying bowl had been moved to the center of the room to use as a focus.

"Oberon, stand there. I want you to go inside with me. Two sets of eyes are better than one."

Oberon took his place across a circle drawn on the floor and filled with arcane symbols and sigils used for protection. Hazrael lay in the circle, the bowl between his spread legs. With a nod from Theodyne, Oberon joined with him and entered the ethereal plane. Down through the layers of consciousness and into the stream of energy that made up Hazrael.

It looked different this time—muddy, murky, unclear. His was a mind in flux. No steady anchor supported or controlled Hazrael. He was cast adrift on a sea of dirty water.

"It's a mess in here, Oberon." Even Theodyne's mind voice sounded as if he spoke underwater. It was hard to hear, indistinct. *"How do we even go about cleaning it up?"*

"One squall at a time."

Hazrael's lack of sufficient memory could be directly contributing to the state of his mental faculties. There was no clear way for the energy patterns to get through, so they stayed stagnant until one or two happened to float to the top or leak out. However, Oberon saw no signatures that suggested any of the mire was constructed or placed by the necromancers.

"I believe we might be looking at Hazrael's defenses. He had no way to protect himself after you tried to contain his talent. I think he tried to drown in order to save his life."

What passed for Theodyne's body on the ether moved in closer to Oberon, treading through the slop. *"You might be right. There are places where it's thick as tree sap."*

"Do you see any trace of the necromancers? I don't feel them at all. Nor do I see any signature that they remain here."

"Me either." Theodyne treaded mud beside him for a moment. *"I'm going to try and disperse the smaller mound over there. We'll see how well it works."*

"You do that. I'll stay here and work on this one."

The eddy before him twirled in a counterclockwise fashion. Bits of debris—thoughts out of time and place—were swept up into the current. Cleaning the fluid wasn't the part that concerned Oberon as much as what would happen to the memories stuck like leaves to the whirlpools. Would they be erased forever or settle back where they belonged once the rest of the mind had been cleaned?

Wasting no more time contemplating the matter, Oberon dived into the center of the churning mass and found the source. One small area was visible where the energy flows were in flux. The unregulated patterns caused a vortex that sucked in on Hazrael's consciousness, making it impossible to break free. With such areas all over his mind, it was a wonder he'd even been able to think and function, much less control his own body.

Oberon swam deeper, to the source of the disruption. An area about the size of a fist was buckled up and outward, an explosion waiting only for a fuse with which to blow asunder. He reached out to smooth the uneven area down, and he shot back up to the top of the pool.

He lay there disoriented and shaking. His hand—though on the ethereal plane it wasn't a physical hand—burned as if he'd tried to capture lightning in his bare fist.

What in all the hells had caused that?

He dived back through the murk. Sediment rose up from the spot in tendrils of darker oil-slicked mud. The festering stench of pure evil permeated the black ribbon. Not the necromancers, though they were the root cause. This stream of vileness was created by guilt and self-loathing. For each act of unspeakable horror Hazrael had inflicted on humanity in the name of the necromancers, his unconscious mind had railed against what his body could not control. Liquid punishment poured from the crack in the flooring of his consciousness, unable to be contained.

"Theodyne. This is worse than we feared. The poor man is going to self-destruct."

"I know. And I don't know how to fix it. This is beyond even my healing abilities."

"I don't think there is anything we can do—not until he forgives himself and lets go of the pain."

Theodyne appeared again. The color streams used to represent his body were dull, faded. He'd used too much energy trying to control the cracks in the floor. *"How is he going to accomplish that if he can't remember?"*

"I don't know, but I'd hate to be a necromancer when these dams finally break."

Chapter Eight

A BAD taste filled Hazrael's mouth. Smells of rotted meat and hot garbage attached to the inside of his nose. Gods and demons, it was hard to get away from the stench.

He rolled over onto his side and looked up at Oberon and Theodyne. "What did you do to me? I feel like I've been wading in a shit bucket."

Oberon reached out a hand and helped him to his feet. "Sorry. Some of the residual energy leaked over into the corporeal."

"Did you find anything? Were the necromancers there?"

Theodyne shook his head solemnly. His hands were folded in front of him. "No. But we did encounter something outside my area of expertise. I'll have to consult the archives to figure out a way to heal you."

Even the news that he'd not been healed did not diminish the relief that the necromancers did not remain inside him. Hazrael put a hand to his chest and sagged against the table. "That's a relief."

Oberon frowned. "A relief?"

"Yes. I was only worried that they still had a hold of me in some way." He waved a hand in front of his face. "I trust Theodyne will find a way to cure the rest. It will take time is all."

Theodyne gave a fractured smile. "Your faith in me is appreciated. I shall endeavor not to fail you. Now if you'll excuse me, I believe I hear food and sleep calling me."

Hazrael watched Theodyne leave and waited for the door to close before he turned to Oberon. "He's disappointed he didn't have the answers."

"We both are. However, healing is not my first calling. I believe it is with Theodyne, though he came about it in a most unusual way."

"Prison?" Hazrael guessed and was not surprised to see Oberon give a thoughtful nod of acknowledgment.

"He learned a lot of skills useful to the alchemists during his incarceration."

Hazrael didn't doubt that for a moment. The alchemists were masters at finding those who would prove *useful* to the brotherhood. Every student who ever walked through the elemental-infused walls of the Gold School had been deemed useful to the art of alchemy. It wasn't an altruistic act that brought practitioners into the fold, but one of survival. If there were no longer those willing to learn the craft, it would simply die out, making room for some other form of magical discipline to take its place.

Rather than contemplating a future that had not yet come to pass, Hazrael started for the door.

"Where are you going?" Oberon called out behind him.

"To the yard. I might be able to at least help a little today." As it was, Nico was going to think Hazrael had taken the lazy way out of doing as he'd promised. That was not the case.

"It's near dark. They'll have gone in by now."

Hazrael glanced to the window. The sun was a large ball of orange on the horizon.

"I have to go."

Oberon started after him but then seemed to think better of it.

Was he not coming along to guard the prisoner?

Not willing to waste the opportunity to move about freely, Hazrael started running, tearing down the stairs from the tower as if the hounds of all the hells nipped at his heels. He'd not done one thing he'd agreed to since he'd woken in a strange time. The drawings were only rudimentary, and the catapult design pulled from another's imagination centuries ago. What had he contributed but confusion, strife, and fear? Not one thing that improved the school, students, alchemy, or defenses.

By the time he arrived in the yard, twilight spread across the grounds in dark fingers. All the students had gone inside, and the materials were covered for the night. The wagons had been returned to the barn.

Disappointment poured through his body, as the air he drew into his lungs. He bent at the waist, trying to catch his breath. His breath sounded harsh in the quiet yard.

The schematic!

Hazrael looked around, but the animated charcoal rendering was nowhere to be seen. Panic speared him, paralyzed him momentarily. He doubted Nico or Journeyman Lorelli would have allowed the picture to remain outside—not at night when there was no one there to watch over it.

He went back into the school and straight to the dining hall. There had to be someone there at this time of evening—someone to tell him where the—

Lit globes exploded as he walked. Each time he passed one, it burst into fragments. Flames shot higher. The tiny elementals inside shook their flickering fists in umbrage.

Fear took to the air in waves of crystalline spores. He backed up out of their way. The manifestations followed him, chasing after him. He swatted at the little creatures, not knowing how to make them leave him alone. Something moved out of the corner of his eyes. A ghost of a person. Something neither alive nor dead but caught somewhere in between.

It took him a moment to realize the person was him, his reflection in the glass of a curio cabinet.

His brief view in the mirror a few days before had not prepared him for the overall effect of how he now appeared in whole. Transformation from boy to man had happened in the blink of an eye. His body was no longer that of a callow youth, but an adult who had experienced the cruelest of fates imaginable. Evidence of his corruption showed in every jagged line and wicked sigil carved on his body.

The tiny crystal bubbles flickered in the lights from the globes that remained. They no longer tried to attack him, but hovered around his head as if they too inspected his reflection.

He looked like something from a child's tale. Long white hair streamed down his back, the sides tied out of the way with a leather thong. Pale skin glowed eerily in the low lighting. Silvery scars shone with an inhuman luminescence.

Hiding his face, he turned away from the reflection of the stranger he'd become. No wonder those who saw him feared him so. He was wretched and hideous to look at.

The crystals continued to follow him, a flock of trained birds flying with their master.

"You should probably hide. No telling what the others will say if they see you."

They didn't pay attention to him. Maybe they didn't respond to verbal commands, but only emotions. Hazrael allowed himself to be still, both in body and mind.

It didn't work.

"Oh well, it was worth a try. Come on, then."

He turned down the corridor that led to the dining hall. Journeyman Lorelli was there, speaking with a couple of apprentices Hazrael recognized from the build. One of them tapped Journeyman Lorelli on the arm to get his attention.

Relief washed through the man, only to be replaced moments later by puzzlement. "What are those?"

"Crystals manifested by emotion, I gather. Pay no attention to them." Hazrael tried to redirect the conversation, but all three students stared at him in wonderment. "Have you seen Master Nico?"

Silently Journeyman Lorelli pointed into the dining hall.

Hazrael entered. The students followed him inside, along with the crystals. Diners stopped to stare. Conversations quieted. Hazrael chose to pretend the tiny beads were not swirling around his head like planets in orbit around a giant sun.

Nico sat in a back corner with Theodyne. They leaned in, having an intense conversation, if Hazrael read their body positions correctly.

He approached the table with his hands folded in front of him, head down in a show of respect. The only indication he had that they'd noticed him was the startled exclamation from Theodyne. Either from the crystals or the fact he was not accompanied by Oberon, he didn't know and rightly didn't care at the moment.

Nico rose. "Can we do something for you, Hazrael?"

"The drawing, it's no longer in the yard."

"I assume you mean the one you sent spinning." Nico pointed to a small box on the table. "It's inside the box. We will take it out again in the morning."

"Has there been much progress on the wagons?"

"Almost finished." Nico picked up the box and handed it to Hazrael. "We'll need that at the grounds early."

The tightness faded from Hazrael's chest, and the crystals dissolved with a tinkling of ice hitting the frozen ground. He clutched the box tightly. "Do you think we can start on the catapults tomorrow?"

"I'll ensure the materials are in the yard."

Hazrael bowed. "Thank you."

He turned to leave, and Theodyne called after him. "You can join us for a meal if you would like."

For once, Hazrael wanted nothing more than to be alone and contemplate what had happened during the course of the day. Not to flog himself with regrets and recriminations, but to contemplate how he could use them to his advantage in the future. With the elementals no longer speaking to him, he had to find other ways to integrate. To study and relearn those skills he'd forgotten.

"I thank you for your invitation, but I believe I'll take a tray to my room. If I may be allowed to have more paper and ink, I would be much appreciative."

Nico made a gesture to Journeyman Lorelli. "Make sure he gets everything he needs."

"Yes, Master Nico."

Hazrael didn't wait for them to ask any questions or make comments. He bowed to bid them good evening, then crossed the dining hall to the sideboard. He ladled up a bowl of soup and took a hunk of bread, then poured a goblet of watered-down wine. It was a meager meal but all he wanted at the moment.

Journeyman Lorelli walked silently beside him, a wraithlike escort, up to the cell where Hazrael lived. Odd how he would seek refuge there now. He doubted he was safe from the necromancers, no matter where he went, but at least the room had grown oddly comforting and familiar. For what he planned to do, he wanted no one to interrupt. Hazrael had no idea if the plan was dangerous or even feasible.

At the door he thanked Journeyman Lorelli and stepped inside. This time alchemical keys didn't jangle in the lock. Hazrael turned to stare at the door. Had his guard forgotten, or had Nico had a change of heart? It didn't matter either way. He didn't plan to go anywhere other than his bed and desk.

Hazrael set his tray and the box down, then stepped to the middle of the room and flung his arms outward. Nothing. How to make the tiny crystals materialize on command? Not through body movements alone.

Perhaps if he tapped into the panic he'd felt in the corridor. Were they tied to that emotion? If so, then why hadn't they manifested before? He'd been panicked plenty of times since waking and had spent that time without the benefit of so overt a display.

Fire began to glow in the fireplace behind him. Hazrael turned and stared into the dancing flames of Anjufer's face.

"Sent to spy on me while I work? I wondered why they hadn't locked the door, but I hadn't expected my keeper to come through the flue."

Anjufer didn't answer; he only blinked what passed for eyes.

"If you'll excuse me. I want to work in private."

Elementals were often stubborn and single-minded. Anjufer was no exception to the rule. He remained in the fireplace, watching with those glowing eyes.

Hazrael turned his back on the elemental and swung his arms above his head. No crystals.

Heat and flame roared behind him. Anjufer came out of the grate, rising up in attack. Hazrael spun and lifted his arms, one to guard his face, the other outstretched in a defensive gesture. Thousands of crystals exploded from the palm of his hand and fit together like tiny bricks, blocking Hazrael from Anjufer's flames.

The fire elemental diminished and bowed. "You needed a bit of help to manifest the crystals."

"How did you know what I intended?"

"Just because you can't hear us, does not mean we can't hear you."

Hazrael moved his arm, and the wall constructed from the crystals slid to the side. "As I suspected—spying."

"No. Evaluating. How else are we to know if you have been redeemed?"

"Redemption is a long way off for me, if it's even possible." He walked around the crystal wall, staring up at it.

It appeared to be a solid piece of unblemished glass. There was a slight reflection, as with any other piece of similar substance. Hazrael raised his hands to touch the surface. Though it looked solid, his hand moved through the plane and to the other side.

"Extraordinary."

He pulled his hand back and moved around to the opposite side. "Come at me again."

Anjufer rose, high and hot. His fiery body hit the crystal wall and bounced off. "It will not allow me access."

"Is it because you are flame and the crystals are of the earth?"

"Those crystals did not manifest from the earth, Hazrael. They are from spirit."

Hazrael staggered under the knowledge. Even at the height of his alchemical powers, he'd never been able to raise a substance from thin air. In this case perhaps not so thin. The energy contained within the human spirit was endless. However, he'd never tapped into that side, nor had the energies come to his defense.

"I need to test this against a human opponent."

"You need to test it against a necromancer."

Hazrael raised a brow at Anjufer. "We are a bit short of them at the moment. An alchemist will have to do."

"Allow me."

Before Hazrael had time to agree, Anjufer had gone up the flue and into the school. No telling where he'd go or who he'd bring back, but that was probably to Hazrael's advantage. Test results were more conclusive if done without prejudice.

He lifted his hand and closed his fingers. The wall collapsed into its individual parts. Crystals formed lines behind Hazrael, straight enough to make an army general proud. He twirled his finger to see what they'd do, but the command went unnoticed. Why did they respond to some commands and not others? He tried a few more hand signals, to no avail. They were as stoic as the stones that made up the school's foundations.

The door opened, and a bolt of lightning shot inside the room. The crystals formed a shield. The current hit with tremendous force, pushing Hazrael back a few feet. The shield held.

Theodyne stepped into the room. "Quite impressive."

"Try to put your hand through it." Hazrael watched with interest as Theodyne came across the same problem as Anjufer; his hand didn't pass through.

"Amazing. What are you going to do with it—them?"

"I don't know. I want to see the range of what they can do and how I can control them before I do anything with them. I'm not sure if they work independently of my will or not." If anything they were a combination of both. "I can throw them up and out if I'm threatened, but I can't direct them in any capacity when there isn't one."

Theodyne rubbed his jaw. "We need Oberon's expertise on this."

Anjufer, who had taken up his former spot in the fireplace, left again. Hazrael supposed it was to go and fetch the headmaster.

"I'd intended to work on this alone," Hazrael lamented.

"Judging from what you just told me, you weren't having much success alone."

"But it seems to be headed into the realm of group project."

Theodyne raised a brow. "Aren't most? We are stronger together than we are as one."

"I know the doctrines. I only meant that in this instance I wanted something solid to show to the Adepts' Council before I made my experiments known."

Without warning, Theodyne struck out again. This time with a material weapon. The shield shimmered and elongated to protect Hazrael's head.

"All right. So your friends are serious about helping to protect you from harm, but they haven't struck out in defense."

Hazrael considered the problem for a moment. "Perhaps if it were a barrage of hits and not just a singular strike they would rise to the challenge."

"Good thinking. But you would know they are coming, and if you control them, then you'd be ready for it and not necessarily evoke the response we're after." Theodyne rubbed his chin in thought. "I'm afraid it's going to have to come down to you being attacked when you're unsuspecting of the action."

Hazrael knew he stared at Theodyne, but it really couldn't be helped. He did manage to close his jaw.

Oberon entered the room to the utter quiet of Hazrael's disbelief. "I sense something has gone afoul?"

"No. Not at all." Hazrael moved away from Theodyne. "The master here was just giving his opinion on how best to proceed in testing my defenses."

When he reached the other side of the room, Hazrael turned and unleashed a jolt of current straight at Theodyne, who jumped out of the way, but not before volleying a similar bolt back. Crystals glittered in the air, dispersing enough to send the charge ricocheting off the fragments. Both Theodyne and Oberon ducked to get out of the way of the stray energy.

"Impressive, but that's still not defensive." Theodyne rose.

Oberon looked appalled. "What are you trying to do?"

"Get his minions to defend him."

Oberon turned to Theodyne with a frown. "Should he even be doing this right now? Give him a chance to heal."

Theodyne held a hand to his chest in offense. "It wasn't my idea."

"Leave him alone, Oberon. I came up here to work on unlocking what these crystals can do." The room had never felt smaller to Hazrael. All he wanted was to work on getting the crystals to comply. He didn't want to have to go through the entire Adepts' Council in order to work with a substance he produced. How was that even helpful?

Oberon gave Theodyne a look, as if the reprimand were his fault.

Hazrael grew weary of the company and made a shooing motion toward the door. "Out. Both of you. Let me work on this alone."

"Hazrael," Oberon began, but Hazrael held up his hand for silence.

"Go. I will see you in the morning."

They both left, leaving him alone with the fire elemental that remained in the grate.

"They are not pleased you sent them away." Anjufer crossed what he used for arms.

"I can't help that. They were going to stand here and argue about the course of my healing, training, or integration back into the order, and I'd get nothing from the night but pain in my head." Hazrael sat down at the desk and picked up the spoon he'd brought up with his tray. Hungrier than he'd expected, he tucked into his meal.

"What you need in order to control the crystals is already there inside you."

Hazrael filled his spoon and took a bite, considering Anjufer's words as much as the source. He swallowed. "Why are you helping me?"

"Because we watched you try and protect the drawing infused with your energy. You risked your life to get it back without thought to self. It was a noble act. One performed by the part of you that remains an alchemist." Anjufer blinked and moved out of the fireplace to hover

over Hazrael. Warmth from the body of flames licked at Hazrael's skin. "Because we have seen your memories and know of your torture."

"I would prefer you stay out of my head unless you plan to start talking to me again." He took another spoonful of soup, not caring if Anjufer agreed or not. Did they not see that by invading his mind but not allowing him access to them, they were as guilty as the necromancers?

"I will consult with the others, but I make no promises."

"Then neither will I."

There had to be a way to keep them out of his head unless he wanted them there. He'd just forgotten the mechanism.

He finished his soup and drank the wine, then crawled into bed. "If you wouldn't mind diminishing, Anjufer. I want to sleep."

Anjufer lowered his flicker to a small flame but stayed in the grate. Hazrael didn't know whether to watch over his sleep or to ensure he didn't move from his bed, but it didn't matter. As soon as he rolled over and put the covers over his shoulders he fell into a deep, dreamless sleep.

Chapter Nine

OBERON LOOKED over the files the journeymen had been going over from the Agia's prisons. All students studied the canon of laws set down by Akabar Kolhen. It was imperative they know and understand that even laws set down by men who governed the Dominicál city-states were integral to the fabric of their lives.

Journeyman Lorelli touched the top folio. "This case is very interesting."

"Why is that?"

"Asgarian is a cleric of some renown."

Oberon opened the file and skimmed through the abstract written by the students who had reviewed the case. Rodderick Asgarian had been the cleric attached to the Agia household three years before. He had written to his *desan*, requesting aid from the basilica in Gusan.

"He requested aid, and for that he was imprisoned?" Oberon glanced through the file, stopping to read that the official charges were conspiracy to usurp a seated *prolate*. "I believe I will go to the cathedral and have a talk with Asgarian."

The trip down the mountain was unsettlingly quiet. He'd chosen to take first-level master Celsi with him on this most important task. Celsi had gained his masters' robes a few weeks before Hazrael returned from oblivion. He was new to the position but was very well versed in the running of the Gold School and had served in the capacity of secretary since Oberon's elevation to headmaster.

Celsi turned a speculative glance Oberon's way. "The trees are uneasy."

So was Oberon. Too many curious and distressing events had unfolded in the last few weeks—not least of which came out of Hazrael's fingertips when he felt threatened. Oberon had never seen anything like it in all his years with the alchemists.

"Keep to a steady pace. If the necromancers wanted us dead, we'd already be so."

Celsi held his reins in white knuckles. "If the master was killed at the Agia's, then why are they still an influence and threat? Shouldn't their minions have perished after the conflagration?"

"That is assuming the *prolates'* forces were able to kill the *Necromon*—the primogenitor of them all. If he is still in play, then he can resurrect his forces. It was never a permanent solution, no matter what Nico would have you believe." Oberon felt mildly uncomfortable about speaking so about Nico to another master, even a first-level one. "Don't get me wrong, I believe he did that to ease the fears of the apprentices and journeymen. A general panic is not conducive to study."

"It's not conducive to protecting ourselves from danger either." Celsi's blue eyes flashed in annoyance. "I'd rather know all the information to better understand the enemy and plan a strategy."

"Master Jolen's testimony from his time in Gusan is very specific about the abilities of the necromancers to construct beings from the blood, flesh, and remains of the fallen. Whole persons are not required to configure legions of soldiers." The thought alone was enough to make a person ill. It defiled the senses.

Oberon had not been to Delaneux since the night of the conflagration. Reports had not been forthcoming with anything close to regularity or accuracy. There was too much turmoil. Too many concerns left to twist in the wind. Oberon didn't like it a bit, but it was outside the purview of the alchemists and in the hands of the *prolates*. It was up to them and their guards to appoint a new *prolate* and see order come to the city-state. At least this trip would afford Oberon a chance to see for himself how much the *prolates* had accomplished or if their promises had been empty.

The mood of the town when they reached the gates of Delaneux was subdued. Guards from both the Houses of DiCarni and Rinni stood at the sentry box, checking papers before people entered the city proper.

The guard wearing the colors of the DiCarni hit his mate on the arm. "It's the headmaster from the Gold School. Open the gates."

The gate swung open, and Oberon nodded in thanks as he and Celsi rode through. At first glance the streets looked no different from those of any other town in the city-state of Calabris. People were walking along the open-air market purchasing food for their table or materials for clothing. The only difference was the unusual quiet that pervaded the square. For a market day, there were hardly any noises from the crowds. All transactions were concluded in near whispers.

Celsi turned to Oberon. "I don't like this one bit. It's unnatural."

That was the exact word Oberon would have used to describe the scene.

"Can you feel anything untoward in the elementals? Do they sense a disturbance?"

Celsi frowned and shook his head. "No, not that they will admit."

Oberon left it at that. Elementals talked when and if they wanted and not until. "Let's go straight to the cathedral. We'll take a tour of the town when we're finished there."

They guided their horses in the direction of the cathedral. Spires rose up above the tree line, calling the faithful to commune with the Gods. As they passed the Agia family graveyard, Oberon reined in his mount.

The wrought-iron fence had been torn down. Holes peppered the ground where the posts had once stood. Even the crypts were gone. The mound had been leveled and dirt tilled under. White covered the ground like snow.

Oberon steered his horse through the gates and to the area where the crypt used to be. He dismounted and bent down, then lifted up some of the substance to study it. "Salt."

"They've purified the graves of the Agia's family line." Celsi jumped down off his horse and came to bend down near Oberon. "I wonder who ordered this?"

"The *prolates*. I don't believe this order came from Master Nico. Not this way." Three years ago they'd confronted a necromancer in this very spot—one who had tried to resurrect the remains of Headmaster Donando.

"Could have been the clerics. Don't they have a ritual that uses salt to purify places of evil and keep those same influences from crossing the boundaries of a salt circle?"

Oberon raised a brow. "I seem to remember something along those lines, but I've not heard of such a practice in a long time." He brushed his hands together and rose. "Maybe we can put the question to Asgarian when we speak with him."

They were both deep in private contemplations when they mounted and rode on to the cathedral. Guards from several different houses patrolled the town, keeping the peace and ensuring the people were safe and secured. It had to be unsettling to know their *prolate* had been toppled by his brethren. How many citizens of Delaneux were as corrupt as her *prolate* had been? How many had been in league with his heinous activities?

A barracks of a fashion had been constructed outside the cathedral. There were bars across what few windows there were, which proclaimed the spaces were used for the liberated prisoners and not the visiting guards. Oberon wondered if they'd find Asgarian inside or if his brother clerics had taken him back into the fold.

The *desan* came down the steps and narrowed his eyes at Oberon's robe. "Headmaster?"

"Desan Olig."

The Delaneux *desan* was one of the more corrupt men of the cloth in the area. He should have been taken down when the Agia and his cronies had fallen. Not that Oberon had the stomach for such things, but if there was corruption within the ranks of the local clerics, it trickled from the top on down.

"We've come to speak with Rodderick Asgarian."

Desan Olig narrowed his cruel, beady eyes. "Why do you wish to speak with him? He's a heretic."

"According to your canon so are we, so I do not see the problem in letting us interview him."

"He's already been corrupted by one Godless influence. You'll only further the rift between his soul and the church."

"Then I shall petition the *demigoge* to have Asgarian released into the care and protections of the Gold School." It was a threat that Oberon did not make lightly, but he needed to use any leverage he had to speak with Asgarian.

Desan Olig sneered at the threat. "That ineffectual old woman? I doubt the new *demigoge* could even manage to stop hiding long enough to hear your case."

Oberon smiled knowingly. "Your candidate failed to win the Heavenly Throne, I take it. You know jealousy is a failing we strive to overcome in the study of alchemy, along with a host of other vices. You might want to explore that as you're thumping your book of holy writ at night."

The *desan's* face turned a horrible shade of red, then purple. "Begone! Begone, or I'll call the guards to have you arrested."

It might have been ill-advised, but Oberon laughed. "Do you honestly believe that the guards are going to arrest the Headmaster of the Gold School and take the word of a *desan* who—if my intuition is correct—has turned this city into his own personal fiefdom? That was never part of the *prolates'* plans."

The color rose higher in Desan Olig's face, if that was possible. "All evil must be stripped from the land and cleansed. That includes you demons in your so-called school."

Oh, this was a dangerous situation.

The *prolates* needed to move on elevating a new family to their ranks before they lost the whole of Calabris, and Delaneux in particular, to evangelical rantings. The *desan* shook with righteous indignation.

The local priest came out of the cathedral and clasped his hands together. "Headmaster Oberon, the Hierophant would like to speak with you, if you please?"

Oberon and Celsi exchanged glances. The Hierophant here in Delaneux? She hardly ever left her cloistered abbey on an archipelago located near the island city-state of Nequan.

Where the *demigoge* was the father of the holy order, the Hierophant was both mother and conscience. She was the keeper of church myths and mysteries, with the power of a seer. Wise and benevolent, she was said to possess powers that made most men tremble in fear.

Oberon started up the stairs, only to be blocked by Desan Olig.

"You will defile her supreme presence. I will not allow such in my city-state."

Oberon took a step closer, putting them almost nose-to-nose. "Your city-state? I had not heard the *prolates* had awarded you the seat. My congratulations on your appointment."

From the corner of his eye, Oberon saw the priest roll his eyes heavenward before he put his hand on Desan Olig's arm. "Come, it is almost time for prayers, and you know how Brother Benedict tends to spill the sacred feast before he manages to get it on the platter at the altar."

"Useless man. He needs to go to a silent order somewhere in the barbaric colonies." Desan Olig threw off the priest's touch. "As soon as I turn my back that heretic will be inside. I won't have it."

"It is not your decision, Desan Olig." The voice came from the top of the stairs. The timbre was feminine but low and throaty. The tone, commanding.

Oberon swallowed and stared. She was nothing as he'd imagined—she was more. She was a tall woman, with the presence of a battlefield general. Her long white robes covered her from neck to feet. A cowl came up to cover all but the front of her gray hair.

Desan Olig turned on her. His face was awash in shock, either at being caught abusing his power or blocking Oberon's path, he wasn't sure.

"Your Grace, I had not meant to imply—"

She cut off his words with the wave of an imperial hand.

She came down the stairs, proud head held high, balance perfect despite the fact her eyesight had been taken years before in a ritualistic blinding ceremony. Two attendants, in the pale blue robes of their order, walked behind her.

When the Hierophant reached them, she inclined her head in greeting. Her hands were folded in front of her, hidden in the bells of her flowing sleeves. "Walk with me, Headmaster Oberon. We have much to discuss."

"Yes, Your Grace."

Oberon fell into line beside the Hierophant. Their attendants trailed them at a discreet distance. The Hierophant's steps were slow yet assured. She did not walk that way because she had to, but to measure her steps as she did her words.

"Please do not look on the *desan* with anger. I fear his thoughts are muddled through disease." It wasn't the opening Oberon had expected her to make, but it explained a great deal.

"Do you fear he's been tainted by the necromancers?"

"No. Something grows in his head, but it is biological in nature, not metaphysical." Her milky gaze stared straight ahead. "I am having him sent to a monastery for reflection and study." At this she turned to Oberon with a crafty smile.

"I fear he won't like that, Your Grace."

"Perhaps not, but it will happen."

They walked through the heart of Delaneux and came to a stop at the place where the Agia's palace once stood. The yard was awash in white, a displaced snowstorm at the end of the summer. How much of the precious commodity of salt had been wasted, poured back into the ground to purify an area that had already been done so by fire?

"You see this as waste, Headmaster Oberon. You feel there were other ways to handle this situation without the bloodshed."

"It was not my decision to make. That rests on the heads of the *prolates.*"

"Ah, but your heart was against the act. It circles you as the moon revolves around the earth."

Her insight was as accurate as it was unnerving. Oberon didn't bother to deny or rebut the charge.

"No matter your feelings, it was the correct choice."

"Is that direct from the oracle where you receive your advice, or some other venue?"

Her serene expression never changed. "Mystic teachings of the oracle from the days of the Great Purge were written and recorded. My predecessor from that time wrote extensively on the return of the necromancers and the rift within the ranks of the church. Your order must hold firm, Headmaster Oberon. The alchemists hold the key to defeating the necromancers in this time."

A cold whisper shimmied down his spine. Hazrael. The Hierophant spoke of Hazrael.

It was no surprise to Oberon, since the alchemists had planned to utilize that strategy. Knowing the Hierophant was aware of Hazrael's significance was quite another matter.

"We will meet the challenge head-on and oust them from the city-states once and for all."

"I have no doubt." She raised her hand. "Send *him* to me."

"Your Grace, I fear he is not well at times."

"Then I shall go to him."

What was he supposed to say to that—disallow her to make the journey? No one with an ounce of sense or logic would dare refuse a request, or demand, from the Hierophant.

"As you wish, Your Grace."

Nico was not going to be pleased by this development, but knowing his penchant for gleaning information from every resource possible, Oberon had no fear Nico would use this unprecedented visit to the alchemists' advantage.

"We can be ready to travel back to the school upon your return. Your interview with Asgarian will give us time to prepare." She turned and started back for the cathedral. Her attendants fell into line behind her.

Celsi stood in astonishment. Those who didn't know the man well would not be able to tell from merely looking at him. Oberon knew, though, and it was telling. The first-level master had gone stock-still, as if under some kind of spell that turned him to marble.

Oberon brushed past Celsi. "Come, let us make good use of this time and do what we came here to do."

"Shouldn't I ride ahead to prepare the others for the Hierophant's arrival? She and her entourage will need overnight lodgings." Celsi had a point, but he was needed as both witness and reader during the interview.

"Under normal conditions I'd say yes, that would be proper, but I need you to read the elementals as I interview Asgarian."

Celsi began to walk beside Oberon back to the prison. "Master Nico is not going to thank you for blindsiding him and the rest of the Adepts' Council with a visit of this magnitude."

"No, but he will survive it and move on, as will we all."

"Are you forgetting what happened three years ago when Headmaster Donando let clerics into the school?"

Oberon stopped and spun on Celsi. "No. I don't need to be reminded. Donando was my friend and mentor, and his loss still pains me. You will do well not to lecture me on the particulars of his folly."

Celsi paled a bit. "I meant no offense, Headmaster, only to urge caution."

"There is a big difference between a group of clerics controlled by the Agia, and the Hierophant. Her position within the church—her very spiritual body—is incorruptible."

Celsi rolled his eyes. "No human is completely incorruptible. If that were the case, then as alchemists we've failed in our quest for perfection and enlightenment by forswearing oracles and ritual blindings."

Oberon wasn't offended; instead, he started walking again, considering Celsi's charge. "You are correct of a fashion."

"You agree with me?" Celsi seemed shocked by the fact Oberon might share the same view.

"Most earnestly, but then I wasn't speaking of the alchemists. We have chosen a path to enlightenment to the higher self by careful study in the physical world. By virtue of our path, we admit we are imperfect creatures. Hierophants are not the same—they are other—better. Born of a union between an oracle and a spirit elemental. Such a birth only happens once an age."

Oberon turned to see if his words showed impact. Celsi had to know this information. It was taught in classes on world religions. Perhaps the older, more obscure teachings were no longer part of the curriculum. He would have to check and make sure, though if that had been dropped, it was during Donando's tenure.

"How long do hierophants live, then?"

Oberon gave a low chuckle. "It is bad form to ask a human woman her age. Do you think any man brave enough to ask a hierophant?"

Celsi smiled. "Stop teasing. Do you know the answer?"

Oberon thought about it for a moment. "Spirit elementals are immortal beings, and oracles can live for hundreds of years. The product of such a union would be long-lived, but not immortal."

Celsi seemed to relax a bit. "That makes me feel better somehow."

"Why? The Hierophant only reports what she knows from readings put down by the oracles of old. Her task is to interpret those visions and apply them, not have visions of her own."

Celsi shook his head. "It is all very curious."

By the time they arrived at the makeshift prison, one of the clerics, and not Desan Olig, waited for them at the entrance.

The cleric bowed. "Asgarian awaits you in the rectory."

"Thank you."

Instead of going into the temporary prison, they were escorted to the living quarters of the local parish. It seemed Desan Olig had lost more than his mind.

Asgarian sat at the head of a long table, holding a cup with steaming liquid between his hands. He was a craggy-faced man of middle years, with dark hair shot through with silver. His eyes were so dark it was hard to tell pupil from iris. There was wisdom in those eyes—wisdom and anger.

He glanced up as Oberon and Celsi entered the room. "Ah, the headmaster." He narrowed his eyes and studied Celsi's robe. "And a first-level master, if my knowledge of robe nomenclature is correct."

Celsi bowed. "You are correct. Master Celsi at your service, Cleric Asgarian."

Asgarian made a dismissing motion with his hand. "Do not fall back on formality. I've spent three years in the Agia's prison. I know nothing of formality these days. Please, sit with me and have some tea."

They both said thank you and took places on either side of Asgarian. The fallen cleric poured both alchemists tea and then sat back against his chair. "Now, what can I do for you?"

"What can you tell us about the Agia's associates three years ago? Any information you can give us will be helpful in defeating the necromancers."

Asgarian raised his brow. "You cut right to the bone, don't you, Headmaster?"

"I don't believe in using subterfuge when so much is at stake. It wastes precious time."

Asgarian let out a pained laugh. "If only I had known that three years ago, I would have gone straight to the alchemists and bypassed my own order."

"It's a bit late to admonish or lament the mistakes of the past, but you can help now." Celsi leaned forward and offered comfort in the form of a surplice he pulled from his pocket.

Shock moved through Oberon. He hadn't known the young master carried such an item.

"I believe this is yours."

Asgarian gave a grunt of sound and reached for the embroidered material. "I doubt I have a right to even wear this. I've left the order.

It's the least I could do when they failed to back me or ask for my release."

Oberon canted his head. "Who refused?"

"Desan Olig. He was as thick with the Agia as Cesare Medovin and the *Necromon*."

"The Hierophant says the *desan* is not infected by the necromancers."

Asgarian lifted a shoulder. "I agree. He's not under their influence, but he's been changed by them. My guess is that instead of taking him into their fold, they chose to destroy his mind to make it impossible to get any of their secrets out."

Oberon had to know the answer to one basic question. "Why not kill him?"

"Oh, no. That's too neat. Too clean for the necromancers. They believe in causing chaos and dissent wherever they tread. Place a *desan* of limited judgment back into the fold and watch the church try to hush rumors of conspiracies and collusion."

Celsi raised a brow and brought his palms together on the table. "The church is guilty of that already."

Asgarian nodded. "True."

Oberon redirected the conversation. "What do you remember from your time in the Agia's household?"

"A terrible weight seemed to settle about the palace. The air was too thick to breathe. I can't say for sure how many of his staff were under the influence, but there were times when I feared I was the only one who recognized the peril. Strangers came and went at all hours of the day and night. Hooded figures who smelled of the most vile stenches imaginable." Asgarian made a face as if the stink remained up his nose.

"When you told your superiors, they turned the other way?"

"Worse. Didn't want to hear it." Asgarian looked down at the surplice in his hand. "I even tried to go to the *cardgrans*. It was felt that there wasn't enough evidence to proceed with in inquiry. It was my word against my *desan*. Politics as usual in the church."

Oberon placed his hand on the table. Palm flat. "Can you think of anything specific that might help us to defeat the necromancers? A weakness to exploit?"

Asgarian frowned in thought. Then his face lightened, as if he remembered a long-forgotten fact. "There is a strange phenomenon that happens when the necromancers are en masse. The temperature plummets by tens of degrees in only a few moments. Air becomes so cold it crystallizes. Fine, small ones, like grains of sand. Every breath drawn into your lungs hurts. Fear that the next one will be the one that shatters your insides like a hammer smashing ice."

Oberon had noticed it that day in the yard when Hazrael tried to claim the drawing. The wind had whipped fierce and bitter cold. The information was both blessing and curse. He'd hate to become suspicious of every cold snap in weather that might be naturally occurring, but if it helped to keep them safe, to help detect necromancers in the area, it was worth the apprehension.

"Is there anything else you can think of?"

"Only to ask how long I will continue to be incarcerated? I've done nothing wrong."

"I will discuss the matter with the *prolates*. The ultimate decision of who is to be released rests with them."

"Very well. I shall endeavor to survive." He seemed resigned to the fact. "I will say this much, our accommodations are much better now than they were under the Agia."

"I asked that you and the other inmates be housed in the cathedral until we sorted out your cases and reviewed the facts. I had no notion they'd build another prison." Shortsighted of Oberon, but he had other crises on his mind that night.

Asgarian waved his hand, dismissing the awkward apology. "It's of little consequence. I do have some friends who remain in the order, and some not without a bit of influence." At this a secret smile played along the edge of his mouth. "I have had word from those close to His Holiness. It seems he is taking the advice of Master Nico and having his guards tested. Those who pass are going into a special order he's named the *Sulith*."

The very name was taken directly from alchemical writings. The *Sulith* were those who had protected the elementals who worked to carve the principles of the *Elementica* onto the ruby tablet. How fitting the *demigoge* would use that to name his guards, loyal to him. Jolen had said that His Holiness was sympathetic and understanding of the alchemists. Perhaps with Demigoge Alexandre there might be a bridge built between the orders.

Oberon studied Asgarian's expression. He'd not revealed all. "What else?"

Asgarian pursed his lips, drew a circle on the table as he weighed his words, stalled for time. "He wants to include alchemists in the ranks of the *Sulith*. Their identities would be unknown by the other members as a means to keep them all safe from necromantic infection."

Oberon and Celsi's gazes collided.

Asgarian nodded. "I know. The news is huge. Shocking even. But while the concept may surprise, the reasons for the precautions are sound."

"I don't deny that, Asgarian. I only wonder if anyone has bothered to inform Master Nico."

Chapter Ten

HAZRAEL STOOD in the yard watching the catapult construction. So far he'd not been allowed to help lift any of the heavy pieces into place. He was relegated to directing as the biggest, brawniest of the students performed the physical tasks. Did they think he was too frail to complete the process? He might look as if a strong wind would knock him asunder, but he had more muscle than appeared.

A student in the robes of an apprentice came hurrying across the yard as if the hounds of all the hells were after him. "Master Nico! Master Nico!"

Nico took off to meet the frantic messenger halfway. Hazrael tried to hear the conversation, but their voices were lost to the sounds of hammering that echoed through the yard.

"Hazrael!"

He turned, apprehensive of the note in Nico's voice. What had he done now? He'd been standing outside in the yard since morning, in full view of students and faculty. Surely there wasn't anything to accuse him.

"It appears I'm being summoned." He handed the schematics to Journeyman Lorelli. "Keep them working while I see what it is I've done now."

Journeyman Lorelli scratched the side of his face. "I'm sure that isn't the reason he called you."

"Don't be so sure." Hazrael walked over to the tiny knot of people that seemed to grow around the apprentice. "What is it?"

Nico's expression of consternation was a new one for Hazrael. "You have a very esteemed visitor to see you."

"Me?" To say he was shocked at the news was not overstating the case. Who did he know who was considered esteemed and didn't already reside in the school?

Hazrael's stomach fell. One of the *prolates*. It had to be. What did they want with him?

"It seems the Hierophant has taken an interest in your plight and has come to see you."

Hazrael might have blinked a few times; he really wasn't sure. The only thing he knew was a sudden roaring in his ears and the inability to form a coherent thought. The Hierophant? Why would she leave her island sanctuary in order to come here? To see him? Had he caused some rift in the fabric of her heightened senses?

"I'm not sure why she should." Hazrael fell into step beside Nico as they started for the school. "I keep waiting for all the horrible things I did under the direction of the necromancers to come home to roost. A meeting with her is sure to break them loose."

Nico raised a brow and studied Hazrael as they walked. "Does that scare you?"

"Terrifies me."

He didn't know if that was what Nico wanted to hear, but it was no less the truth. With every word, action, and intent being weighed by those around him, he'd rather say nothing than lie.

When they entered the school, Master Rhone was frantically ordering apprentices around.

Nico approached the harried under-headmaster. "Where are they?"

"I put them in the atrium."

"Ah, yes. Good choice." Nico motioned for Hazrael to follow him. "I'm not sure if you remember where the atrium is located. It was only placed in the school a year before you were taken from us."

No, Hazrael remembered the room with a clarity that nearly choked him. He and Oberon had sneaked down there for a romantic tryst after the rest of the school was abed. Oberon had taken him up against one of the glass walls as moonlight filtered in, splashing across the floor and making the room shine with an otherworldly glow.

They entered the room that connected two of the older buildings. It had once been a breezeway, but now the sides were filled in with alchemists' glass. Exotic plants and flowering trees lined the edges of the room. Tables and chairs were set up along the colonnade for students to sit and study. The Hierophant and her entourage were seated at one of the tables. Oberon was there, as well as a first-level master Hazrael did not recognize.

The Hierophant rose, turning to him though she had no ability to see him. "Come, my child. Sit with me."

Hazrael shot a glance to Nico. He gave a subtle nod.

The Hierophant waved her hand in a dismissive manner at the others. "Leave us. I will speak with Master Hazrael alone."

Though Oberon and the other master appeared nervous, the entourage bowed and left without a word. They were no doubt used to the holy woman's eccentricities. Wanting to meet alone with a man who bore the marks of the necromancers was a risky proposition for one as important as she. Did she not fear for her safety, or had one of the prophecies she'd read told her the outcome of this meeting? It was hard to tell with a person who was the offspring of a spirit elemental and oracle.

Hazrael approached the table as she turned a graceful hand to indicate the chair.

"Sit. I will not crane my neck to look at you."

He did so, even as he found the sentence odd.

A smile curled the corner of her mouth. "What? You think because I cannot see in the physical sense of the word that I can't see you at all? I assure you my sight is better than most people who have two working eyes."

A shiver of wariness traveled down his spine. He must tread lightly with this woman.

"I would never presume to know what it is you see or do not see. It is not of my experience."

"A good, if evasive, answer." She folded her hands together. "The lines on your body bind you to the necromancers. The scars work as if to brand you in flesh and blood to them."

Hazrael turned away from those milky eyes that saw too much. "They tortured me to place them. I fought them, but it was useless. They had me and my powers subdued before I ever woke to find myself in their clutches."

"I know." The Hierophant bestowed a benevolent smile on him. "Your pain is as dear as my own. The marks are called the Kiss of Death and work very much as a lodestone."

"If that is true, then why didn't Masters Oberon and Theodyne find the link?"

"Because it is like no other one the necromancers use. They were simply not seeing it."

How many other cases were there that the alchemists had missed? Cold surrounded Hazrael, drove into his heart as an icy spike. He tried not to react, but those unseeing eyes of the Hierophant noticed. "How do I get rid of them?"

"You don't. Not yet. I came to warn you that to allow your brethren to remove the marks at this critical time will be detrimental to their mission in defeating the necromancers. The Kiss of Death must remain on your skin for now. Use them as a way to draw them to you when you are ready for the confrontation."

"How do I protect myself and the rest of the alchemists until such a time? Surely the necromancers use them daily to gain intelligence on our plans."

The Hierophant raised a hand in caution. "Not necessarily." That same graceful hand indicated the walls that surrounded them. "You are well fortified here. The necromancers will only know where you reside but will have no way to penetrate the barriers of the alchemists' spells. Your fellow alchemists have already learned how to remove influence from the minds of infected students. The necromancers will no longer use such means to invade your ranks from within. The next attack will be full frontal and without mercy."

Hazrael leaned forward. "What have you seen?"

She frowned as if looking into a memory long ago and far away. "Prophecies, portents, and visions are not written in stone. They are scrawled on paper or animal hide with ink or charcoal. Some are passed down verbally and are contained within the catalogs and volumes of a Hierophant's mind. They can be erased with the simple act of one man."

Hazrael begged to differ. There was nothing simple about the actions of any man. Not of the alchemists, *prolates,* or clerics.

"My function is to let the prophecies be known so countermeasures can be set in place and the future altered."

Hazrael frowned. "How do you know if the actions meant to defeat the necromancers will, in fact, cause the future as you see it come to pass? Every action and reaction has a consequence. Oftentimes they are unintended, unforeseen, and detrimental to the cause."

She gave a cagey smile. "You are wise beyond your years, Hazrael."

"I only wish I could remember what I did during those seventeen I missed."

Her expression turned grim, and she reached out a hand to rest on his arm. "Do not be so quick to want them back. The spirit elementals protect you from the knowledge for your own good. Allow them to do their part to shield you from the truth."

Hazrael felt himself pale by degrees. His head spun as dizziness washed over him. He tried to swallow, but his mouth had gone dry. So they hadn't completely deserted him as he'd thought. They were only blocking him from himself. Was that what Oberon and Theodyne had found when they tried to see if it was the influence of the necromancers? But wouldn't Theodyne, as a *terrathant,* know the spirit elementals when he saw them?

Honestly he resented the interference without words. The elementals had always spoken to him before. He'd known of their presence in his soul since he'd been very small. Now, nothing, and yet apparently they were as much a part of him as they'd always been.

The Hierophant turned to a large cast-iron stove that heated the room during the cold winter months. "If you wish to eavesdrop, Anjufer, do not be so foolish as to believe I will not know you are there."

Flame grew to life in the belly of the stove. Bright eyes blinked out at them from the wavering tongues of fire. "The years have been kind to you, Astara."

She nodded in acknowledgment of the compliment.

Hazrael sat very still, not wishing to invade what looked like a private reunion. Was Anjufer so familiar with the Hierophant he used her birth name?

She waved her hand in an imperial manner to Hazrael. "You may return to your duties. I shall speak with the fire elemental at length. Please tell my entourage and your brothers I will not be disturbed but will send for them when I am ready to go to my chambers."

Hazrael performed a slight bow, feeling in some way she probably saw him. "Yes, Your Grace."

He went to the end of the atrium and through the door into the school proper. Several masters, journeymen, and a few apprentices, along with the entourage, stood in the hallway. When he exited he was immediately accosted by the rush. All but the entourage. They stood back from the crowd, a serene pool in the middle of a stormy sea.

He turned to the Hierophant's entourage. "The Hierophant is in a private conversation with the fire elemental, Anjufer. She wishes not to be disturbed at this time."

The others deferred to a tall woman with power behind her blue eyes. She bowed her head in acquiescence. "As she requests."

Nico, Oberon, and the first-level master he'd seen before flanked Hazrael. They all talked at once, trying to gain information from him.

He put his hands up to ward off the verbal assault. "I'll start by saying I will not discuss what she said to me, only that for now, and as long as I stay inside these walls, I am safe."

Nico frowned. "You are a target as you suspected."

"I'm a bit more than that." He scratched at his face, then belly—everything itched at once. It was maddening. "I seem to remember a spell from one of my earlier lessons that allowed a protective cover to form over an area. Is there a way to erect one on the school grounds?"

A look passed between Oberon and Nico. "Yes, there is. Why do you want to know?"

"Because each time I step outside to direct the building, I place myself and the rest of us in immediate danger. With a shield, I'll be able to continue to work and not place us at risk until we're ready for me to do so."

Oberon frowned. "Ready for you to do so? What do you mean by that exactly?"

"I would think it is obvious. My place is not only to help you to understand and learn how to defeat the necromancers, but to get them where you want them for the final battle." Oddly enough, Hazrael didn't feel anything close to the panic he'd believed he would, but instead a sea of calm kept him centered, filled him with purpose. If his fate was to sacrifice himself in order to bring peace to the Dominicál city-states, so be it. It might even bring him a measure of penitence for all the wrongs he'd done under the necromancers' influence.

In order to defeat the necromancers, they had to build the tools of war. Surely there were other substances to be had besides the catapults and crossbows they'd already contemplated. There had to be something more, a specific need they had yet to fill.

Hazrael turned to Oberon. "Did you ever get your scrying bowl to work?"

Oberon frowned at the sudden change in topic. "There hasn't been time to test it again."

"Then I suggest we go to your workroom to do so. I also have an idea that might make it easier to communicate though ranks and troops without having to stop and pull out a scrybowl."

The idea had come to him as he'd watched Oberon with the large golden bowl, then coalesced when he'd worked with the crystal manifestations.

"All right."

Oberon and Hazrael started for the workroom.

"Hazrael? Aren't you going to finish overseeing the catapult building for me?" Nico called after their retreating forms.

Hazrael turned. "I dare not go back into the yard until the barrier is raised. Once it is in place, I'll spend every day under the sun building you an army of catapults."

Nico gave a quick nod. "Do you mind if I join you? I'd like to see this new idea you have."

Hazrael smiled. "I would never be so bold as to ban you from going to a room in your own school. That's beyond even my arrogance."

They climbed the stairs to the workroom at the very top of the tower. Oberon opened the door, then moved out of the way to let them inside.

Quickly Hazrael lifted his hand and let the substances he needed call to him. Gold, water, sand. He hurried and collected the ingredients, then picked up a small bowl while Oberon and Nico took up places beside him.

"My idea was to take your storm spheres, Nico, and use them as small devices for communication. The gold flakes will give you greater distance. The water is the connection medium. Since the sphere will be closed, there will be no evaporation." Hazrael dropped a thumb-sized amount of sand along with a pinch of gold flakes into the bowl.

With a quick, efficient hand, he swirled the contents, lifting them from the shallow bottom to create a perfect sphere about the size of a robin's egg. One end he left open to pour in the water. Hazrael submerged the sphere into the water. Bubbles rose to the surface, displacing the air inside the sphere as it filled.

When it was full, he lifted it and ran his thumb over the hole, closing it off. He handed the sphere to Nico. "You take the first one. Let me make another one, and then we can test them."

Nico held it up to the light coming through the window. "If this works, you will have revolutionized the way we communicate with our brothers. Not only over distance, but to make it portable enough to slip into a pocket or purse."

"And not have to worry if the person you wish to communicate with is at the bowl at the moment. Or expend the energy to communicate over distances on the astral plane." Oberon leaned in and watched as Hazrael added the powders to the dish to make a second scry sphere.

When he'd completed the tiny device, he filled it with water, sealed it, and handed it to Oberon. "Now I suggest you go to opposite ends of the school and make sure they serve the purpose I've intended. If not, we'll try until we get it right."

Oberon took the sphere and weighed it in his palm. "It's so light. If I didn't feel the solidity of it, I'd never know it was there."

Nico squeezed his sphere. "I'll return to the yard and see about the building. Expect a report from me shortly."

Hazrael watched Nico as he walked from the room, and a sense of satisfaction he'd not known in a long time grew from a tiny kernel to a bloom.

"You've done a wonderful thing here."

Oberon's voice cut into Hazrael's contemplations. Hazrael looked into those deep green eyes he'd loved so well and felt a tinge of loss. Since he'd been returned to the fold, Oberon treated him as if there had been nothing between them but friendship. Quite the bitter pill, but not unexpected. Who would want to give his heart to someone whose skin was etched with the sins of his past? He'd be best served if he concentrated on what he could do for the alchemists in the short time he would be with them again, and not on what he'd lost.

There was peace to be found in knowing his end was near. It wasn't even a question that the necromancers meant to kill him when next they met. Death permeated every aspect of his life now.

He finally turned to Oberon. "Let's wait and see if it works first. I'd hate to excite anyone's anticipation with a device that might not even work."

"It was an inspired idea."

"I have to do what I can in the time I have left. I have so much to make up for, so many years spent laboring under a necromanical agenda without having a voice with which to protest. It's the least I can do."

Oberon's gaze softened, dropped to Hazrael's lips. "Did the Hierophant tell you of your death?"

"She didn't have to. I can feel it creeping up on me like shadows." Hazrael glanced down at his arms. "Am I really alive now? I was held by the necromancers for so long, am I nothing more than a walking corpse?"

Oberon's look of compassion nearly undid Hazrael. "By virtue you can even ask the question, I have to conclude you are very much alive."

Hazrael took Oberon's hand from where it rested on the worktable and placed it against his chest. "Can you feel my heart beat? Or is that only my imagination?"

Oberon's gaze warmed. The space between them shimmered with desire. Oberon cleared his throat. "It beats strong."

Hazrael covered Oberon's hand, pushing it closer to his ruined flesh. "It's been so long since I've known a loving touch."

Oberon looked away and tried to pull back.

Rejection cut through Hazrael like an icy blade. Perhaps he was wrong. He could still feel pain, still hurt. Still wanted and needed love, even if it wasn't to be. The feeling left a hollow pit in the core of his soul.

Heartbroken, Hazrael let Oberon's hand fall away. He put space between them and gave a sharp nod. "I'll leave you to your work on the communication bowl. I'm sure there are other things I should do to prepare. Have Nico alert me if the small sphere fails."

He barely made it from the room before tears swam in his eyes. He bit his bottom lip to keep it from trembling. Experiencing Oberon's rejection was worse than waking and knowing he'd lost seventeen years of his life to the necromancers. His body and soul might be tainted by his actions, but he was trying to make amends, trying to live by the codex as set down in the *Eye of Truth*.

He hurried down the stairs and turned at the corridor that led to the library. There was no one to watch him now, no one to keep him from searching the stacks for a way to cure himself of his faulty memory while maintaining the scars on his arms and body. Each scar was keyed to a particular memory, he was almost sure. Judging from the way they lit up or bled when a particular recollection surfaced, it had to be some form of necromanical spell that kept them active. Not merely as a lodestone, but as a record for what they'd done to him.

Before he ever touched the doorknob, the library opened to him. The heavy doors swung open without the normal creaks of wood and hinge. A host of spirit elementals stood in the center of the cavernous room, awaiting his arrival.

Music streamed in the sunbeams that poured through the windows. Notes, sweet and light, danced along the bookshelves from paper, leather, and ink. It was a tease in the worst possible way, as the song swept around him, generated from the spirit elementals, but did not come from inside him. Not as it once had.

Hazrael walked toward them. "If you mean to taunt me with your music, I hope you realize it is beneath you."

They looked to one another as if trying to determine the source of his bitterness. As if they didn't already know.

"I'm going to find a book that will help me unlock the memories buried in the Kiss of Death. Now you can either assist me or leave me."

The being standing before him raised a hand and sent a blast from an upraised palm that hit Hazrael square in the chest. The impact sent him flying back into the now closed doors.

He sat up and shook his head. His ears rang, but not from music this time. Perhaps it was impolitic to correct a full elemental, but they weren't perfect creatures. They had flaws and foibles like any other sentient being. Hazrael hadn't had time to raise his hand to send up a crystal shield in defense.

The circle of spirit elementals advanced on him. They stood, towering above him, their shimmery images fading in the light. *Do not think to tamper with the Kiss of Death.*

"Not tampering, accessing," Hazrael corrected those assembled.

He rose to his feet, facing off against their anger as if it meant nothing to him. The pit of despair ruptured by Oberon's rejection split wider, engulfing him. The Hierophant had been wrong. The elementals had not wanted to protect him. They wanted to torture him as the necromancers had.

He started forward again. "Either I find a book to proceed in a safe fashion, or I discover my own method. Either way I'm going to do it."

The center spirit elemental lifted her hand, and Hazrael raised his, but no crystals shot into the air. He was alone. Defenseless.

This time the bolt hit him hard enough that he awoke in his bed hours later.

His chest ached as if he'd gotten kicked by an angry horse square in the sternum. Full night had fallen, but flames from the fireplace sent a golden light through the room. He sat up on the bed and looked down at his chest, pulling his shirt away. A dark purple bruise radiated out in a starburst pattern.

All right, he hadn't gotten a book. He hadn't even been allowed into the stacks, but at least he truly knew where he stood with the spirit elementals. It was worse than a forsaking. They had declared themselves his enemy. This time they had attacked. Hot tears burned behind his eyes, but he bit them back and reached for a center of calm. No matter what he had to do, he had to persevere. There was no room for vengeance in that quarter. He'd just have to try and avoid them in order to reach his goals.

He'd have to learn how to work around them in order to help the alchemists. Doubt that the protective crystals were made from the spirit elementals rose. But then again, perhaps they were. They'd not raise a hand to their own kind. That was why the blast had been allowed to reach him. They probably wanted the privilege of killing him themselves instead of letting an outside influence do so.

Nico had probably already heard of the incident. Whoever had carried him up and put him to bed had probably seen to that. And he hadn't even gotten a chance to explain. Now his actions were going to be misconstrued as a means to use the library against them. This was such a tangle.

Comfort came in the knowledge it was going to be of short duration. After he delivered the necromancers into the alchemists' hands, his life would cease, and he'd be only a memory to those whose lives intersected his. Let him rest there for eternity—the man he used to be.

Easier said than done when his heart ached with a need to belong.

But then, didn't everyone's?

Chapter Eleven

OBERON STARED into his wine, blocking out most of what the Adepts' Council debated. He had no stomach for it at the moment. The only thing he wanted to do was go to Hazrael's chamber and check on him.

"The process is simple. It can be shown over a long-distance scry bowl, and other schools can make their own. We will only be responsible for outfitting this particular branch." Nico lifted the carafe and poured another mug of mulled cider. He'd taken to drinking unfermented beverages at about the second hour of the meeting.

Oberon glanced at the candle that marked time. That had been about four hours ago. They'd discussed everything, from the Hierophant's visit to Hazrael's attack in the library. They'd finally gotten around to talking about the success of the scry spheres.

He closed his eyes and tried to push away the look of dejection that had filled Hazrael's face. The underlying dignity with which he'd extricated himself from the situation had almost cost Oberon to lose his countenance. It wasn't that he didn't want Hazrael—by the elements, he still loved him—but in this atmosphere, it was dangerous for both of them to become involved in anything more than a mere association.

How he wished he was able to say that appearances didn't matter, but they did. He'd learned that the hard way when Hazrael had first arrived. In order to maintain control of the school and the students, he needed to be seen as a man of strength and integrity. His support of Hazrael needed to stem from how Hazrael stood now, not as the lover who'd been taken from Oberon.

It was a fine distinction but one he felt important to make.

To make the others think he had distanced himself, his love for Hazrael had to appear to grow over time. Not come in a heated rush. Still, it was difficult to stay away when all he wanted to do was hoard every moment with Hazrael, tuck it away as the precious commodity it was. He'd never thought to have this second chance with him—a gift he did not want to squander.

"How was the clarity of the device? It seems it would be hard to hear in so small a space." Master Fenelli turned the sphere around and held it up to the light, looking through it.

"Good enough to see the face of the person contacting you, though they are small, as drawings in a book. The sound is clear, distinctive. I expect the conduction properties in the gold flakes have much to do with that." Nico gave a triumphant smile. "Hazrael has designed a wonderful device that will improve communication immensely. My only regret is that I didn't think of it first."

Master Rhone narrowed his eyes. "How do we know he didn't slip anything into those devices to send all our communiqués directly to the necromancers?"

Theodyne raised a brow. He'd never liked Rhone, and Oberon didn't care much for Rhone at the moment either.

"We don't. We just have to trust him." Theodyne practically bit the words out.

"I don't like it. I won't use it." Rhone crossed his arms over his chest like a petulant child.

Nico shrugged. "Suit yourself, but you will be left behind, because I'm making carrying these a mandate for anyone who acts as an agent to the alchemists or wishes to join the fight."

Oberon could keep quiet no longer. He sat upright from his relaxed position. "Rhone, if you make your own damned sphere, you'll have no reason to believe Hazrael tainted any of the product used."

Rhone shot Oberon a look that should have quelled the younger man, but it didn't. Oberon might be at least twenty years Rhone's junior, but he was his superior in the school hierarchy. "I'll do that. And I suggest those of you who have a possibly tainted one replace yours with some of your own making."

Oberon waited for Nico to say something to defend Hazrael, but he said nothing, making Oberon believe that perhaps Nico had already done so.

"I still say he was up to no good in that library." Rhone banged the tip of his finger against the table.

Master Fenelli rolled his eyes in dramatic fashion. "Yes. We all know how you feel about the situation, but that doesn't mean you are correct. I'd trust Anjufer's deposition of events as given to him by the spirit elementals involved before I'd trust your suspicions."

Rhone narrowed his eyes. "You'll see I'm right, and you'll be sorry."

"If I am, I will apologize most humbly. However, if you are wrong, then I expect you to do the same."

Oberon wanted to reach across the table and kiss Master Fenelli. Anjufer had gotten an account from the elementals involved and now watched over Hazrael as he slept. By all accounts, the spirit elementals had knocked Hazrael ass over teakettle for daring to enter the library. Oberon just wanted to know if Nico had a hand in asking them for such protections of the sacred texts, though the request would have to come through Theodyne. Nico, like Oberon, had no elemental blood.

"If I am wrong—which I don't think I am—I'll gladly lead the charge against the necromancers."

Oberon guffawed at the mental image that promise evoked. "Rhone, the only charge you'll ever lead is the one to accuse him of wrongdoing. You were not built for bravery on the battlefield."

Rhone had the audacity to look offended. "I beg your pardon."

Oberon stood and placed his hands on the table. For him the meeting was done, and he was not going to stay and listen to the other adepts for a moment longer. "Let's face it, Rhone, your talents extend only to the intrigues and accusations that stir others into frenzy. You are a master craftsman when your own neck isn't on the line. You did the same thing to Theodyne when he arrived, and he has proved you wrong time and again."

To the others he inclined his head. "I bid you all good night."

He left the room without a backward glance. If Nico wanted to reprimand him, let him. The spheres were an inspired idea that would save both time and labor. In the upcoming conflict, that might be the difference between life and death.

The alchemists had Hazrael to thank for that advantage.

Oberon entered his room and found a projection playing against the wall. It was a static image of Jolen. What was this?

"Jolen?"

The image didn't move. It didn't blink or appear animated in any way, shape, or form. He went to the bowl and touched it with the stirring wand. The image wavered, then began to move.

"If you receive this, it means that my experiment was a success and I've been able to send a message for you to retrieve at a later date. It might prove a useful ability, though if the news that reached me earlier regarding the tiny personal spheres made by Hazrael is true, I believe this may be obsolete before it's ever implemented." Jolen gave a self-deprecating smile. "Please touch the scry bowl again, and it will alert me that you are available. I have some important news to share."

Oberon was stunned. He'd have thought Jolen would contact Theodyne before anyone else at the school. Those two had gone through the better part of hells together in Gusan and forged a bond stronger than brothers.

He tapped the bowl, and the static image cleared, superimposed by one of the real Jolen. "There you are. A rather late night, Headmaster?" There was a teasing glint in Jolen's eyes that Oberon was more than appreciative to see. It seemed like a long time since anyone had actually joked with him about anything—the fact it was Jolen was doubly surprising. He'd been very close to the child Hazrael had killed in the catacombs.

"Adepts' Council meeting." Oberon ran a hand through his hair. "Elements save me from self-important masters."

"I can guess easily who you refer to."

"Aye." Oberon didn't want to go over it again. He'd spent enough time in that stuffy council chamber with alchemists who had a penchant for panic to last him into the next decade. "You had some news for me I believe?"

"Yes. The *prolates* have chosen a successor for the Agia."

At least the night might end with good news. However, that all depended on who they chose and why.

"They are reinstating the Darium family into the *prolates'* circle. Belari Darium will take the seat."

"What do we know about him?"

"Estobán says he is a good man. Knew him at university. The family has spent their exile from power growing olives and raising cattle. It has been a very lucrative business." Jolen said this with a raised brow. "If Estobán believes he is the right man to take the position, then I'll stand by his judgment. Most importantly, I checked him for influence by the necromancers and found none. He and his entire family are clean."

That was good to know. At least the *prolates* had taken precautions to ensure the family was untainted by the death dancers. The fact it was a family who had once held a *prolatial* seat might give some citizens pause, but it actually made perfect sense to Oberon.

"The installation ceremony is going to be in Gusan. Blessed by the *demigoge*. Estobán wants you, Nico, Theodyne, and a few of the others to attend."

"Getting away might not be so easy at present. There is a lot going on here at the moment. Preparations to be made."

"Aren't you at all curious to see the new *prolate* for Calabris? He will be presiding over the lands occupied by the school."

The taunt fell short of the mark. Technically the lands were owned by the Valencia family—and in turn, Nico. They were situated in an area of the city-states that was more of a no-man's-land than an actual geographical location incorporated into Dominicál. The land had been claimed by Mercurian Dante when the city-states were still enjoying a time of eastward expansion.

"And what do you presume we do with Hazrael? We can't take him to Gusan with us, and I dare not leave him here in the school alone."

Jolen made a face of distaste he had a hard time hiding. "I don't know. I would suggest you do bring him here, but I'd be afraid the guards and clerics who remain infected by the necromancers might see him as a bridge and unlock whatever memories Theodyne was able to suppress in him."

Oberon considered hiding what he knew about Hazrael, what they'd learned from the Hierophant, but decided full disclosure in this case was probably the best policy. "Hazrael is afraid to leave the school, even to go outside. The scars he bears are used to track him. He doesn't want to bring the necromancers down on us prematurely."

Jolen rubbed his jaw, considering the problem. "Then we take a stand at Gusan. The longer we draw this out, the worse it will be. What are we waiting for? It's time to end this now."

Nico might have something to say about that. Oberon could just see them rolling into Gusan with wagons filled with catapults, spheres, and angry alchemists. It would not go over well.

"I will bring up the matter with Nico and see how he feels about making the wait of shorter duration."

"He will agree because he'll see the logic in it and because Theodyne will convince him it's a good idea."

Oberon wondered for a moment if Jolen had a visit from the Hierophant as well. Too many people making prognostications lately to give him any comfort.

They ended the connection after bidding each other good night. Oberon was exhausted physically, but his mind raced with seven hundred and twenty different ideas, worries, and postulates. He left his room and walked up the staircase to the workroom. Up here he could be alone with his thoughts and attempt to solve some of their problems. Hiding in his room made it appear as if he tried to disassociate himself from his brothers. He'd never do that or forsake them, but they'd made it awfully hard to work with them lately.

When he entered the workroom Anjufer waited in the hearth.

"I thought you'd set up post to watch over Hazrael?" Oberon addressed the fire elemental wavering in the fireplace.

"He woke, looked at his chest, then lay back down."

"Then he's all right?"

"He appears so." There was a suggestion to Anjufer's voice that made it sound as if the fire elemental wasn't sure of Hazrael's health.

"Are you going to elaborate?"

"I'm thinking."

Worry crept down Oberon's spine in a slow crawl. If Anjufer was at a loss for words, the situation was grave. He tried not to react to the possibilities. Leave the topic alone and perhaps Anjufer would find the right words.

Oberon began to set out supplies to create a box to catch the necromancers in—a trap of some sort. There had to be some way to seal them from the rest of their brethren. Once they were killed in an elemental backlash, their brothers could still reanimate the remains and create another being. This had been proved on several occasions and in many battles with the necromancers. It was prudent to create something to keep the remains away from those who might resurrect them.

Oberon glanced to the hearth. "Was there more you wished to report?"

The flames that composed Anjufer's brow furrowed, flickered. "Only that he seems... defeated."

Oberon's hands stalled as he poured lead powder into one of the bowls. "How so?"

"I don't know how to explain it. The set of his shoulders, expression on his face." Anjufer gestured with a fiery hand. "I will say he was no less determined. I felt it flowing around him in a protective field."

Oberon set the canister down on the worktable. "I was afraid of this. Those damn meddling spirit elementals did something to him when they attacked. Other than knocking him shit limber."

Anjufer shook his head. "They have closed ranks and are not even sharing their intent with the rest of the elementals."

Hazrael probably felt more abandoned and alone than he had in a long time. Oberon had only succeeded in making matters worse. His gut tightened when he thought of the look of hurt he'd placed on Hazrael's face.

"Is this a dangerous situation? Do we need to protect Hazrael even here in the school?"

"I don't think so. As long as he doesn't go into the library, he might be all right. He even might be all right if accompanied by you, Nico, or Theodyne. There wasn't a problem before when he looked into the stacks for books on weapons." Anjufer wavered a bit. "They wouldn't even let him get into the stacks. He'd barely stepped through the doorway."

"What did Hazrael say to them? Was it anything that might provoke them?"

"That he was looking for a book to unlock the scars on his body, not to use knowledge against anyone."

Oberon frowned. "Maybe they're afraid once he does that he'll use what he learns to bring the necromancers to us."

"He has only to step outside to do that—as he's proved."

And yet the necromancers had only descended on him in the form of a storm that one time. It was almost as if they were letting him and the rest of the alchemists know they could grab him whenever they wanted. So what were they waiting for? The alchemists to get into a position advantageous to the necromancers and their minions?

Oberon poured lead into the bowl. He added binders of ground quartz and diamond to strengthen the compound. Instead of swirling his hands above the mixture, he moved them as if forming a small chest. The particles rose, creating the box before his eyes. As he repeated the motion, more of the dust rose, sticking to the growing structure. He left a small slat on the top open in which to pour the remains. With his thumb, he traced the sigil for the Gold School across the top, along with a warning sign should the box ever be opened.

Anjufer rose from the grate to hover over the worktable. "I'd not mark it like that if I were you."

"Why not?"

"Because the sure way for someone to open something they aren't supposed to is to put a warning against it on the top. Centuries from now someone will find the cask and decide the warning is only a superstition and that they know better than a primitive alchemist, and they'll open it, releasing death and destruction upon the land."

Oberon plucked the cask from the air where it hovered. "And you've seen into the future?"

"No, I've lived the past. It's nothing new to this age or the age that will come after this. It's a universal truth. Man is a curious beast and will grow more arrogant and less tied to his past as the world progresses." Anjufer sent a flaming finger over the top, erasing both the alchemists' sigil and the warning. "Simple and unadorned means no one will be curious enough to open the cask. It will be nothing more than an odd metal brick."

"I wonder how many of these I should make?"

"It depends on how many of them you are willing to kill."

"All of them." Oberon's heart was most decisive in this.

"Including those who are merely under their influence? The basilica guards? The unsuspecting agents?"

Oberon hesitated as he started to prepare another mixture. He looked up from the bowl. "No. Not them."

"When you say all of them, you must be specific who it is that occupies that function. Most of those working for the necromancers do so without the benefit of their own intellect. You will need to sort them out before you cast the necromancers to the void."

As they had not done so for Hazrael, he'd been bound to his masters and suffered greatly when they died, but he had been raised with great powers of his own. The average basilica guard had none.

"All right. I take your point."

He made another few boxes before he decided to call it a night and head to bed. The day had been a long one. He'd not wish to repeat it for anything in the world.

Oberon sneaked down to Hazrael's room. He tried the handle but found the door locked. There was no key in the lock and no one around standing guard. Who had locked the door? Oberon hadn't ordered it locked, and as far as he knew, neither had Nico.

He hadn't come prepared with his set of keys. The damn alchemical lock would not allow material alteration even from one of his experience. Oberon slipped into the ether and crossed into the room to look down at Hazrael.

Hazrael lay on the bed, curled up, his head resting on his arm. His long white hair streamed out behind him like a river of pure moonlight.

The man before him looked nothing like his Hazrael. Only the eyes, and then they were no longer that same guileless shade Oberon remembered. The necromancers had stolen Hazrael from him in every conceivable way. For that alone he wanted to see them obliterated.

How could Hazrael ever think for one moment that Oberon's heart didn't bleed for the man he'd been, the one who had died that day in Delaneux?

"It's hard to sleep when being stared at." Hazrael's voice cut through the dark with all the precision of a well-honed blade. "If you've come here to reprimand me for trying to get into the library, you needn't bother. I am fully determined to find the secrets of these marks. The library was only a logical choice for finding information. It is, by no means, the only place."

Hazrael sat up. His shirt fell off one shoulder. He brushed that long fall of hair from his eyes. The action was quietly sensual, mesmerizing Oberon.

He should have known Hazrael might sense his presence. He slipped into Hazrael's mind just enough to speak. *I didn't come here for any such reason. I only wanted to check on you. Ensure you slept well.*

"Didn't Anjufer tell you?"

Oberon smiled. *You knew he was here?*

"Yes."

Oberon lifted his arm and leaned his head against the wall. Tenderness swept through him. He tried to push it back. *"It has been suggested that we should accelerate the timetable and confront the necromancers in Gusan."*

"I wish you luck and good travels."

"You would be going with us."

Hazrael glanced up sharply, as if seeing Oberon's spirit in the ether. "I thought I was relegated to this cell again. Isn't that why you sent Anjufer to watch over me and had the door locked?"

"You couldn't have it more wrong." Oberon let his essence hover closer to the bed. *"Let's see the mark."*

Hazrael dipped a shoulder, ran a hand across his chest, and turned away. "It's nothing."

Shut out, Oberon wanted to persuade Hazrael to show him the injury but decided to change the subject.

"What will you do tomorrow?"

"Work on the crossbows. While the others make the two-man versions in the yard, I'll make single-user models that are portable. Those can be assembled inside one of the workrooms. I won't need the yard." Hazrael yawned. "Do you mind if I try to go back to sleep?"

"No. Not at all." Oberon didn't want to leave but could think of no reason to stay. *"Good night, Hazrael."*

Oberon pulled his essence back. He'd send someone down to unlock the door. At this point, Hazrael had more than earned the right to walk freely through the school. It was about time for the other alchemists to let him.

Chapter Twelve

HAZRAEL SAT in one of the larger workrooms on the classroom level. Pieces for twenty crossbows were separated and piled in a circle. He intended to work from one side to the other. It might take him days, but the industry, working with his hands, would be good for him. Of course, there was always the possibility someone would take his assemblage of the weapons to mean he was going to turn against them. He kept waiting for an irate adept to charge into the room and demand he be returned to his cell.

So far that hadn't happened.

Hazrael had managed to stay out of trouble and avoid both alchemist and elemental alike. Except for Anjufer. Hazrael hadn't gone anywhere in the school the last few days where the fire elemental hadn't followed him through the flues. What bothered him more was that his plans to work on the crossbows the morning after the library incident had been thwarted by his physical inability to move without extreme pain. He'd lain in bed a few more days to allow those injuries time to heal a bit. He only wished he'd gotten as good at ignoring physical pain as he had emotional.

Anjufer stared at him from the fireplace.

Hazrael had gotten well-versed at ignoring him too.

No progress had been made on unlocking the secrets of the Kiss of Death. Those evil lines hid information until they were ready to reveal it, either that or he hadn't found the right mechanism to unlock the memories.

Sensing someone watched him, he glanced up from his work. Theodyne lounged in the doorway, arms crossed and head tilted to the side. "Seems a lot of work for one person."

Hazrael gave a shrug. "It will go faster once I've done a couple."

"I haven't seen you around the last few days. Where have you been hiding?"

Hazrael gave a nod to the fireplace. "Ask Anjufer. He doesn't even leave me long enough for me to take a piss in private."

Theodyne gave a low chuckle and pushed off from the doorframe. "Do you plan on taking a meal or drinking anything?"

"I have been."

"Sneaking down to the dining hall after mealtimes to grab a few crusts of bread and rinds of cheese is not what I mean. I want you to eat full meals, three times a day, until you build your strength. You've lost a lot of weight and muscle."

"How can you say that when you didn't know me before?" Hazrael screwed a long metal bolt into place to fasten the lathe to the tiller.

"I've heard accounts."

Hazrael glanced up. "Are you the same man you were seventeen years ago?"

This time Theodyne didn't laugh. He shook his head solemnly as he came deeper into the room. "No. Not even by half." Theodyne traced the scar on his face. "Though I wouldn't change the path I've taken. All experiences teach us important lessons we take into the future."

"Maybe this is the way I'm supposed to be now. The course my life was meant to take. If I hadn't lived through my experiences with the necromancers and been liberated from their hold, I wouldn't now be in a position to help the alchemists."

"That's true enough spoken." Theodyne's expression cleared. "It doesn't, however, mean you need to starve yourself until you meet them on the field of battle."

"I'm just not hungry. I'll eat something later." Hazrael moved the tiller to add the nut, trigger, and other pieces of metal hardware. "I want to get a few of these done before I do anything else today."

Theodyne looked around. "Why isn't anyone helping you?"

"I would think that's obvious." The screwdriver slipped, and Hazrael busted a knuckle open on the sharp side of the nut assembly. He dropped the tool and shook his hand, then placed his finger in his mouth. The taste of blood hit his tongue. Memories surfaced, sharp and hot.

"You will do as you're told, etherealthant.*"*

Hazrael turned away from the stench of the breath that bathed his nostrils. He'd yet to see his tormentor's face, but the gray robes looked as if he had been buried for hundreds of years before exhumation. "I will do nothing you command."

"You will, or you will die, and we will use your body without your consent."

"With my death the spirit elementals leave with my soul. Not even a necromancer can hold on to a soul—or an elemental without the Elementica. I'm afraid without that relic, you really are lost."

The backhand from that skeletal hand sent him tumbling backward. His head hit the stone wall of the cave. He bit his tongue. Blood filled his mouth. Scabs had fallen off the etchings on his skin. They might try to bend him, but they wouldn't break him. He was an alchemist.

Hazrael's vision cleared.

Theodyne held his hair back from his face. Concern filled his amber eyes. "Another memory?"

"Yes, but this one is confusing." He sat back from his work and gazed down at his busted knuckle. "I must have fought their influence for a long time. Even through the torture of having the Kiss of Death imprinted on my skin."

"I'm sure you did."

Hazrael ran a hand through his hair. It shook. Little crystals dripped from his fingertips, hitting the ground with soft music. "Why did I finally give in? Where or what was the turning point for me?"

"I don't know. Only you can answer that." Theodyne picked up the crystals on the tips of his fingers. "I wonder if we can use these to arm the bolts?"

"I don't even know how I produce them. I can't do it on command, and I can't seem to get them to defend me when I really need it, like when I'm being attacked by the spirit elementals." He raised a hand. "I'll see what I can do, but I can't make promises where those are concerned."

"Understood." Theodyne moved to one of the other crossbows. "You want some help with these?"

"If you have time to offer."

The brush with his memories had given Hazrael a headache. It always did. Light hurt his eyes, and he only craved crawling into a dark hole and staying there until the pain subsided. Not today. He had no choice but to work through it. No matter if with each heartbeat his vision faded in and out. No matter if the world began to spin and he no longer knew up from down. His nose started to run, and he wiped it on his sleeve, leaving a crimson trail in its wake.

"Is your nose bleeding?" Theodyne came back to him. He pulled a handkerchief from his pocket. "Here, hold this and tilt your head back."

Hazrael tried, but the blood ran down his throat, trying to drown him. He choked and started sputtering and coughing. He slapped at Theodyne's hands. "Let me up."

The pain in his head eased some.

Maybe he only needed to spill some blood to feel better.

The dark thought revolted him. Made his stomach turn and roil. What kind of a monster had he become that seeing his own blood, feeling it drain from his head, eased the pain?

"Hold my hand."

Hazrael glanced up at Theodyne. "What?"

"Take my hand. I'm going inside your mind again."

"You realize you're in there more than I am."

Theodyne gave a low rumble of laughter before he eased his hand into Hazrael's and closed his eyes. As before, Hazrael got swept up into Theodyne's tour. However, this time didn't look like a memory. It more resembled a murky swamp, where little gas explosions burped up from a hot, festering bottom layer of gross.

"Is this my mind?"

"A part of it. Yes." Theodyne moved around the cesspool, skirting the explosions. *"This seems to be the part giving you the most trouble at the moment. Can you tell me what caused the nosebleed? Were you in pain?"*

Hazrael had not wanted to confess it, but it seemed as if Theodyne already knew. *"It's the memories. They cause me pain when they come. The nosebleed actually relieved the pressure in my head."*

"Ah."

Such a tiny word with so much meaning.

"Can you fix it so I won't hurt when I remember?"

"It's not that simple. Pain is a way to tell us something is wrong. It's the body sending up an alert. One you should heed."

That wasn't encouraging. Hazrael just wanted to know everything he'd lost and get it all over at once. No lingering. No spacing it out over days, weeks, or months. *"Is there any way you can just rip a seam open and let the memories fall out? I don't know how much more of this I can take."*

"If I do that, we may never get you back. The trauma to your mind could be irreversible."

And the spirit elementals were unlikely to help him recover. They'd most likely rejoice at his demise.

"I understand."

"The best we can do is to let the pressure release a little at a time to avoid an explosion. But do so in a controlled manner. In other words, we can't wait for you to experience these rips in the protective fabric you've created. I'm convinced that's where a lot of the pain stems from."

Shock reverberated down the stream of their connection. Hazrael knew the exact moment it reached Theodyne from the tiny tremors that rippled the colors that made up his ethereal body.

Theodyne turned. *"What's wrong?"*

"I'm doing this to myself?"

"Yes. It's an automatic self-preservation instinct that kicked in when the two sides of your mind collided. The one that witnessed what you'd done while under the control of the necromancers, and the one that lived for years as an alchemist."

His deeds must have been gruesome indeed for his mind to play such tricks to protect him from himself. If they didn't need those memories of how the necromancers worked, Hazrael might be tempted to let them remain buried. The alchemists—the entire city-states—did not have that luxury.

It was a hard concept to swallow. Despite their rather contentious beginning, Hazrael trusted Theodyne's assessment of the situation.

"Then how are we to proceed?"

"A little bit each day."

"Then pull back another piece of the fabric."

"You've already suffered enough today."

Hazrael squeezed Theodyne's hand. *"The memory gave us less than nothing to go on."*

"You can't look at it that way. All the pieces together will make a cohesive whole."

Footsteps on the stones alerted Hazrael that they were no longer alone. He turned to the intruder and broke contact with Theodyne. Nico and Oberon stood watching the two of them seated on the floor holding hands. At first blush it might appear as if there was something illicit going on, but the bloody handkerchief held to Hazrael's nose told a different story entirely.

"Has there been an injury?" Oberon crossed the space and knelt down. "Say something to offend Theodyne?"

The teasing glint in Oberon's eyes had the desired effect and broke the momentary tension. "No. A rather painful headache that decided to find its own relief in the form of a nosebleed."

Oberon exchanged a glance with Theodyne. "That doesn't sound encouraging."

"It's not," Theodyne agreed. "However, we've come up with a plan to take charge of Hazrael's ailment and were just about to get started when you entered."

Nico brought a few chairs over to the area. "No need to sit on the floor."

Hazrael looked up at Nico. "Oh, I think it might be better for me down here. Shortens the distance of a fall considerably."

"Good point." Nico took a seat and faced the small group. "Is there anything I can do to help?"

Theodyne gave Nico a heated look from under lowered lashes. "Your strength and steady mind are always appreciated, my love. I think the more support we can give Hazrael as I delve into his mind and unravel a memory, the more it will help to stabilize him."

They rearranged themselves with Hazrael in the middle of the other three masters. Light glittered in the corner of the room, materializing from the walls, moving outward.

Hazrael raised a hand to point. Oberon, Theodyne, and Nico turned as one to look at the spirit elementals manifesting around them. Hazrael recognized the one who stood in the center as the one who had attacked him in the library.

Theodyne stood. His face was resolute. Judging from his expression, they communicated directly with him but let none of the others hear the conversation. He gave a slight incline of his head as if granting assent.

They remained in the room. Hazrael wanted to tell them to leave, that this did not concern them. They had given up their right to interfere in his life when they'd forsaken him. To honor his pledge not to interact with the spirit elementals, he closed his eyes. Better to ignore their presence and get on with the healing than to stare at them until they felt the need to retaliate against him for what they might consider insubordination.

Theodyne sat on the floor next to Hazrael. "Take my hand again. We'll get this one done, and then I want you to return to your room and rest."

Hazrael opened his eyes and glanced at the unfinished crossbows. He'd only managed to get through about three-quarters of one. "I can't promise anything. I still have a lot of work to do here."

"Nonsense. Your health is more important."

Feeling useless and more a drain on the alchemists than he ought to, Hazrael closed his eyes again and settled into the rhythm of having Theodyne in his mind. Oberon joined in, hearty and robust. Nico's touch was subtle and light. There was great finesse in the descendant of Mercurian Dante as he touched the rough spots and smoothed them down. It was calming and warm, like wrapping Hazrael's mind in a soft blanket.

"I'm not going to pull a thread that looks as if it's about to give way, but one from the opposite side. Diverting the building pressure will give you more relief in that section and stabilize the base." Theodyne hunted around, assessing the little peaks and valleys of energy fluctuations.

"I trust you to do the right thing." Hazrael tried to relax and take deep breaths. It was hard when he didn't know when the spirit elementals might decide to attack again.

A low rumble of a chuckle shimmered through his mind. *"That is reassuring."*

Nothing happened for another few moments. Sensations not unlike a fluttering of butterfly wings in his brain moved around in his head. It was a bit unnerving, but not painful or unpleasant.

Theodyne's ethereal essence landed. *"All right, I'm going to start working this area free."*

The experience wasn't anything like Hazrael had imagined. Images didn't come to him as they had when the memory forced itself to the surface. This came at him in fits and starts. Sudden flashes out of time and place that gave him neither context nor explanation. None of the scenes looked familiar. It seemed Theodyne had grabbed hold of a cross section of several memories all woven together. One in particular disturbed him the most. Death dancers, moving around him in sinuous, almost seductive, ballet. Repulsion made him look away at first, but the closer they danced on an ethereal breeze, the more he found he couldn't pull his gaze from them.

Energy, raw and sexual, grabbed him in the lower belly, moving down to the seat of all desire. Hazrael tried to turn away from them, but his body betrayed him. Everything good and pure he knew about loving and sex was tainted with the brush of a cold hand. He didn't want this. He damn sure didn't want to remember what it was like to give in when he'd fought so long and hard to resist.

Hazrael tried to disengage from the memory, but failed. It played out as if it exerted freewill.

Hazrael dropped Theodyne's hand and pushed back, trying to flee the circle. He knocked into Oberon's chair and almost unseated him.

"By the elements!" Oberon tried to grab for Hazrael but missed. Hazrael felt the touch of Oberon's fingers through his shirt, and it sickened him. Not because it was Oberon, but because it was someone who was gentle and kind.

Hazrael flipped onto all fours and crawled across the floor, trying to get away from the images that continued to race through his mind. Of his response to their ministrations, of the fact he capitulated when he should have fought on. When Oberon came to him, Hazrael put both hands up to hold him back.

"No! Don't come any closer."

"Hazrael, please. What did you see?"

He let out a breath that ended in a sob. They hadn't seen the memory? How was that even possible? He chanced a glance at Nico and Theodyne. One look at their faces and he knew—Nico had seen nothing, but Theodyne had seen it all.

Hot tears welled in Hazrael's eyes. Heartbeats thundered in his throat. Oh Gods! Breath squeezed off and failed to move. He really was as vile as they claimed.

No. He'd not cry over this. He only needed a moment to push the horror back inside, to tie it back down under the wreckage of his life where it belonged.

The spirit elementals remained in the room, looking down at him with silent accusations. He deserved every one of those cold stares. How could he ever think he was worthy to help the alchemists now?

Theodyne stood. "Leave us."

Oberon turned on his friend. "I will not until I know what is going on here."

Nico pushed up from the chair and put a comforting arm around Oberon, then steered him to the door. "Theodyne wants a private word with Hazrael. I think we should give it to them."

Oberon glanced down at Nico, offended. "And you are going to allow this? We offered to give our support to Hazrael. Why should we turn our backs when he clearly needs us?"

"Because some things are too private to discuss in a group setting."

Oberon moved his arm to encompass the room. "Then tell them to leave."

"I can no more command an elemental than I can move the sun from its current orbit." Nico got Oberon to the door, but not before the headmaster turned a worried expression to Hazrael.

"I wish you felt you could confide in me, Hazrael."

Hazrael brought his knees up to his chest and lowered his face, trying to squeeze into as small a space as possible. He didn't watch Oberon and Nico leave, but heard the quiet click of the door as it shut behind them.

"You can leave too." Theodyne's voice was a gentle command.

Celestial breezes fluttered the drapes and rattled the shutters. The spirit elementals might have decided to leave at Theodyne's request, but they weren't going quietly. When the room grew still, Hazrael uncovered his eyes and found Theodyne still across the room. He'd taken the chair Nico had vacated, holding one of the crossbows between his thighs to brace the tiller as he screwed down the lathe.

"What are you doing?"

"I figured I'd work on some of these until you were ready to unroll yourself enough to talk."

Hazrael watched Theodyne work for a few moments. "You shielded my memories from them. Why?"

"Because I saw where that particular one led, and I didn't think you'd want everyone to know. If they find out, it will be because you chose to tell them." Theodyne tested the lathe for sturdiness. "No matter what you may think, it was not your fault."

"How can you say that?"

"Easily. I knew men in Pallonia Prison who were used so by the other inmates and the guards. They had no more chance of overpowering their attackers than you did. It wasn't their fault either."

"But they probably at least tried to fight back."

"At first. Yes. Some continued to fight up until the point they were killed for it. Others gave in because at the time it was a matter of survival." Theodyne turned to Hazrael fully now. His amber gaze deep, penetrating. "I'm not judging or saying one way is superior over the other. That decision is one for the individual to make. I'm simply saying that the necromancers gave you no choice whether to fight them or die. They were going to get the response they wanted from you no matter what. It's how they work. You were no more in control of your body than you were when we found you."

"How can you exonerate me? I let them turn me because of a few orgasms."

Theodyne hung his head like a defeated man. "I didn't even get to fight off the infection of the necromancers. When they entered my mind, they did so with the barest of looks. In other words, you held out a lot longer than any of us who have felt their touch. For you, it took carvings and pain, blood and anguish. The fact they finally chose pleasure tells me that they had to wear you down and break you before they ever found a way inside. You, my friend, are stronger than you'll ever realize."

Hazrael sat in the corner and rocked back and forth a few times. Strong was a matter of perspective. He had none of that now. The situation was too dire, too fresh. Claws raked his insides, leaving him to bleed. Theodyne might say there was no blame, but when he'd found enjoyment and release from the touch of his captors, that had crossed a line he'd never be able to retreat from.

Pushing the self-loathing away, he stood and went to the crossbow he'd set aside. They worked silently until the bell gonged for midday meal.

Chapter Thirteen

A TERRIBLE quiet descended on the school. The only sound was that of the wind as it whipped past the turrets at the very top of the towers. Rattles and whistles, banging and knocking continued on into the darkness. With each passing hour, the gales became more violent.

Oberon sat in the warm comfort of his room. Letters, notes, and annotations covered his lap and the surrounding bed. Every expression of emotion he'd gotten from Hazrael while they were together was spread out around him. Poetry in rhyming couplets illustrated in flowery imagery Hazrael's love for Oberon.

Words floated off the vellum, morphing into rosebuds that bloomed. Oberon had forgotten about the animated aspect of Hazrael's writings. In those months after Hazrael's disappearance, he'd gone to his room—one he'd shared with Hazrael—and read the papers over and over again, committing each word, letter, and flourish to memory. As if somehow the life in the characters would bring Hazrael back. It never had. Years had gone by; the letters lay in the bottom of a drawer drawing dust and mites. All the while Hazrael had been tormented by the necromancers, living through unspeakable acts of cruelty, and Oberon, Nico, and the rest of Hazrael's friends had been none the wiser. All those who had loved him had let him down. They should have found other means to locate their missing brother.

Now, all these years later, Hazrael turned to Theodyne for comfort. And why not? Theodyne hadn't been here when Hazrael went missing. Hadn't let him down by not finding him soon enough.

The wind howled like a tortured soul seeking revenge. Windows rattled and shook in their casements. Rage from the air elementals disrupted the natural flow of the school's energies. They were seriously displeased.

Oberon set the letters aside and walked to the window to look out. A horrible storm had rolled in, hovering over the school, a vengeful weather system with the power to kill.

A chill ran down his spine as he gazed at the black night. Lightning cut through the clouds, illuminating images scrolling in the swirling, angry mass. He'd seen formations like those before—on the road to meet Theodyne and Jolen.

Fingers pointed in accusation at something above Oberon. He opened the window and leaned out but saw nothing in the darkness. Rain pelted his face. Lightning flashed. A lone figure stood on the battlements, raging against the storm.

Long white hair whipped in the wind. Clenched fists were raised in anger.

What in the name of the elements was Hazrael doing?

Oberon ran from his room and hurried up to the roof. That stupid, crazed maniac was going to get himself killed and the rest of the school along with him.

He reached the roof door and jiggled the handle. Locked. Of course. He'd not want anyone to witness this certain suicide. Whatever he'd seen in that vision earlier had rattled him completely. Oberon could only imagine the worst.

Quickly, he said an incantation to release the levers. It didn't work. The lock clicked closed again. Damn. Hazrael had taken the time to institute a reverse spell on the mechanism. Well, there was nothing for it. The lock would have to go.

Oberon lashed out with his power and turned the metal to its liquid state. It heated through the door and ran down in rivulets. He pushed through the opening, only to find Hazrael taking aim with one of the larger crossbows. He had a spear the length of Oberon's leg in the channel. Hazrael cranked the handle, winding up the tension, and the spear sailed up into the clouds. Like a stick of dynamite thrown at a house of straw, the clouds exploded into fiery shards. The faces of the necromancers contorted in rage.

Oberon lifted Hazrael with one arm and the crossbow with the other and ran for the door. Hazrael yelled, beating Oberon's arm, kicking out with fury at being stopped.

Oberon got them both inside and closed the door against invasion. "What were you thinking?"

"I'm going to kill them!"

"I could see that. Taking them on all on your own was very foolish and ineffectual."

Hazrael looked at him through long, wet hair. He pushed it out of his face. "You saw what happened when I shot the spear at them."

"Yes, but I fail to see how mortal weapons made them respond. Suppose you come with me to a warmer area and explain." Only moments out of the heat of battle, and already Hazrael's teeth had begun to chatter with cold.

Hazrael jerked away from Oberon to avoid his touch. "I used the crystals. It was Theodyne's idea, and he was right. The necromancers don't like them."

Oberon tried to wrap his head around that and failed. Perhaps he was a bit more cautious, but he'd think sending in something that manifested from the seat of Hazrael's talent might be dangerous and could be used against him later.

"Come. We will go to your room so you can change into dry clothes, then meet in the library."

Hazrael stopped. "No. No library. *They'll* be waiting to attack me again."

Oberon let out a weary breath. There was no need to ask who Hazrael feared. "No, they won't. Not if I'm with you."

"I won't go in there again. I mean it." He walked in a jerky, almost paranoid step as they descended the staircase. Every shadow and noise made Hazrael jump and turn and twist.

"What made you go up there in the first place?"

Hazrael shook his head, but Oberon noticed the evidence on the wet nightshirt. Hazrael's scars had ripped open and bled again. Something in his sleep had set him off. More memories must have surfaced when he closed his eyes.

Instead of going to Hazrael's room, Oberon stopped on the level for his own and pulled Hazrael along the corridor by his sleeve. When they arrived at his suite, he opened the door and gave Hazrael a gentle push inside.

"Stand there and don't move. I don't want you dripping all over my furnishings."

Hazrael pulled his arms in close to his body and stood straight as a statue. He stared ahead with his gray eyes dull. His hair was plastered to his head. He looked a sight.

Oberon grabbed a towel from his linen locker and opened it. He started at Hazrael's hair and dried it with vigorous rubs before he moved down his body. "Get out of those wet clothes while I find you something to put on."

He knew his voice was gruff and had a hard time softening it. What was he going to do with Hazrael? The man was becoming a menace to himself and reckless with the school. Each atrocity uncovered brought out another aspect of Hazrael's personality that meant to punish him. Gods and soldiers, wasn't he punished enough?

Oberon found a robe and some pants that were going to be big but would have to do. He took them back to Hazrael and stopped dead. Hazrael had lost weight, but his body was beautifully lean and muscular. There was a wiry strength to him. Every muscle and contour was played and hinted with the candlelight. His odd, beautiful eyes stared out at Oberon as if waiting for a judgment.

Hazrael finally hung his head. An uncomfortable silence grew. "I know I no longer look the same as I once did, when we were young and in love. I don't know why they changed my looks. Perhaps to help conceal me from those who might set me free."

Oberon shook his head. "No. It's the rogue energies they use." He pointed to the pronounced streak of white in his hair among the sea of dark locks. "I got this the day you went missing."

Hazrael looked up. He turned, exposing his nudity in full view of Oberon's watchful gaze. "You did?"

"Yes. We were both knocked unconscious, but when I woke, you were gone, and this was left behind." He ran a hand through his hair now, holding the clothes out to Hazrael with the other one. "I was frantic to find you. Thought my soul had been ripped in two."

Emotions rolled to the surface, seventeen years in the making.

Hazrael slipped the clothes on, looking up at Oberon with curious glances. "It was. When I woke in the necromancers' chamber, chained to the altar, I called for you. I was afraid they'd killed you."

"I missed you so much I wish they had."

"But you can't love me now. Not knowing what you do about me. I saw it in your eyes in the tower."

"I'm conflicted, but I've never stopped loving you. Not for a moment."

Hope rose, then died in Hazrael's eyes. He turned his face away. "You loved the man I was. Not the one I am now."

"Would that be the one who goes up on the battlements at night and tempts the necromancers into striking him down?" Oberon lashed out. "Why would I even try to love someone who is so determined to break my heart again?"

Hazrael took a step forward, his hand out. "I didn't mean to hurt you."

Something broke inside Oberon. All the years of waiting and hoping that Hazrael might return were washed away. Staring at the being in front of him, the one with Hazrael's face and voice, but not his eyes and hair, with scars to mark him as property of the necromancers, Oberon knew he'd run through all the pits of the hells to free his former lover from the torment. If only for him to know love one more time.

Oberon took a few steps, closing the gap between them, and cradled Hazrael's face in his hands. "I forgive you for everything you did while under the necromancers' influence, but by the Gods and elements, I will hold you accountable for all you do now." He brought his mouth down on Hazrael's.

Energy swirled in beautiful patterns before his closed lids, melding and merging until there was no beginning or end. This was how it had looked the very first time they'd kissed. Back when they were both young and innocent to the ways of evil. Before either of them had ever been touched by necromancy.

Oberon swept his tongue along the seam of Hazrael's lips, urging him to open to a deeper connection. Hazrael clung to him. A low, coarse moan rolled from his throat, right before he opened his mouth to grant Oberon entrance.

He tasted different. Pain and suffering were a dark musk on his tongue. Fear painted the flavor in a burned offering. Oberon ended the kiss by placing small ones on the corners of Hazrael's lips. A glance down his body, and Oberon had no chance of concealing his desire for Hazrael. Of how much he wanted him, even knowing his crimes.

That beast the necromancers had created was not *his* Hazrael. Would never be *his* Hazrael. Nor was Hazrael the beast they'd created.

He was a man, newly formed and trying to find his place in a world he didn't remember.

Hazrael's eyelids fluttered open. His lips remained parted as he gazed up at Oberon. "I shouldn't have let you do that."

"Why not? Didn't you enjoy it?"

Hazrael looked away, his cheeks stained a dull red. "I did." He reached out and stroked Oberon's cock through his robe. Oberon's breath caught and hitched. "If you touch me, you'll see I'm just as hard. Just as wanting as you."

Oberon took the words as invitation and laid a gentle knuckle against the rigid outline of Hazrael's cock. It was true, and the thought of how he'd aroused Hazrael nearly undid him.

Hazrael let his hand trail away and turned from Oberon. "But you see, my body can be easily fooled and manipulated. It has known and responded to the touch of the necromancers, so it cannot be trusted when dealing with the baser emotions."

So that was what had him on the battlements, raging at the bastards. Oberon had expected as much. But seeing the broken, haunted look in Hazrael's eyes over the knowledge made him wish to run up there into the storm and fight alongside him.

"I wish I could erase that from your mind. Make it so it never happened, or you never remembered. It isn't a condemnation of your body or guilt of your mind." He stalked to the bed where he'd left the words Hazrael had written long ago. He held up the vellum for Hazrael to see. "These are the words my lover wrote to me. He wrote about passion, hearts, and love never ending. He promised them to me, and then he was taken from me."

Hazrael's clear eyes rounded, and he reached for the pages. "You kept my letters?"

"Of course I did. When I told you I loved you, I meant it forever. That never changed. Not one day. I am the man I am today because I was loved and loved deeply by one such as you." Tears filled his eyes. His heart broke as if afresh. "You might not look like my Hazrael, or even move like him. But in your heart, you are still the same man I fell in love with. It's time you started acting like him."

"I doubt I could write about the pure love I see in these poems." Hazrael's gaze skimmed the pages. "I don't even recognize myself in these lines, though I remember very clearly writing them."

Oberon gave a brief smile. "And there we are evenly matched. I no longer recognize myself as the recipient. We have all grown and changed. Perhaps your growth took a different road than mine, but we are together now. We fight on the same side. We can come to an accord and love again."

Hazrael tipped his head as if considering. "You aren't disgusted with me and what I am? What I was forced to become?"

"I hate what they made you do, but I also know if you had been in charge of your faculties, you never would have been a party to them."

Hazrael seemed to consider this. "So you don't find me repulsive?"

Oberon smiled. "Would I have kissed you like that if I did?"

A smile peeked from the corner of Hazrael's mouth, and for an instant it transformed his face into the young man he used to be. Then, like a flash of lightning against the night sky, it was gone.

"Thank you for the dry clothes. I will leave you now."

"Oh no you don't." Oberon took Hazrael's hand and pulled him back to the bed. "You are going to stay here where I can watch you and make sure you aren't running up to the battlements again."

"I won't. I give you my word."

"Yes." Oberon turned away and poured them each a glass of wine. "Here. Something to calm you."

"What will the others say if they know I've spent the night in your room?"

"I don't particularly care what they say." Oberon sat on the chaise and leaned against the back with his wine balanced on his stomach. He held it with a loose hand and looked over at Hazrael. "Go on. You take the bed. I'll be perfectly comfortable here."

"No, you won't. Your feet are dangling off, and you've never been able to sleep on your back."

The intimate little detail sent heat coursing through Oberon's body. Only someone who had slept a number of nights with him would know that detail. It had happened when he was a young boy. He'd taken a fall from a horse and hurt his back. He'd spent months in bed recuperating, as pain ate away at his spine. It seemed forever before he was allowed to do anything more than turn. By then he'd had horrible bedsores that festered. He'd spent another few months on his sides, getting rid of the sores. It was a long and uncomfortable experience.

Since then he'd not been able to sleep on his back for fear of getting bedsores again. Even though the rational part of his mind knew they were not likely to occur after only one night, his body remembered the pain and refused to let him sleep on anything but his right or left.

"I can just as easily sleep on my side here."

"You're too long. You'll have to put your knees around your ears." Hazrael hit Oberon on the leg. "Get up. I'll take the chaise. You take the bed."

"You won't leave?"

"I should, but I'll not make you mad at me for something else. One taste of your fury today is enough."

Oberon reached out for Hazrael's hand and closed his larger one around it. "Let's get something straight. I only feared for you. I wasn't angry."

"Put out?"

"Annoyed," Oberon corrected. "You are making friends here, Hazrael. Good friends who want to see you well again. Those who know you still have a lot to offer."

Oberon finally got up and gave Hazrael the chaise. He waited until Hazrael had drifted off to sleep—which didn't take long—and then covered him with a blanket.

In the light of a single candle, he sat down on the bed, surrounded by the proof of Hazrael's love, and read until his eyes blurred from strain.

Chapter Fourteen

THE MORNING dawned with the sounds of birds filling the parapets. Rainclouds were nowhere in sight. Blue sky stretched far into the horizon. Hazrael twisted on the narrow bed and looked around. He didn't know this room. The surroundings were unfamiliar.

He sat up. A blanket fell from his shoulders, sliding down the front of his chest. The clothes he wore were not his own. He'd not been given back his masters' robes.

He brushed a hand over the embroidered collar and felt an essence brush against his. Oberon.

Memory returned on a heated rush. He'd been up in the battlements, provoking the necromancers to fight. Oberon had run up there in the storm to rescue him.

A quick glance around the room showed that Oberon was no longer in the suite. He must have risen earlier and left to begin his morning duties. Hazrael let out a sigh and rose. He folded the blanket and left it on the chaise. His clothes were dry and sitting on the edge of the desk. Quickly, he changed, then crept from the room, careful to make sure no one saw him leave.

Oberon might not think it a bad thing to be caught leaving the room, but Hazrael wasn't so sure the other masters would agree. Some of them might remember what he and Oberon were to each other, even if it was a long time ago.

A tingle moved around the edge of his lips. He placed his finger there, tracing the pattern. Oberon had kissed him. He'd become aroused while holding Hazrael in his arms. Not the way Hazrael used to be, but him *now*. White hair and lacy scars.

His heart did a flip. A smile filled his face. Warmth spread throughout his body in brilliant radiance. Could Oberon learn to love the man he'd become? Was there a place in Oberon's life for one who did not fit completely in the alchemists' mold?

Hazrael took a deep breath and continued walking down the stairs to his room. Whatever the new emotion Oberon had for Hazrael, it must be taken slowly and be allowed to grow. He did not wish to scare Oberon away or give him reason to question his feelings.

Once in his room, he changed into day clothes and went to the dining hall to find something to eat. For the first time in a long while, he felt the unfamiliar pang of hunger gnawing on his belly.

Voices came from around the corner, their owners out of sight from where Hazrael stood.

"When should we be ready to go?"

"I want the wagons loaded and packed by the end of the week. We have a lot to accomplish in a short time. I believe Jolen is right. If the necromancers are going to strike, it's going to be at the new *prolate's* installation ceremony."

"Which brings me to another point, Nico. What are we going to do to get Hazrael there without confronting the necromancers before we're ready? They'll have the advantage."

There was a slight hesitation. "If we spelled something as big as the school, why not the wagons? We attach it to the wheels, canvas tarps, the entire structure. If we anchor it, he can ride inside and not be felt by his former masters."

The voices moved away. Hazrael stuck his head around the corner and looked. Nico and Theodyne moved down the hallway, unaware that their conversation had been overheard or that Hazrael had found their plan genius. That might be the only way he could ride through the country to Gusan.

He was somewhat amazed that they still wanted him to accompany them to the holy city. Knowing the way he reacted whenever his wounds reopened was enough to make even Hazrael hesitate. It didn't mean he was going to go back on his word. On the contrary, he felt a responsibility to see this through to the end.

Hazrael hurried to the dining hall and loaded a plate with food, then grabbed a carafe of juice before climbing the stairs to the workroom he'd used the day before.

A quick bump with his hip and a word said under his breath and the door swung open to admit him. The piles of wood and metal fittings were no longer there.

Had he gotten the wrong room?

He stepped back out and looked up and down the hallway. No. He was definitely in the right room. What had happened to all the crossbows? They had been here when he'd returned to get the one he took to the battlements. Had Oberon returned to collect the materials to keep Hazrael from making more of the weapons?

Of course he had. Who else would have come up here and taken supplies and moved them? Irritated but not defeated, Hazrael took his plate to the worktable and sat down. He might as well eat his meal and then find some materials to make more of the crystal bolts.

He dug into his food, taking a moment to actually taste the offerings. Flavors exploded across his tongue, rich and delicious. It seemed so long since he'd enjoyed a meal just for the sake of sensory pleasure.

Meals at the school had always been good. Physical nourishment was as important as those that filled the metaphysical channels. He stuck a piece of sharp yellow cheese into his mouth and chewed. The door opened, and students filed in.

They stalled, not bothering to take their seats or even stand near the worktable. Instead they all stopped to stare at Hazrael with eyes wide and mouths open.

Hazrael stopped chewing and stared back. The first-level master who had traveled with Oberon the day of the Hierophant's visit came into the room.

"Odd place to eat your meal, Master Hazrael."

Hazrael picked up his plate and carafe. "I apologize. I came up here to finish work on the crossbows only to find them gone. Thought I would eat before I left. I hadn't realized this room was scheduled for instructions."

"The crossbows are being loaded onto the wagons."

"Thank you." Hazrael left the room, feeling the stares of the students on his back.

They were young ones. First-year apprentices if the wide-eyed look of innocence was any indication. No wonder they looked at him as if he were an apparition. So far the youngest students had been kept away from him. Fear of exposing them to the necromancers no doubt in the forefront of Oberon's mind.

Hazrael didn't blame him. There was enough time for apprentices to know the cruelties in the world. No sense in exposing such young minds to the extent of evil he'd known before they were ready to handle the knowledge of such atrocities. Hazrael hadn't been ready, and he'd been a first-level master.

He carried his plate and carafe to another room. One on an upper level, away from the classrooms. There was more chance of being able to eat in peace there and contemplate the best way to construct the crystal bolts.

This particular workroom looked out over the vast school grounds. Floor to ceiling windows gave a panoramic view of the mountains. It was a scene that calmed as well as inspired.

He set his food down and went to read the containers stored in the corner. There were a few materials that he could use to create the shafts before he laced the points with the crystals.

But what should he use to construct the bolts? It had to be durable enough to penetrate the necromancers' bodies and magical fields yet flexible enough to destruct on impact. No trace should remain of the materials, lest the necromancers use them to construct their own weapons later.

A thought—more an essence of a thought—niggled at the back of his brain. Faded images of the necromancers moved against his mind's eye. It was as if he looked at the image from the bottom of a pool. Visions shimmered and shook.

Hazrael took a slow, deep breath. It was best not to push the memory, but to let it unveil itself naturally.

He took down a few of the jars and found a basin to place a mixture in. Glass. It was durable, flexible in its states of matter when placed under pressure and heat. The crystals would adhere to the point without being visibly noticeable. The best part of using glass bolts was that he could, if needed, make them during the heat of battle. Sand and soil around Gusan would give him plenty of material to work with if pressed to do so.

He filled the basin with sand, then frowned. The bolts needed to be bigger in order to fit into the weapon. He tipped up the basin and poured the sand on the table, then closed his eyes and began to shape it, changing its state to harden.

The door opened. Hazrael sensed a presence, but not who had entered. He kept his eyes closed, working to try and complete the first bolt in their arsenal.

He moved his hands down the length of the sand, seeing the finished product in his mind. Fashioning the end into a lethal point. If there was only some way he could dribble the crystals throughout the length of the shaft, increasing the potency of the spell. However, short of being able to exude the crystals at will, which he'd been unable to do as yet, he didn't see a way around the problem.

Hazrael completed the first bolt and opened his eyes. The weapon gleamed in the shaft of light coming through the window, sending multiple colors across the table.

He glanced up at his visitor, surprised to see Journeyman Lorelli waiting patiently for him to finish.

Lorelli nodded in the direction of the bolt. "I suppose it's probably not a good thing that our weapons are as beautiful as they are deadly?"

"Even beautiful things have the potential to be lethal." Hazrael lifted the bolt. The glass was warm from the transmutation. He closed one eye and stared down the length of it, making sure it had fashioned straight.

"I was sent to help you in whatever tasks you were taking on today. Headmaster Oberon said you had a hard night."

Hazrael raised a brow. "Oh, did he now?"

Lorelli raised a shoulder. "I'm sure he meant nothing offensive."

"I have no doubt of his sincerity." Hazrael looked to the sand. "Do you know how to fashion instruments from their granular components?"

"Yes."

"Good. Set up over on that table and start making bolts." Hazrael held the one he'd made between his palms. "Make them this length and width, and ensure they are straight."

"Yes, Master Hazrael."

Lorelli collected his materials and went to work. They had a significant pile before the door opened again and Oberon entered.

Hazrael heard the clink of glass tapping against glass. He kept his concentration focused on the bolt he worked on. When he finished, he gave a nod to the ammunition. "We've made some inroads."

"So I see."

"They'll have to be packed carefully in crates with straw. I'd hate to see them broken before we have need of them."

Oberon picked one up, much as Lorelli had done when he'd first walked in. "That's a nasty piece of business."

"I've made improvements on the design. Given what I observed last night, I think we need to go with a substance that will completely disintegrate on impact."

"Agreed." Oberon ran his thumb over the tip of it. "No crystals?"

"I'll put those on later."

"How many do you think we need?"

Hazrael glanced up from pouring more sand on the table. "I have no idea. As many as we can make and transport."

"So a tall order." Oberon put the bolt back on the table and retired to a station across the room. He grabbed a few jars and placed them on his worktable.

"I've also used minerals we can find in soil no matter where we go. We'll be able to manipulate the material to make bolts as we need them."

"That's the best news I've heard yet." Oberon went to the cabinet and started to pull other materials out, then brought them to the table that sat adjacent to Hazrael. "I suppose I can fashion some of these."

"We need to make as many as we can now, before we leave. Just because we can fashion them anywhere doesn't mean we should rely on it. I'd rather not expend the energy on the battlefield."

Oberon looked up at him. "Anything we can do to conserve energy on the field against the necromancers we need to institute. They are too clever by half when it comes to finding extra stores, then converting them to mayhem."

Hazrael gave Oberon a knowing smile. "A bit more than mayhem."

"I didn't want to offend you."

"I'm past the point of offense. What I need is to get this over and done with so I can break their shackles for good." Then perhaps he'd put his demons to rest.

At least he'd try.

His gaze slid to Oberon. Until last night, Hazrael had believed the best way to be released from the necromancers was with the sacrifice of his life. Now in the light of day, knowing Oberon still cared, it was hard not to cling to the thread of a life, knowing the potential for love existed.

If there was any hope for a life that had known such ruin, it was found in a pair of bright green eyes and the arms of a former lover.

That was the hardest part of this—to him Oberon wasn't former, he was current. It was hard to forget those horrible memories stirred only a day or so ago. If they became intimate again, it was going to have to be slow. One step at a time.

"You're slowing down on your output over there. Are you getting tired?"

"Yes." It was easier to admit that than to tell the truth.

The pile of bolts in front of him had grown significantly.

"Why don't you go and lie down for a while? Rejuvenate some of your energy." The suggestion was made in a quiet voice, full of concern.

"I'm tired of resting. I need to be useful."

"You are being useful. You've given us the tools we need to defeat the necromancers, or at least a bit of an edge."

"We will need more than that." Hazrael turned to the window. The light looked strange to him. Deeper than it should. Ocean water but made from gold rather than blues and greens. Motes sparkled in diamond brilliance as they floated to the floor. An unnatural patina settled over the room.

Imagination or metaphysical illusion, Hazrael wasn't sure. A spinning sensation turned his view upside down. He held on to the table to keep from falling. That was the last thing he wanted to do.

"Master Hazrael, are you unwell?" Journeyman Lorelli's voice came from down a tunnel and far away.

He'd felt this sensation before but failed to remember where or when. It wasn't any time from before he'd been lost, but during that long black absence.

Oberon had come around his table and stood in front of Hazrael, arms out to catch him in case he fell. "Sit down."

"No. I'm fine."

"You're even paler than normal and you're shaking."

"Leave me alone for a moment. Let me think." Hazrael took a deep breath and let it out slowly. "A memory is trying to surface, and I want it to come up naturally. I don't want to force it."

"All right. Do you have an idea what it might be?"

Hazrael put his hand up. Blue light crackled from his fingertips. He turned his hand over to study it, but the light faded. "Did you see that?"

"Yes. Static?"

"I'm not sure."

Hazrael turned back around. The memory dissipated as fog chased away by the sun, the moment lost.

Odd blue light continued to pour from his fingertips, an ethereal goo left over from an experiment gone afoul. He ran his hand over the length of a bolt. The glass rod began to glow, taking on the same eerie properties. Where the stack touched, the infusion spread from one to the next, crawling downward through the bolts until they all glowed.

Oberon and Lorelli stood in mute fascination, watching the process. When all the bolts glowed, Hazrael broke contact and looked up at his companions.

"I have no idea if it will help our plight or not, but I'd as soon try it as not. We already know that weapons infused with the crystals will destroy the necromancers. I am curious as to what this blue energy will do when released."

"It's hard to determine results when we don't even know the base product." Oberon ran his hand along one of the rods. Small bits of blue energy transferred to his fingertips, alchemical stains.

He tried to wipe it off, but it remained.

"It tingles." Oberon ran his thumb over the other fingers.

"Is that all? Do you feel anything else? Numbness? Cold? Heat?"

"No."

Journeyman Lorelli ran his hand along the top. No apparent transfer showed on his skin. "I wonder why it didn't work on me."

"Perhaps the transfer only happens immediately after the energy has been placed." It was only a guess. Hazrael had no idea. "See if you can infuse the pile of bolts you made."

Oberon ran his hand along the length of the one on the top. He hadn't made many before he'd come over to check on Hazrael. The bolt glowed with a very faint light. It failed to do a serpentine through the others.

"It doesn't look as strong as the energy coming straight from my hand." Hazrael studied the difference, analyzing the properties as he turned his hand toward the sunlight.

Where Hazrael's energy was bright and sharp, Oberon's was duller, muted, as if filtered through gauze.

"Interesting."

"What do you think it means, Master Hazrael?" Journeyman Lorelli regarded the variation as if he looked at a mystical puzzle.

"I'm not sure yet." Hazrael placed a gentle hand on Lorelli's sleeve. "Will you please go find Masters Theodyne and Nico? I want to test a theory on them."

"Yes. Of course."

When he'd gone, Oberon gave Hazrael a considering look. "What are you thinking?"

"That it has something to do with having been touched by the necromancers." Hazrael turned his hand over, and the blue energy continued to leak from his fingers in a steady stream. It pooled on the tabletop, some ectoplasmic substance brought through an ethereal curtain. "You and I have both been touched, but by varying degrees. Thus the exudate is thicker, brighter. You were only touched briefly, but enough to turn your hair. You carry their mark in a small way, and your light is smaller, less defined."

Oberon nodded. "And Lorelli has not been so tainted."

Hazrael shook his head. "No, he has not. So the energy had no affinity for him. He is immune."

Oberon's smile was slow to come, but when it did, it was full-blown and filled the room with joy. Then the most miraculous thing happened; he tilted his head back and laughed. It was full and deep and echoed throughout the workroom, filling each corner with untold mirth.

At a loss as to why Oberon found this predicament so funny, Hazrael went back to work, fashioning more of the bolts.

Oberon slapped a big hand on the tabletop, startling Hazrael. "Don't you see?" Disbelief mixed with elation filled Oberon's eyes. The smile remained on his face. "You're brilliant in your assessment and what this could mean, and you don't even understand why?"

Hazrael hesitated, then said, "I do understand, but I think you may read too much into it. If it can be used to more accurately target the necromancers, then I'm afraid they will also find a way to use this energy to their advantage, especially if it is byproduct from having such a close brush with them."

Oberon's smile faded. He sobered. "I see what you mean. Is there a way we can test it, like you did the crystal-laced bolts on the battlements?"

Hazrael nodded. "A small test might be just what we need."

"Just what we need for what?" Nico entered the workroom a few steps ahead of Theodyne and Lorelli.

"To prove we can use the blue energy to our advantage without it getting back into the hands of the necromancers," Hazrael supplied. "They are already formidable foes without giving them an edge they don't require."

Theodyne gazed down at the glowing bolts. "Odd." He held his hand above the area and closed his eyes. "It's air energy."

Hazrael frowned. "Are you sure?"

"Positive." Theodyne closed his hand around a tendril that rose up toward his palm. His entire hand began to glow. "It's protective in nature, with a propensity to build or destroy."

Oberon held up his hand to show Theodyne the slight bluish tint to his fingertips. "Then why am I able to spread it and Lorelli is not? I have no elemental blood."

Theodyne jerked his head to indicate Nico. "You give it a try."

Nico had neither been touched by the necromancers nor held elemental blood. He ran his hand down the length of the rods and came up with nothing.

"Journeyman Lorelli had the same result." Hazrael held up his hand again. "My theory was that only those of us touched by the necromancers were able to use it and to manipulate it at will."

Theodyne rolled the energy into a ball. "You might very well be correct, but it's also composed of a pool of energy that surrounds an air elemental. One that can be manipulated."

Hazrael frowned. "The spirit elementals won't like that. They will find a way to diminish from me."

Nico frowned. "What makes you assume they'd do such a thing?"

Hazrael rubbed his chest where the ugly, angry bruise remained. It had turned a vivid purple-black. "They'd rather see me rot in the hands of the necromancers than to see me survive. I have no illusions as to their minds and hearts where I am concerned, regardless of what the Hierophant or Anjufer might say."

An uncomfortable silence filled the room. Oh, he did not want to relive those moments again. It was bad enough the absence of the elementals left a hole under his heart and through the middle of his soul. Each time he spoke of it, the wound in his heart bled afresh.

Hazrael decided to tackle a new problem. "Theodyne, see if you can throw that ball you just made?"

Theodyne raised his arm and pitched the small glowing orb against the far wall. It hit true and spread outward in tiny ripples of energy. "It appears I can."

"Good. We'll use one of those for our test rather than risking a bolt." Hazrael started out of the room and turned when he realized no one followed him. "Well, are you coming or not?"

There was a bit of confusion before assent rose in the small group.

He brought them down to the yard and out to the walls of the school, then out farther still.

He stopped when he was a good way from the border wall surrounding the yards. "I needed to be out from under the shield and far enough away that if our tests fail, no harm will come to the property. Are we ready?"

Even as he asked the question, the sky began to churn in ominous threat. A feeling of being sucked into a powerful vortex pulled Hazrael from behind.

He turned and saw the portal open across the field. It shimmered and vibrated with the same blue light he held in his hand. A legion of necromancers appeared in the gate.

Hazrael held up his arm across his chest, legs locked in a fighting stance, willing them to come. Without warning he let the blue energy fly in an arc that reached the necromancers.

The portal grew unstable, closing the aperture to a mere pinprick of light across the field.

"It doesn't look like it did much but close the portal." Oberon started for the area where the beam of light originated.

Nico grabbed the sleeve of Oberon's robe. "Don't touch it. It might zap you."

"Perhaps, but if it helps us construct one when all other attempts have failed, I'm going to utilize it."

"I'm almost sure we can manipulate it for that purpose." Theodyne gave his assessment. From the looks of it, he had already moved on to solve another problem. He duck-walked low to the ground, with his hand stretched out before him, brushing above the top of the grass. "A portal pulls life force from the surrounding elements to build power."

Hazrael glanced down. Spots of brown leeched into the green grass, making it look almost as if a circle had been painted in the clearing. It wasn't so much that the color had changed, but the perception of the spectrum on the ethereal. "There would have to be a price extracted to generate enough power for a portal. The reason the alchemists do not use such means of travel is because it is not in their nature to steal such gifts from unsuspecting entities. Necromancers have no similar scruples."

A mischievous glint filled Theodyne's eyes. "True. But we have something they don't."

Nico turned. "What is that?"

"Cooperation from the elementals."

Chapter Fifteen

OBERON SAT with Theodyne and Nico in the library. Hazrael had declined the invitation to join them, citing a need to further test the strange blue energy leaking from his fingertips. First crystals and now light—was it any wonder the poor man seemed half-crazed most of the time? What, besides the obvious torture, had they done to him? Had they bestowed powers on him that were only now beginning to manifest? Surely they wouldn't have turned him into a weapon and allowed him to be unleashed on the world until they were ready to make their final move.

Oberon rubbed his brow and tried to concentrate on the books in front of him.

None of them had given the alchemists much to go on by way of a portal. As a matter of fact, Oberon did not remember once even hearing about such a feat. Unless....

There had been a strange tale he'd read years ago. It wasn't even in one of the books—not a bound one. A scroll. He'd come across it while doing research for a project when he was still a second-year apprentice. At the time he'd only thought it an amusing tale about one of the first alchemists, even before Mercurian Dante founded the Gold School. This story was told before written language transformed to the familiar letters used at present. Back then, script was merely odd cylindrical shapes going in various directions and impressed on wet clay. The clay was then dried, and a pressed papyrus leaf was placed over the slab and rubbed with charcoal. The charcoal was then set with a resin to harden to ensure it was not brushed away and the message or story lost. For all intents and purposes it was a very crude form of a printing press.

Oberon rose from the table. Theodyne and Nico's quiet conversation barely registered on his mind as he went to the sealed vault at the very top of the library dome.

An iron gate closed the door off from curious hands and prying eyes. Odd how the scrolls had been moved to this closed space after Hazrael's abduction. The connection gave him pause. Did the Adepts' Council at the time move the scrolls for mere protection of the ancient works, or had there been some other reason?

He pressed his thumb to the notch in the lock mechanism. It was keyed for only three people: the headmaster, under-headmaster, and Nico. Only Nico knew the process used for adding a person to the lock so it would recognize the person who wished to enter. The metal heated under his touch, causing the wheels inside to begin turning. The gate swung open, leaving him only the iron door of the vault to open. This was no great mystery or magical construct, but a physical lock and key.

He removed the chain from around his neck. The small golden key was attached to the necklace, looking for all the world a lucky charm.

"What are you looking for?"

Oberon jumped at the sound of Nico's voice. He glanced over his shoulder. "A scroll I read in my second year, back when we all had access to these texts without having to be at the upper reaches of our discipline."

Nico made a face at the cutting remark. "Knowledge is power."

"Knowledge is also freedom." Oberon unlocked the vault. The door swung on hinges that had not been used in a very long time. The stench of old paper and mold wafted out of the opening. "Smells like we might lose some of the writings to spores."

"Damn!" Nico pushed inside, reaching for the alchemists' globe at the entrance. "How could they have been so stupid to not protect against the smallest of thieves?"

"After we defeat the necromancers, we'll have to catalog and try and recover every last scroll in here." Oberon began searching the shelves for the scroll he sought. "Did they even think to put in a filing system, or are the stacks made by throwing scrolls on the shelves in any old manner?"

"There is a ledger on the table over by the door."

Oberon was almost embarrassed to admit he'd never visited this part of the library. There had never been a need to before now. All the books he'd ever needed since that day he'd found in the main stacks.

The ledger was written in a fine hand. Donando's handwriting to be precise. Oberon's suspicions grew. Had he known the necromancers had returned seventeen years ago? He fisted his hand atop the pages. Anger put a sheen over his vision, making it hard to see.

If they'd suspected an infiltration by the necromancers, why had they not warned their brethren?

"I've never wanted to go back in time and strangle a group of men more than I do at this moment."

Nico glanced up from where he inspected the stacks for damage. "I don't know if some of these can be saved without putting them through some rigorous alchemical works."

"Maybe they should be unrolled and stored behind sheets of glass."

Nico nodded. "My thoughts exactly."

Oberon tried to tamp down his anger as he turned the ledger pages. Nico had misunderstood Oberon's annoyance as stemming from the ruination of priceless documents. It hadn't been anything that simple or tangible.

He flipped through the pages, looking for the name of the scroll. It took a few minutes to go through the entire book, only to find it not written onto the ledger. Had the former headmaster missed the entry on purpose, or was it simply an honest clerical error when the scrolls were relocated?

It didn't sit right that it was the only scroll in the entire library he needed at the moment, and it was the one missing. At least if others were missing, he'd never realize it.

"It's not registered here."

Nico glanced up from his assessment. "It has to be. Maybe you have the title wrong."

Oberon merely stared at Nico. If there was one thing he always remembered, it was the title of any book or scroll he read. Complete content might be a little harder to pull from his brain, but not titles.

"Then go backward this time. Start at the end of the entries and move forward." Nico gave the matter-of-fact advice as he went deeper into the stacks. "It has to be there. I can't see the former Adepts' Council—some of whom are still seated members—hiding a scroll."

"Maybe not." Oberon looked around him. There was the distinct possibility the elementals had taken the scroll to the hidden library.

They were known to take it upon themselves to relocate books they deemed too dangerous for human consumption. Why not a scroll that illustrated the use of a portal by an alchemist?

So far the only alchemist since ancient times allowed in the hidden library was Theodyne. The elementals had welcomed him into the archives with open arms three years before. Then they had been eager to get the information of the necromancers to Theodyne.

Oberon left the vault and went to the railing and looked down into the main floor of the library. Theodyne remained at the same table, poring over texts.

Oberon cupped his hands around his mouth. "Theodyne!"

Theodyne looked up. "You bellowed?"

"I need you to get into the hidden library for me."

"To look for what?"

"A scroll." Oberon started down the long spiral of the library. He met Theodyne at the entrance to the hidden room. He'd not yet been granted access.

"Any particular scroll you had in mind?" Theodyne waited against a bookcase that looked solid and unassuming.

"It's titled *The Journey of Corwin Crawley*."

"Which means if there is more than one scroll in there, I'm going to have to open and read them all before I find it." Theodyne smiled a devilish grin. "Unless the elementals decide to help me." He rapped a knuckle against the bookcase. "Doesn't look like they are so inclined at the moment."

Oberon agreed. Why were the elementals so guarded with the secret? Surely they saw the advantage for the alchemists to be able to manipulate portals. He was rightly sick of their secret agenda and failure to become involved in the affairs of man until things became so dire it affected them directly.

"All right. Try again later. In the meantime, I need to take a break and walk around. This ineffectual search is slowly making me doubt my sanity."

Theodyne narrowed his gaze, as if assessing Oberon through the critical lens of his healer's talent. "Do you need me to evaluate you?"

Oberon shook his head. "No." He pointed to the upper levels. "When Nico comes down, tell him I've gone somewhere to think."

Normally the library was a calming retreat from the rigors of the day. Not this time. It only proved to be a source of frustration for Oberon. He left Theodyne and Nico to their searches and headed up to his tower workroom.

Part of his frustration stemmed from the fact he had this overwhelming feeling of being out of his depth lately, and without much to contribute to the quest. It wasn't at all like him to doubt his abilities or lack confidence. He'd not been that way since early in his training.

An odd tingle came to his fingertips, ghost prints from the weird blue energy that had infused them when he'd touched the bolts. What if the light wasn't used just to destroy portals but to construct them?

He turned and headed to the workroom where Hazrael had been constructing the glass bolts. An odd blue glow filled the room, shining from under the door. Oberon unlocked the door and grabbed one of the bolts before resecuring the door and heading up to his workroom.

The energy illuminated the dim hallways, negating the need for a candle or globe. Handy little beacons, if they proved of no use for anything else.

The glow once again transferred to his hands. This time to a greater degree, and it penetrated farther under his skin. It burned with all the searing pain of a hot skewer. Yet he held fast to the bolt, hoping the deeper it burned, the more permanent it would become.

By the time he reached the tower workroom, his hand throbbed and his fingers contracted. He set the bolt down on the table.

Fire filled the fireplace grate. Anjufer roared to life. "You dabble in powers you have no control over, Oberon!"

Oberon was unconcerned by the warning and Anjufer's theatrics. "Perhaps, but it must be done, since the elementals have decided not to help."

"The elementals are concerned for the welfare of the alchemists."

"Then they should give us the tools to make it easier to get to the action rather than allowing us to risk our lives by traveling across the country, toting weapons and a person who acts as a lodestone to the necromancers. If that doesn't reek of danger, I have no idea what does." Oberon stalked to the other side of the room to get away from Anjufer. Not that such a move would stop the elemental. He was very determined for an ancient one.

The palm of his hand still burned, though he'd set the bolt down. When he lifted his hand, he could see straight through it, cast in that odd bluish light. Bones and tendons made dark shadows in the depths of skin. He tried moving it, but a slice of agony traveled up from his palm, passed his wrist, and went straight up to his shoulder. If he didn't know better, he'd swear his bones had splintered. No, fractured like ice hitting stone.

That was what this burn felt like—cold, frozen, not a burn from heat but one from an icy hell.

He didn't know quite how that would help him in his endeavor, but he was going to push through the pain and try. Now the first step of any alchemical experiment was to call on the Grand Matter to intercede.

As above, so below.

To think of the problem logically, how was opening a portal from one point to another any different than changing the state of matter of any other substance? It was, after all, only shortening the distance between two places. They had been coming at the problem in entirely the wrong manner. Rather than railing at the heavens and elementals for not giving them the power to manipulate distances, they needed to look at it as any other experiment the order had conducted over the centuries.

Based on what he'd read in that scroll years ago, it had been a power granted to the alchemists, then allowed to die out.

Oberon turned to Anjufer, who still burned bright, watching him as he drew a doorway in the air with his glowing hand. "Why was this skill suppressed?"

Anjufer narrowed what passed for his eyes. "You know why."

"As a means to control the alchemists?"

"*No!*" Anjufer blazed outward into the room. The heat of his anger bathed the side of Oberon's face.

"Turn down your temper. It is wasted on me." Oberon glared at the elemental. "I, too, have reason to be angry at your kind. Over the years the secrets the elementals keep has done more harm to the alchemists than any benefit it's brought."

"It is done out of love. Out of protection." Anjufer's hissing, crackling voice took on a note of pleading. "You are our children."

"Not all of us." There was no mistaking that some alchemists had only human blood in their veins. Oberon was one such example.

"Yes. All of you." Anjufer diminished some, but did not fall all the way back into the grate. "Even if you have no elemental blood, we see you as one of our own. It is the way of things."

If it was, then why had they turned their backs on Hazrael? Oberon wanted to know the answer to that but decided instead to stay on task.

"You should speak with the others about making portals accessible to the alchemists. It might make things easier, but know in advance, we will crack the trick and make it work for us regardless of what your kind decides."

"I cannot betray my nature and give you the answer, Oberon. I can, however, bend the mandate and tell you that you are currently headed in the right direction." With that Anjufer diminished and shot up the flue.

Validation sang in Oberon's veins. Over twenty years of practicing the arts of alchemy had not failed him; he'd only been blinded for a short time.

The doorway he'd started to trace before Anjufer's interruption continued to glow in the center of the workroom. Now, how to make the place he wanted to go appear on the other side? That was the real trick. Shortening distances between two points could only come if one had altered the space occupied by an object, in this case everything between the origination and destination.

He'd try something close, within the school proper this first time. He knew all the hallways and rooms as he knew his own heart. There was no mistaking them or landing in a place unsecured or unknown.

The energy held strong. Oberon concentrated on the area inside the glowing border. A shift here, a change there. Slowly, he let the interior of the image morph to show him the lower level of the library.

Chairs and tables, books and shelves came into view a little at a time. Nico and Theodyne sat poring over the volumes they had left earlier. Theodyne looked up. Eyes wide and wild. He hit Nico, who turned around in his seat.

Oberon stepped close to the portal, but did not go through. Not yet. He waved to his brethren. The energy began to fluctuate and die. It was hard to hold the images steady. They faded and snapped closed.

Oberon's legs went out from under him, and he sat on the hard stone floor. His head swam and eyes watered. A splitting headache made him groan. Maybe it would be best if he just lay down for a moment.

He must have fallen asleep. A tap of an insistent hand on his cheek woke him a bit later. His eyelids fluttered. The strange blue light in the room still shone but was now augmented by candlelight. Theodyne stood over him with a worried expression on his face.

"He's coming to."

Nico was at his other side, helping him to sit up. "I'd yell at you for taking chances by yourself, but I'm too excited at your breakthrough to make it very forceful."

Oberon shook his head to clear it. A buzzing plagued his ears, and his eyes swam, convincing him that his head was full of water. Was that a normal reaction to creating a portal? If so, it was a singularly miserable experience. "I think the blue energy came directly from portal building."

Theodyne winced. "You don't have to shout, Oberon. We can hear you."

Oberon pointed to his ear. "Buzzing. Can't hear."

Theodyne turned Oberon's head to either side and looked in his ears. Judging from the expression on his face, he didn't see anything untoward. "What's wrong with your palm?"

Oberon glanced down. The light had faded, but the burn remained. In its place was the perfect image of an eight-sided star. The skin was shiny there, the lines smooth. "I carried one of the bolts up here and it burned me."

Nico frowned. "The bolts can generate enough energy to open a portal?"

Oberon questioned how much to tell the others about the events right before Hazrael opened his hand to reveal the odd light that poured from his fingers. It was another sign Hazrael's time with the necromancers had transformed him into a being none of them understood, including Hazrael. Though, in all truth, Hazrael had already told him that the power originated inside him.

Oberon ran a hand through his hair. "Right before Hazrael began to manifest the energy, he had one of his spells. Not a bad one. He managed to stay upright, but he'd gone even paler than normal, if that's possible."

Theodyne latched on to the confession. "What was he doing? How was he standing when it occurred?"

"He was making the crystal bolts, then turned to the window and stared at the sunshine as it streamed in. As for what was going through his head, he didn't say. When I asked if he was all right, he got rather defensive."

"Defensive how?" This from Nico, who had brought a chair over and sat down. "Angry?"

"No, more frustrated with himself. Worried that we see him as weak because he can't work for long without getting assailed by some memory that makes him falter." Oberon's heart bled every time he thought of it. Hazrael had once been the best and brightest of them all. His place on the Adepts' Council assured once he moved to the highest level of master. He'd been robbed of his health and future. Under those circumstances anyone might feel frustrated.

Nico grew pensive. "I wonder how any of us would hold up if faced with the same trials."

Oberon swallowed. "There are times when he is quite in despair. I fear what will happen if he ever learns he killed a child."

Theodyne looked away. He had been there and witnessed the death, unable to stop the horrible murder. "It will surely break him as nothing else has. I am hoping his sense of self-preservation is strong enough to keep that suppressed."

Nico shook his head. "That's not good enough. Other painful memories have leaked through. We have to do more to ensure he never discovers that painful truth."

"I'd hate to go back into his mind and try and fix it again. It seems every time we do, it only makes his symptoms worse." Theodyne had a point.

The golden bowl in the corner flashed with shimmery lights.

"Someone is trying to come through the scry bowl." Theodyne rose and went to the bowl as Jolen's face reflected off the mirror on the wall above. "Jolen."

Either the image was bad or he looked horrible. His eyes had dark circles under them, his hair was a mess, and there was a cut along one of his cheeks. "The situation in Gusan is deteriorating fast. You must...."

A blinding explosion lit the field behind Jolen. The connection severed.

Theodyne banged on the bowl. "Jolen! Jolen!"

Nico was already up and moving. "Assemble those traveling to Gusan. We must leave immediately."

Chapter Sixteen

DISQUIET FILLED Hazrael. All around him shadowy images leaked through the walls of his room, trying to get to him from the ether. Threats circled, closing the space between him and safety. He raised his hands. Defensive crystals shot out, building a wall, blocking him from his tormentors.

Vibrations shook the school. Was it thunder or quake? He wasn't quite certain, but either menace was the work of those elementals trying to kill him.

The door to his room swung open, and Oberon entered. The beings retreated into the walls again. He looked at the clear wall around Hazrael and shook his head. "Get out of there. We have to leave. Immediately."

"What's happened? Are we abandoning the school?"

"No. Why would you ask that?"

Hazrael stilled. The vibrations had stopped. Were they ever there? He ran his hand in an arc across the wall and the crystals fell to the floor. "Then why are we leaving?"

Oberon glanced to the defensive manifestation as the crystals hit the floor with a soft tinkling sound. "We've had news from Gusan. The holy city is under siege, or at least that's what it appears. We lost contact with our agent there."

Hazrael moved around the room collecting what he might need for a journey to Gusan. There wasn't much he owned, but what he had, he treasured. "When are we leaving?"

"As soon as we are all assembled and the horses harnessed."

Praise to Nico for having the forethought to have the wagons packed ahead. It would speed up the process.

"Are there any details on what happened?"

"No. Nor have we been able to reestablish contact." Oberon looked out at the hallway as someone walked by. He summoned the person into the room. It was Journeyman Lorelli. "Wait here for Master Hazrael. I'm going to gather the others."

"Yes, Headmaster."

When Oberon stepped away, Hazrael turned to Journeyman Lorelli. "Did you feel any odd currents in the school? Vibrations?"

Journeyman Lorelli shook his head. "No. When did this happen?"

"Right before Oberon entered." Hazrael glanced around the room. Had he felt what happened in Gusan down the cord of his connection to the necromancers? It was possible, he supposed. The Kiss of Death on his skin hadn't glowed or bled.

Journeyman Lorelli took a turn about the room, his hand outstretched. "I don't feel any stray energy or signatures on the air. Could the problem have been physical?"

Hazrael didn't believe that to be the case. No, he'd seen beings leaking through the walls, trying to get at him from the ether. Better not to mention that aspect. It might not be physical but mental. At the moment he didn't know which was worse. Either could incapacitate him, making him useless to the alchemists. He'd not risk being left behind on this important trip to Gusan.

Hazrael held up his hand. "Forget I mentioned it. Whatever the cause, it seems to be gone now."

"I will get your bag." Journeyman Lorelli picked up the small fabric sack that contained the clothes Hazrael had been given since arriving at the school. There were no formal masters' robes in the pack. He'd not been reinstated in such a fashion. When he went into battle against the necromancers, he'd do so as a separate entity.

As Hazrael left the room, he swore he saw those same beings convening in the shadows.

He pushed the experience from his mind, knowing there was nothing in there the necromancers could use to call him forth. Everything they had of him was etched in the lines on his body. Those same lines began to itch as he walked behind Journeyman Lorelli to the lower level of the school and out into the drive.

The wagons were filled and the horses harnessed. Nico stood in the center of the confusion, directing apprentices and journeymen with last-minute instructions. He glanced up at Hazrael and pointed to the lead wagon.

"I've made a place for you in here. The wagon is already protected with shields."

"Can I do anything to help prepare?"

"We are almost ready. I'm only waiting for the last of the riders to arrive, and we will pull out."

Hazrael took his sack from Journeyman Lorelli and climbed up into the wagon, feeling a bit useless. Now he knew how a hammer or chisel felt. They were tools to be used and then left to sit on a shelf until needed.

The wagon was his own personal shelf. He was more than a mere weapon to be unleashed on the necromancers. He had arms and legs to carry or support. They need not only call on him when they needed the firepower of his odd talents.

A small pallet of blankets was situated between crates. The spot didn't provide a good deal of room for him to move around, but then he didn't need much. Snuggled among the weapons, he doubted he'd even be seen by anyone inspecting the wagon bed.

Vibrations started under his feet, moving along the ground, rocking the wagon. He stuck his head out and looked around the drive. No one else stopped to consider the odd tremor. In fact the other alchemists didn't even seem to notice.

"What is it?" Journeyman Lorelli stood by a large bay stallion next to the wagon.

"Can you feel that? The ground is shaking."

Journeyman Lorelli stilled. He remained that way for a full minute before he shook his head. "I feel nothing, Master Hazrael."

Hazrael jumped back down from the wagon. Perhaps the wheels were unstable and he'd mistaken the movement for the odd vibrations he'd felt in his room.

Nothing.

Hazrael put his hands on his hips and looked down at the ground. All right, he'd clearly gotten confused.

This time the rumbling started in his core and moved outward, knocking him off his feet. Heat from a blast washed along his left side. He screamed in agony. The Kiss of Death lit his skin as brightly as any firefly's tail.

"Master!" Journeyman Lorelli bent down over Hazrael, trying to help him. "Master Theodyne! We need you over here!"

Hazrael tried to crawl from the pain, but he couldn't get far enough away from it. Over the ragged roar of his voice, he heard the shuffle of feet moving beside him, felt the gentle hands of Theodyne as he assessed the etchings, heard the speculative murmurs of those in the yard.

"He complained of feeling vibrations." Hazrael heard Journeyman Lorelli explain. "He thought a quake was upon us."

"No. It's not that at all. He's feeling the backlash of power from the necromancers all the way from the holy city." Theodyne placed a cool palm over the angry scars. "It's traveling along the connection they share and using him as an end point and grounding for the power."

It was a grim diagnosis. Theodyne need not say anything more— it was enough to know that it was magical in nature. If the power became too much for Hazrael's system to control, he'd disintegrate from the inside out.

With muscles and skin aching, Hazrael tried to push up to his feet. "Get me up into the wagon. I'll devise a way to channel this outward as we travel."

Theodyne gave a sigh as he helped Hazrael to his feet. "You are a determined one. What will you do to counteract the effects? The Kiss of Death gives them direct access to you."

Hazrael had no idea at the moment. The pain blocked his ability to think, to plan, but he wasn't going to give up without a fight. He wasn't going to let them win by eating away a bit of his will with every blast down the line of their connection. To sever it at this point was to lose the opportunity to draw the necromancers in as they'd planned.

He settled in among the boxes and weapons. Comfort escaped him. The nap of his shirt rubbed against the scars on his chest, causing a fresh wave of pain to erupt along his side. He gritted his teeth and peeled the fabric up to look down on his torso. The angry tracks of the intricate markings were beginning to fade. Whatever had caused the blast had injured one of those who had been present when the Kiss of Death was carved into his skin. Though the reaction along the connection was strong, Hazrael doubted it was the knife bearer who had been injured.

Enough with the worry and speculation. What he needed was to find a way to narrow the connection so he no longer felt their peril.

Unfortunately, severing a cord of that magnitude would also make it harder to use it to call them forth once the alchemists reached Gusan. For now, he'd have to bear it the best he could and hope they didn't use him for a true shield. At this point the grounding might all be unintentional, but if the necromancers realized part of the energy backlash flowed directly to Hazrael, they might channel it all to him and overload his mind.

Hazrael had been used as their channel too many times to want to go through it again. His mind was littered with murky flashes of all the sins the necromancers had visited on him, and he'd as soon not add to the burden.

If he was to go back into the darkness, it would be on his terms. Now he knew the reason for his pains, he could divert the energy and maybe even use it to his advantage. The strategy might kill him, but he'd go into the afterlife with enthusiasm if he knew he'd done so with honor. However, he'd not go until he made good on his promises to the alchemists. There had to be a way to get to Gusan faster than by caravan. All his experiments into using a portal, or even constructing one, had failed. Yet he knew the blue energy was part of the equation. He'd not been able to make it work for him. Frustration had transformed the blue goo into crystals. There was no controlling what substance manifested and when.

He was sure he'd used portals before, made them of his own accord. Somewhere locked inside his mind were the answers he sought, and yet he was almost afraid to dig through them and unleash the agony. He needed to be clearheaded and cognizant when they reached their destination. He might have to strategically think and plan. A much harder proposition when his head thrummed like a kettle drum.

The wagon flap opened, and Oberon looked inside. "Feeling better?"

"Still tender, but the burn is subsiding some." Hazrael raised his shirt to inspect the flesh beneath. It was still bright pink, but the lines had stopped glowing. "You don't understand how I long to confront the monsters who made me what I am. To have the chance to wring some vengeance."

Oberon's expression hardened. "We all do, and I fear that way leads down a dark path."

"Then we will all travel it together." Hazrael lowered his shirt. "I can't make a portal. I've been trying all afternoon. I think they might have stripped that skill from me somehow, afraid I'd use it against them."

A mischievous light came into Oberon's green eyes. "I managed a very faint one. It didn't look stable enough to cross through, but I was able to wave to Theodyne and Nico on the other side of it."

Hazrael sat up. Excitement sang in his veins. "You managed one?"

"Don't sound so surprised. I am a decent enough practitioner."

"You misunderstand me, Oberon. I can't build one myself, but I can help to power one. Don't you see? Together we can get the caravan to Gusan tonight." Hazrael scrambled to the edge of the wagon bed and started to climb down. Oberon held his arm to steady him.

"You can't be serious." Oberon kept hold of Hazrael as he started away to find Nico. "You'll risk us all if the portal is unstable."

Hazrael held himself a little taller. "I'll go through first and wave the rest of you to proceed if it's safe. If not, then you'll see the results for yourself and...." He scratched his side. The burn had started to tingle and itch. "No, that won't work. If I'm helping to power the portal." Ideas tripped over one another in his mind as he worked out the logistics of moving so many people and wagons through a portal. "Yes, it will work. I'll power it from the other side. Hold it open for all of you until you can get through. You stay here and power from this side."

"It's not that I lack courage or even talent, but when it comes to raw elemental power, I have none."

Hazrael swatted Oberon's reminder away. It was less than unimportant. "And yet you were the one who was able to open one. Not Theodyne. Not Nico. Not Rhone. Not any of the others. *You.*" The last word was said with a poke of a finger into Oberon's chest. Maybe that would get through his thick skull. "Now hurry before Nico gives the order to pull out."

They found Nico standing near his horse, getting ready to mount. When he saw Hazrael and Oberon, his frown was very telling. "I thought I told you to get into the protected wagon."

"Forget that for now. I think I know a way to move us all through a portal to Gusan without wasting time on the roads."

Nico only blinked a few times. Slowly he came back into his mind. He let his hands slide down the side of the saddle. "How are you going to accomplish this, and how long will it take to set up?"

"Not as long as it will take to travel to Gusan." That was, if the rumbling Hazrael felt under his feet subsided. If he got hit with another blast from the necromancers before the gate was complete, the potential for fatalities increased exponentially.

"That's not helpful, Hazrael."

Hazrael turned around and blazed a look of irritation at Nico. "I haven't timed myself while conducting such an elaborate setup. I apologize."

Nico gave a sigh. "No. Of course you haven't. Where did you want to set it up?"

Hazrael turned to Oberon. "How did you construct the portal?"

"With my hands. I used the blue energy from the bolts to trace a doorway."

Hazrael nodded. "We'll need something a bit more permanent if we're going to get all these people and wagons through. It will take less from us that way, and we can anchor the structure." He turned in a circle, trying to remember the layout of the school grounds and surrounding areas.

The portal needed to be attached to someplace convenient, but one that posed no immediate threat to the school should the necromancers manage to take control of it before they were all through.

"The gates of the school grounds. We can affix it to the archway and have one of the Adepts' Council release it once we're through." Nico waved to Rhone. "Your assistance, Rhone."

Master Rhone's eyes rounded. There was a moment or two of indecision where it appeared as if he might turn and run before he stepped forward in a slow walk. "Yes, Nico."

"Since you have chosen to stay behind during our excursion, it falls to you to remove a portal from the gates once our party is through."

Even before Nico finished giving his instructions, Master Rhone shook his head.

"No. I will not. That is power we cannot control or wield, and I'll not be a tool used to do its bidding." Master Rhone backed away with hands raised.

Nico's nostrils flared in anger. "I will deal with you when we return." He turned to look around the drive and spotted one of the other adept-level masters helping to strap down the pieces of a siege machine to a wagon bed. "Erhnheart. Attend me!"

The master looked up and nodded. He finished securing the straps and ran over to Nico. "What can I do for you?"

"Masters Oberon and Hazrael believe they can send us to Gusan through a portal. We need someone on this side to release the energy once we're through. Are you up to the task?"

A mischievous glint filled Erhnheart's eyes. "To surprise those death-dancing bastards in Gusan, I'm more than up for the task. What do I need to do?"

Hazrael bent down and scooped up some dirt in his hands. He rubbed it together, concentrating, fashioning it into a long glass rod. When it was finished, he held it out to Master Erhnheart. Instead of glowing blue, this had a faint green light in its very core. "Use this. The energy of the portal will become attracted to the earth elemental in the rod. Once you've managed to gather all the blue light, ground it. Oberon will take down the portal on the other side once he's through, so hopefully the necromancers will be unable to use it. However, the anchor must be taken down, or you—we—risk allowing them to erect one using our energy."

The glint left Erhnheart's eyes, replaced by one of purpose. "Understood."

Now to try and create a stable portal.

OBERON GAZED down at his palm. The burns were smoothed over, the power gone. "I'm going to need another one of the bolts to hold."

Hazrael glanced up as he worked quickly on the gate. "No, you won't. You're going to use the energy I lay down. I'm placing it at strategic points along the construction. You'll need to fill it in and work it from there."

"I haven't been to Gusan in years. I'm not sure if the place I remember entering the city is even still there or looks the same. It will make visualizing the other end of the portal difficult." It also created a problem on where exactly they came out. Without knowing at the moment where the heaviest fighting occurred, they had no way to know if they were going to drop directly into the middle of a battle or out on the fringes.

Hazrael cocked his head. "I have no clear memories of being there either. Theodyne was there recently, correct?"

Oberon nodded.

"Then you two will have to work together to visualize the exit point." Hazrael twirled his hand as if it was of no consequence. "You've worked together before. It should be easy."

Reservations continued to fill Oberon's mind. This was probably one of those decisions he was going to regret the rest of his life. Attempting a portal in the middle of the school was one thing, but bringing their entire strike force through one that had not been tested was foolhardy. For Nico to approve it, well, there weren't enough words in the Dominicál language to express Oberon's shock. Yet he was going to go along with it, because even though it didn't seem a prudent move, it was the shortest distance to get them to Gusan.

Hazrael placed the finishing touches on the archway. "Now, where is Theodyne?"

"I'll go get him," Celsi, who had been standing to Oberon's right, offered. He hurried off into the crowd that had gathered at a distance to watch the spectacle of the portal being erected.

Alone with Hazrael, Oberon leaned close to him. The spicy tang of cinnamon and herbs hung heavy about his skin. It was the way he used to smell, before the taint of the death dancers. Oberon took a deep breath, assailed by memories both painful and sweet. "Please be careful when you cross over. I don't want to lose you a second time."

Hazrael's clear gray eyes rounded, the pupils dilated. "Oberon." His name came out as a harsh whisper full of longing.

Unable to stop himself, Oberon closed the space between them, only enough to brush his lips against Hazrael's. When he pulled away, Hazrael's eyes had slid shut, his face immobile. Slowly, he opened his eyes.

Color filled Hazrael's pale cheeks. "You probably shouldn't have done that, Oberon."

"Why not?"

"Because if something happens to me, it will hurt twice as hard this time."

Panic seized Oberon. He clamped a hand on Hazrael's shoulder. "Did you see something? A prognostication that you will not come out of this?" His heart took a plunge and almost stopped beating. "The Hierophant *did* tell you something, didn't she?"

Hazrael laid a slender hand on Oberon's cheek. "I have no way of knowing what the necromancers have in store for me. They will either try to take me back into the fold or kill me. Those are their only choices. The chances of me coming out of this fight alive or intact are very slim at best and always have been."

Oberon wouldn't accept that as an outcome. He squeezed Hazrael's shoulder tighter, as if a punishing grip would protect him. "I won't allow that. The only outcome will be the one where you return with us once the necromancers are put down."

Hazrael gave him a sad smile. "With the Kiss of Death on my flesh, their destruction ensures my own."

There had to be a way to free Hazrael. "We'll take it all away, sever the connection once we are over and they've been called."

Hazrael gave a bark of laughter. "Oberon, I love you, but you fool yourself. There won't be time, and to take it in order to heal my scars will be wasting resources needed elsewhere."

"You sound like you want to die." The idea was so foreign a concept to Oberon he couldn't even wrap his mind around it.

"No. You mistake me." Hazrael ran his hand down the front of Oberon's robes, stopping at heart level. "I don't want to die, but I am resigned to it if it means saving the alchemists, clerics, and the *prolates*. I've killed under someone else's will. Now let me save them under my own."

Who was Oberon to deny a man the right to die on his own terms? To sacrifice himself to save others? Perhaps it was what the Grand Matter had planned all along for him to atone for crimes not of his making.

Oberon wasn't going to let it end this way. He leaned in, brushing Hazrael's hair back from his face, then lowered his mouth so their lips touched, soft and passionate.

Hazrael's hands tightened in the folds of Oberon's robe. A deep, sensual moan purled up from Hazrael's throat, vibrating against Oberon's tongue. He took the kiss deeper, tasting and savoring Hazrael, wanting the moment to spiral out until it touched forever. If this was the last moment they were to be together, he wanted no questions to remain about his true feelings.

A discreet cough behind them, and Oberon broke away. He touched his forehead to Hazrael's before turning to whoever had interrupted the passionate moment. He finally glanced over his shoulder to find Celsi and Theodyne behind them.

Celsi was studying his shoes, and Theodyne gave Oberon a questioning look. Oberon ignored both reactions and stepped away from Hazrael.

"He says we need to join so you can give me a detailed location of where best to place the exit point for the portal."

"Ah." Theodyne touched the stones that composed the archway. "I know just the place, and we will be within the walls of a secure villa."

Oberon raised a brow. "The Medovin's Gusan residence?"

"Yes. He has a couple of sizable gardens to choose from that can support the wagons." He pulled out his personal scry sphere. "Let me see if I can contact anyone within to let them know we're coming."

Oberon held out no hope. They'd been unable to raise any of their contacts in the holy city for hours.

The sphere lit. A connection grew to life, then flickered out.

"This is Master Theodyne of the Gold School. If you receive this message, please respond." He placed the sphere back into his pocket. "I am not going to say anything unless I get someone to answer back. If the Medovin villa is overrun by necromancers, it's best not to let *them* know we're coming."

Hazrael waved off the need. "I can let you know if it's safe after I go through the portal."

Oberon didn't like the thought of Hazrael going through without one of them to go along. "Take Celsi with you."

Hazrael turned from where he made finishing flourishes on the energy placed on the archway. Each palm-sized disk now had a tail extending outward that Oberon could use to spread the substance.

"Ready?" Hazrael rubbed his hands together. There was an eager look in his eyes. Either from the fact he was close to getting his revenge or because the experiment might bear fruit, Oberon wasn't sure. What he did know was fear gnawed at his belly.

Chapter Seventeen

HAZRAEL CLOSED his eyes, concentrating on the small eddies and furrows of the patterns when Oberon and Theodyne joined their ethereal essences to find the location of the Medovin's villa.

Seeing the city through Theodyne's memories brought back visions from his own. Ugly, distant ones, hidden behind the black veil of excess and degradation. So much energy moved through his fingers and body, rusty and foul as old metal against his tongue. He spit onto the ground to try and rid himself of the flavor.

There were too many people in the garden of the Medovin's villa. At least at the time shown in the memory. A grave marker. A small casket.

Hazrael felt the blood drain from his head. He stood holding on to the archway. Sweat beaded his face and the back of his neck. Why did seeing that grave affect him so?

He waved Oberon to the archway. "Hold the image in your mind and spread the energy." His voice was thick, deeper. It was hard to get the words out.

Standing so close to the origins of a forming portal, the Kiss of Death began to heat, radiate. He pulled his clothes away from his body.

Oberon stepped to the archway, hand raised. Thank the elements, Oberon was concentrating too hard to pay attention to Hazrael's problems. He'd as soon deal with this on his own than drag Oberon into why that grave seemed important.

Air shifted around him. The Medovin's garden appeared on the other side of the archway. Hazrael sent power into the structure, helping to hold the image, bring it closer into focus.

Theodyne stepped forward and touched the portal. It lit up brighter than a campfire. Medovin's garden could have been located on the very spot where they stood.

Theodyne gave a nod to Hazrael. "It's not going to get any sharper than it is now."

Hazrael didn't see any activity that could be considered suspicious. As a matter of fact, he saw no one in the area. The villa appeared abandoned.

"We need to get the wagons moving and go now. There's something wrong."

Theodyne placed his fingers in his mouth and let out a loud whistle. He waved his arm in a forward motion, calling for the wagons and mounted alchemists to begin coming toward the portal.

Hazrael started through the entranceway. Memories swamped him. His body remembered the sensation, even if his mind did not.

Sound pounded at his eardrums, a roar loud enough to deafen him. Wind battered his body with all the ferocity of a hurricane. As he stepped through the energy storm, the sensation of falling nearly brought him to his knees. He stayed upright by sheer will alone.

He came out into the Medovin's garden and looked around. Guards poured out from the shadows, lances and firearms pointed at Hazrael's midsection.

He raised his hands in the air, maintaining contact with the side of the portal. "I bring the alchemists with me."

Master Celsi stepped through the portal, shaking his head, unfamiliar with the sensation.

"Put your hands up, Master Celsi. Let them see you mean no harm."

A stocky man with dark hair came through the door into the garden. Power radiated from him, but not of the magical variety. This man had to be the Medovin. There was simply no other explanation.

"What's the meaning of this?" When his gaze fastened on Hazrael, his eyes narrowed. Rage seethed behind his dark eyes. "You."

Hazrael kept his hands in the air. He felt a presence behind him, and the Medovin's gaze shifted.

"Estobán, please. He's with us. The alchemists."

"Theodyne." There was relief in his voice. Medovin turned to his men. "Stand down."

Hazrael lowered his arms and moved out of the way so the wagons could come through. Theodyne crossed the yard to where the Medovin stood. They began to speak in quiet tones. Hazrael wished he could hear the conversation but decided it might be best to be seen as helping rather than standing around feeling the unwelcome intruder.

Hazrael turned to Celsi. "Let's get the others through. Oberon won't be able to hold the portal open for much longer."

Already those on the other side were faded, the image hazy. Hazrael put his hands up, touching the very edges of the portal, infusing it with his power. It might be an odd source, but it seemed to hold the portal steady.

Nico rode through the portal on his horse; behind him were the string of wagons.

The Medovin broke from his conversation with Theodyne. "Bring them over here. As far as you can go, and we'll be able to fit them all."

"Speed it up!" Hazrael called. "We can't hold the portal too much longer."

Nico dismounted, handing the reins to one of the Medovin guards. "You heard him. Get those wagons moving."

Medovin guards helped get the wagons into the garden, leading the horses away. Within minutes—which seemed like hours—the alchemists were inside the garden and unloading the wagons.

Oberon stood on the other side of the portal. Master Erhnheart was directly behind him, waiting with the rod to close and ground the portal.

"Come on, Oberon!" Hazrael urged. He held up his hand, reaching out for Oberon. "Take my hand. I'll pull you through."

Hazrael didn't like Oberon's color. His skin was ashen. Sweat matted his hair to his head. His breath came fast and hard. This exercise had taken too much out of him. It had to happen, though. Oberon had been the only one of them to successfully complete even a partial portal.

Oberon stood there, still as a statue, save for the tremors Hazrael noted in his hands. Hazrael turned to Celsi. "I have to go back through and get him. He won't come to me. Hold on to my shirt in case the portal starts to collapse before I make it back."

Celsi grabbed the bottom of Hazrael's tunic and held on. "It doesn't give you much room to move."

"It will have to do. There isn't time to find a rope to tie around my waist." Time ran down. The edges of the portal began to curl inward.

Hazrael lunged forward, pulling Celsi along with him as he lurched through the energy field. He grabbed Oberon by the sleeve and yanked.

Master Erhnheart caught what Hazrael meant to do and gave Oberon a shove. Hazrael opened his arms and caught Oberon as he fell into the garden. Hazrael scrambled to his feet, then bent over and lifted Oberon under the arms to drag him clear. The portal winked out of existence.

Hazrael lay back on the ground, exhausted. His heart galloped.

Theodyne was with him in a moment.

Hazrael waved away the assistance. "See to Oberon. He's in worse shape."

He closed his eyes and covered them with his arm. He just needed a moment to rest. To fight the effects of stepping through the weightless void. Not once, but twice. How did the necromancers do it repeatedly? Were they immune to the effects because they only lived a half life?

All around him the sounds of men working and equipment being unloaded from the wagons filled the garden. They had so much to do, and he needed to be a part of it, yet his body refused to move.

Scents of flowers, herbs, and unspent magic tickled his nostrils. Someone among the gathered had tried to turn a spell but was unsuccessful. It was enough to make Hazrael throw off the mantle of fatigue and sit up.

He gazed around the garden, trying to determine the direction the odd working came from, but it seemed to permeate the air. Everyone appeared busy unloading the wagons, except he, Oberon, and Theodyne.

"Do you feel that, Theodyne?"

Theodyne looked up from assessing Oberon. He sniffed the air and stuck his hand out, shifting through the atmosphere. "I do."

"Can you name the source? It feels odd to me."

Theodyne made a face. "It's elusive. I've not felt it before either."

Hazrael was about to make a comment when it became apparent the fighting had stopped. There had been no new vibrations storming through his connection to the necromancers. All felt calm, but not settled. Perhaps a cease-fire while both sides regrouped.

The door to the villa opened again, and the Hierophant stepped into the garden, accompanied by an older gentleman dressed in the robes of the *demigoge*.

Hazrael sat back on his heels. Air closed off in his throat. He knew that face, knew the man. Had spent time in his presence, but did not recall any of the details.

The *demigoge's* eyes narrowed when they lit upon Hazrael.

"Tell me what offense I've made against the *demigoge*."

Theodyne went back to looking over Oberon, who was now sitting up, though he remained hunched over onto his knees. "You poisoned him."

Hazrael's eyes went wide, and he turned to Theodyne. "Are you sure?"

"Positive. I was the one who treated him."

So many people with reasons to hate him. Did they even realize that no matter how much anger or resentment they felt for him, it would never come close to the amount he felt for himself?

So many crimes. So many sins. His spirit would never be washed clean.

"Master Jolen is on his way back to the villa." This from the Hierophant, who stood as a calm eye of the storms that brewed in the garden. "The necromancers have receded for the time being. It is not finished by half. You have time to get your weapons into place, Master Nico."

Nico stalled while helping to pull a catapult off one of the wagons. "And the city? Does it still stand?"

"The walls have not fallen, save those that housed the Agia's local palace." Here the Hierophant gave a slight, satisfied smile. "As it should be. Recompense will not be paid without destruction of some kind, followed by the rebuilding."

Words struck like arrows into Hazrael's heart. The warning was for him as much as the city of Gusan. He doubted if he lived to be her advanced age, he'd ever truly pay for all the crimes he'd committed while under the necromancers' influence.

She turned to Hazrael. "Well done, Master Hazrael. You managed to get the alchemists' forces here without losing any of your party."

He waved a hand to Oberon. "Thank him. He's the one who opened the portal. I only powered it."

A rush of sound enveloped him. Wind blew him back against the wall. He shook his head to clear his thoughts, but it was hard when something choked the very life out of him.

Hands around his throat cut off his air. He struggled, trying to get his assailant off him. It was no use. He was pulled up off the ground, his feet dangling helplessly. He looked into the eyes of hate and saw his own death staring back at him.

Theodyne held the young man by the shoulders, trying to pull him off Hazrael's throat. "Jolen! Stop!"

Regardless of what Theodyne called him, this was *not* Master Jolen. This being wearing Jolen's face was other—a construct. Hazrael had been around enough to remember the reek of it when it got up his nose. He tried to alert them that this was not their beloved brother of the robe, but the words choked off. He lifted his hand and touched the middle of the construct's chest with the blue energy.

Lights exploded behind Hazrael's eyes. Sparks showered off in all directions. The thing screamed. A giant maw opened, turning the head inside out as it melted. The Medovin yelled in grief.

Hazrael shook his head, but the residual power from the construct's fingers remained clamped around his neck.

Black dots peppered his vision. He was going to succumb, and he didn't care. He'd gotten the alchemists this far, and he'd seen the machines made to destroy the necromancers—they no longer needed him to call the fight, as they'd gone to it.

"You miserable bastard! I will see you dead this time." The voice came from the Medovin.

Hazrael's eyes closed. Sound stopped. Heartbeat slowed. No, he had to stay awake, had to make them understand that was not Jolen he'd killed. Death held him down, and there was no more surfacing to make.

Motion.

Hazrael hurtled back through time. History—his life—unfolded before him. Not the one he lived, but the one denied him when he was captured. All the things he'd lost and would never recover were unveiled in vibrant colors. Why torture him this way? Now he'd never know that sweet life or make amends for the one he did live. Even the Grand Matter hated him and meant to tease.

At least he now knew there was an afterlife, something beyond the veil of death that even the necromancers did not control.

Question was, how would he be judged? By the actions of his heart or those he was forced to take? Was the fact that he did not fight his captors harder going to make him pay the same price as one who went into their arms willingly?

Perhaps to the Grand Matter it was all one and the same.

As above, so below.

"HAZRAEL?" OBERON'S voice broke. Tears blurred his vision and dripped off his nose, splashing onto his lover's face. "Hazrael?"

He held Hazrael's lifeless body against his own and rocked him, trying to bring comfort to the empty shell. A hand squeezed his shoulder in sympathy and support.

"I am so sorry, Oberon." Nico didn't sound much better. He might have had his reservations about Hazrael, but they had been close friends once.

Oberon glanced up, looking at the pile of gel that had once been Jolen. Portal energy shouldn't have done that to an *aerothant.*

The Medovin wiped tears from his eyes. His sobs echoed through the garden.

"What's happened?" A voice came from the villa door. Jolen stood there, rumpled, disheveled, but whole and alive. His gaze fastened on Estobán, and then he was in motion, going to his lover to wrap him in a comforting embrace. "By the elements! Bán, love, what is it?"

The Medovin looked up, momentarily confused. His gaze fastened on Jolen, followed by a hand to his cheek. "We thought Hazrael had killed you."

Only then did attention return to the fallen Hazrael, lifeless in Oberon's arms. "It was a construct, created in your image, Jolen, to fool us."

"A construct, here, in the villa?" Panic and concern filled Jolen's face. He pushed to stand, but not before giving the Medovin a hard kiss. "Captain Fessen, come with me."

Work in the yard continued around them. One dead former necromancer was nothing to the guards. For the other alchemists, it was a mixed emotion. Oberon knew. The currents ran as an undertone through the garden. No one seemed to care that Hazrael had given his life in such a stupid and careless way. Why didn't the Medovin have someone at the physical gate to keep the necromancers from breaching the entrance?

Both the Hierophant and the *demigoge* had been removed from the scene of violence. However, the Hierophant's attendants remained. One crossed the yard and bent down over Hazrael.

She leaned closer, smelling of an exotic flower that Oberon could not place. "Bring him into the villa. His story is not over yet. There is life in him still."

Oberon glanced up, meeting her cool gray eyes. "He does not breathe."

"The Kiss of Death keeps him alive. It is his only link to our world. You must exploit that connection to bring him back to you." She placed her hand over Hazrael's heart. "Even now he looks for a way to return. Show it to him."

Incredulous but willing to try, Oberon pushed up from the ground, Hazrael in his arms. Nico held on to them both, steadying them.

"Theodyne, attend us," Nico commanded as they passed by the knot of people gathered around Jolen, getting instructions to secure the villa.

Theodyne hurried to them. "We need to establish a shield over the entire residence."

"I agree." Nico grabbed Theodyne's shirt. "But the Hierophant's attendant believes Hazrael can be saved."

The attendant never turned as she guided them into the villa. "He can be. But we must work fast."

She guided them into a room where the Hierophant waited. Candles lit the room around the perimeter of a circle.

The Hierophant raised her hands. "Place him in the middle of the circle. Master Oberon, you take his right hand. Master Nico, his left. Master Theodyne, I want you placed at his head, as you are the strongest and have brought him back from the brink in the past."

A chill swam down Oberon's spine. How had she known about the night the Agias were killed? About the risks Theodyne had taken to pull Hazrael out of the wasteland where he hid? Her powers were magnificent indeed if she had seen the events carried out on the astral plane.

"If you would all please connect to Master Hazrael."

As they did so, shadows in the corners of the room began to shift as spirit elementals stepped closer to the circle. Oberon closed his eyes and squeezed Hazrael's hand.

"Come back to us. You know the way."

His words faded as he slipped into the ether. At first he didn't see Hazrael. It was nothing more than a barren landscape where trees grew in crooked disarray, devoid of leaves or bark. Jagged rocks made the terrain difficult to navigate. If he had been in his corporeal form, the sharp pieces of stone would have cut right through his shoes to the flesh beneath.

Panic rose. Oberon didn't see Hazrael anywhere. Not among rocks or lifeless trees. The sound of ocean waves breaking against the shoreline echoed in the air around him.

"Hazrael!"

No answer returned. The wind picked up, carrying the crashing of the waves away from him. He headed to the cliffs, afraid Hazrael might have tried to pitch himself off the ledge. The result might not be corporeal death, but it would place Hazrael deeper into his own mind and therefore make him harder to reach.

However, if he believed himself to already be dead, how would that impact the search? The scene shifted, changing from a desolate cliff at the sea to one inside an abandoned graveyard. No matter where Hazrael fled, he was always alone. The knowledge broke Oberon's heart. Hazrael had never been alone, not truly. There had been so many of his fellow alchemists who had mourned him when he'd been lost. So many who had wanted nothing more than to see him back in the fold. Didn't he realize that? Hadn't he made himself a valuable asset once again?

A dark shape loomed up ahead. Not a person, but a structure. Large with a gabled roof. A statue stood out front, a deity with arms uplifted in entreaty. The face was sculpted in a vision of twisted agony, depicting the horrors of death. Though Oberon didn't see their likenesses on the ethereal plane, he felt Theodyne and Nico beside him. Were they seeing the same images?

Fear made a pit in his stomach. Nothing good ever came of weeping deities.

He looked past the sculpture and into the mouth of the crypt.

No. Not a crypt. A cave.

Oh, Hazrael, what have you come back to?

It was dark, ugly, and frigid. A stench of rotting flesh filled the tunnels, making Oberon's ethereal form want to gag. This was a place where evil magics crushed hope and tortured happiness. He continued to walk, moving faster now, following the low moans of pain echoing through the chambers.

Lights were only pinpoints along the walls. None of them truly bright enough to illuminate the dark passage, and yet Oberon saw everything in vivid and gruesome detail. What he'd thought were stones along the way were skulls embedded into the cave walls, each one looking out at him with blank sockets and open maws.

So many questions tumbled over in his mind. Things he needed and wanted to ask Hazrael about this construct. It told a story that shredded Oberon's heart with every step he took deeper into the recesses of the dark. The tunnel bent around a corner and came out into a chamber. Hazrael lay on a slab, naked. His skin rent in thousands of tiny spirals, bleeding down onto the stone. His eyes were glazed as he stared at the ceiling.

Oberon closed his eyes, turning his head away from the scene. This was not some construct of a troubled mind, but the memory of a torture so heinous it had scored Hazrael's soul as surely as it had his flesh.

"Oberon? Where are you?"

Oh, by the elementals, it was a knife thrust to the heart hearing Hazrael's cries go unanswered.

Not this time. He pushed off from the wall and crossed the chamber. He leaned over Hazrael, moving his hair from his face. *"It's all right. I'm here. I've come to bring you home."*

"Oberon. I thought they'd killed you." Tears leaked from the corners of Hazrael's eyes, running into his hair. *"We have to hurry before they return."*

"They won't return. Not here. Not now." Oberon went to work, releasing Hazrael from his chains.

Hazrael sat up, rubbing his wrists. *"How did you know where to find me?"*

There was no way in all the heavens or the lowest rings of hell Oberon was going to tell Hazrael the story. Not now. Not before they made it to the material world again. *"I followed the trail."*

The explanation seemed to mollify Hazrael until they started out of the chamber. At the entrance, he turned and stared up at Oberon, shaking his head. *"No. This isn't how it happened. No one ever came for me. I wasted and rotted and allowed the necromancers to have me."*

"You allowed nothing! They used you, and if we don't move from this place, they will use you again. Please, Hazrael. I beg you to follow me."

"We can't change the past."

Oberon grabbed for Hazrael's hand, but it slipped through his, becoming even more elusive. *"We aren't trying to change it. We're trying to save you now."*

Hazrael's expression changed. His face fell. *"You came here for me?"*

"Always."

Hazrael began to move. The walls began to shake, the floor, ceiling, and archways trembled. The entire structure began to shift. Was that real or merely the protections he'd erected around his memories coming down? It didn't matter. They had to flee, had to make it outside and back to the material world before the entire structure crumbled.

He felt hands on his shoulders, but no one was there. Oh hell. It was the material leaking over into the ether. *"Hurry!"*

They made it to the opening and into the graveyard. Wind swirled from every direction, catching them up in the cyclone. Death dancers began to fill the scene, moving forward to claim their brethren.

Oberon raised his arms in front of them, blocking the necromancers' access to Hazrael. *"You will not get him."*

"We will take him, either in this world or the next." The voices were a chorus of angry hisses, circling around them.

Hazrael shot a hand out from under Oberon's raised ones. The blue light arced outward. When it hit the necromancers, it lit them up like cannon fuses before they exploded.

"Now, Oberon!"

They linked hands and passed into the material.

Chapter Eighteen

HAZRAEL WOKE to a fuzzy world. His head pounded, and his eyes felt swollen. The vibrations had returned, except this time they came from all around him. He glanced at his surroundings. The pungent scent of tallow along with the stink of sweat and despair filled his nose. Where was he?

Oberon held his hand, as did Nico. Above him, Theodyne looked down into his face. "How are you feeling?"

"As if I've been run over by the caravan." The words came out low, husky. His throat was sore, and it was hard to breathe around the lump in it. He placed his hand there and was not surprised to find the skin was tender.

Master Jolen had strangled him. Wait. No. Not Jolen. A construct made to look like Jolen.

Why, then, was he alive?

He sat up with some help from Oberon. One of the Hierophant's attendants held out a cup of water. He nodded in thanks before he took it. How had they managed to pull him back from the grave?

Another concussion, this one closer, rocked the villa.

"The necromancers are using the *demigoge's* basilica guards to fire upon the *prolates'* villas," Nico answered the unasked question.

"Of course. We bring magical weapons, and they use their agents to fight with mundane ones." Hazrael tried to stand but found his legs would not hold him. "I think I need to go back in. I've brought them to you. Now you must fight them in this plane. I'll fight them on the other."

Oberon rubbed a hand down Hazrael's back in comfort. "You are in no condition to fight on any plane, be it material or otherwise."

Dizziness swept over Hazrael, and he leaned heavily against Oberon. "I don't think so either, but I have to try. There's no time to wait until I feel better."

Oberon brought his arm around Hazrael's shoulder, then kissed his forehead. "Rest for now. The *prolates* are not without their protections."

Nico placed his hands on his hips, brow raised. "Though I fear there might be nothing left of the basilica when this is over."

"Buildings can be rebuilt and repaired. The fabric of Dominicál society will take a lot longer to heal." This from the soft-spoken attendant. She made a calling motion to indicate Hazrael should follow her. "Come, we have prepared a healing bath and place for you to rest."

Being so close with the Hierophant, she probably knew quite a bit about Hazrael that the others did not. He tried to push up from the ground, but once again his legs failed to hold him. "I'll need assistance."

Oberon took him under one arm and Nico the other.

As they followed the attendant through the villa to a bathing chamber, Hazrael became more apprehensive of the rite. "What all does a healing bath entail?"

Either she pretended not to hear the question, or she was told not to give an answer should he ask. That did nothing but spike his anxiety higher. "Please understand I'm not unappreciative of the Hierophant's efforts to help me, but I've spent a lot of years being subjected to others' use of my body as they saw fit. I won't do it again. Not even for a healing."

The attendant stopped and turned. "You need this. By hiding from your pain, you've damaged your ability to heal. The parts of you that were born human will not be completely well again nor integrate with your *etherealthant* side until you embrace the past."

Hazrael gave a rusty laugh that caused pain to throb in his head. He squeezed his eyes closed as a wave of nausea rolled over him. "The elementals want nothing to do with me. I might have been born full human."

Engulfed by a pregnant silence, Hazrael opened his eyes to look at the attendant. Confusion marred her pretty features. "You have never been more mistaken."

She turned and pulled a sheer curtain back. The bath was more a pool, the kind which accommodated several bathers at once. Steamy air filled with the scents of eucalyptus curled through the room. One lungful cleared the chest and head, making it easier to breathe.

Hazrael was guided to the edge of the pool. The water wasn't clear, as he'd expected, but black, shiny, and murky. There was an odd opalescence to it that brought greens, purples, and blues to the roiling surface.

"Is it safe?"

Another blast, farther in the distance, rocked the ground under them. Oberon and Nico tightened their grips on him.

The Hierophant stepped from behind a curtain. "It is. The question is, are you courageous enough to heal?"

It was a good question, an important one. Courage wasn't something he lacked. He might doubt, second-guess, and vacillate, but he did not lack courage. Strength, now that was another matter.

"Masters Theodyne and Oberon have tried to heal me and found it might do more damage than good."

The Hierophant turned her eerie, sightless eyes to him. "No disrespect intended to the masters in question, but they are not the Hierophant."

"No, but then you are a mystic seer, not a healer."

She smiled knowingly and put out her hand. "Please disrobe and climb into the pool."

Another blast, this one closer, rocked the entire villa. Glassware shook, and mortar crumbled and fell from the ceiling.

Hazrael looked up. "This might not be the best time for a healing."

"You will do your fellows and Dominicál no service by fighting when your thoughts are scattered and you have no idea how to use your pain to your advantage. You must channel that anger and use it against them, but you must know and understand how and why."

Hazrael stood his ground. "If this is so important, then why didn't you do this when you were at the school? It could have saved me time and torture."

She was resolute in her stance and insistence that he obey. "You weren't ready then. You are now."

Odd, he didn't feel any more ready at this juncture than he had when they last met, despite her assurances. Spirit elementals folded out from the mist, advancing on him.

"Do what the Hierophant requests. We command you." Their chorus echoed off the walls, reaching into his body with every breath.

Anger gave him unexpected strength. "I am no longer yours to command! You saw to that when you turned your back on me. When you attacked me in the library. Do not pretend you want to see me anywhere other than the ground."

He felt rather than saw Oberon and Nico react, urging him not to go on the defensive.

Candles' flames jumped, growing higher.

"No! We protected you from yourself. From the destruction of your soul you seemed so bent upon."

"What?" The one-word question came out meek, shocked. Hazrael blinked a few times, hoping that might help him to understand what the spirit elementals said. "You've left me alone in my despair. Not even reaching out to comfort me when I was found and cut off from the necromancers."

"We have been with you. Always."

At the moment, he didn't see it, but he felt it. First as a tiny bud in the middle of his chest, right under his heart. Then it grew larger, more prominent. It exploded along his nerve endings, inciting tingles to erupt under his skin. He wanted nothing more in that moment than to crawl out of his epidermis and leave the meat shell behind.

He started to scratch.

With every touch of his fingers against his scars, they lit with the same odd glow he'd experienced in his hands. Portal energy.

The Hierophant turned her head. Her sightless eyes searched the room. "Hurry! Into the pool."

The elementals circled him. Hazrael didn't even bother to try and remove his clothes. He dived for the pool, but before he reached the sanctuary of black water, he was snatched back through a portal and thrown on the ground in the middle of the catacombs, surrounded by a legion of necromancers.

OBERON GRABBED for Hazrael and came up with air. He was gone! Vanished.

By the elements, the necromancers had gotten him. Plucked him straight out of a villa, and without the benefit of healing, without knowing all the horrors they had visited on him. Now he had only to hope Hazrael didn't succumb to their influence before they found him.

Oberon turned to Theodyne, who had a look of panic and determination on his face. "Where would the necromancers have taken him?"

"Either the basilica or the catacombs. There are no other places I can think to look at the moment."

"Good enough. We'll start there. If we can't find them, we'll cast a larger net." Oberon hurried from the room. The others trailed behind him. His long strides ate up the distance as he moved through the villa. "We will have to travel on foot. I don't think I have enough power to even make a partial portal."

They came out into the garden. Oberon went to the wagon carrying the crossbows and the bolts. He took one of the weapons, along with several containers of ammunition, and strapped it on his back. He found a pack and shoved some of the lead casks into it.

Jolen came across the yard, followed by a contingent of guards. "Where are you going?"

Oberon looked over his shoulder. "To kill the fucking necromancers who just pulled Hazrael through a portal."

"I want to come too." He started to reach for a crossbow, but Oberon placed his hand over Jolen's.

"Stay here and protect the villa."

"I can track the necromancers."

"Yes? So can Theodyne, and if Hazrael needs to be healed when we find him, Theodyne will already be there." Oberon left the wagon and stalked across the garden. He stopped and threw over his shoulder, "Besides, I don't want to have to worry that if you get separated from us that they've made another construct of you."

Jolen stalled, hands on hips. "And how about if they make constructs of you?"

"We need a code word for verification."

They stared at each other for a few moments before Oberon smiled. "Krutarch."

"Good choice." Jolen held out his hand. "You all take care."

"Same to you."

The Medovin stood with an elaborate firearm in his hand, loading it. "Take some of my guards with you. They've fought the necromancers before and know how they work."

Oberon didn't bother to point out the fact the guards had battled Hazrael under the influence of the necromancers. There was no telling how different the experiences might be, but if it was manpower they needed, he wasn't going to dismiss trained guards.

"Very well." He slid a sidelong glance to Jolen. "But make sure your lover stays put. I am very uncomfortable about leaving your residence unprotected."

"Headmaster—"

Oberon held up his hand. He didn't have any more time to waste. Hazrael had been gone too long for Oberon's peace of mind.

Their small band headed out into the streets. Full night had fallen, painting the city in horrific shadows. Explosions lit up the night on the other side of the city, the battle having moved away. It was an odd, fluid type of warfare. First raining down on this part of the city, then falling on a section a mile away. Still the stone streets vibrated underfoot, rocked from the concussion of the cannon fire.

Some of the blasts were so violent Oberon's teeth rattled together. Smoke billowed up into the night. Flames flickered in a far-off district. Oberon wasn't sure if that area contained the homes of the *prolates* or the peasants.

But everywhere the air was filled with the taste of burned flesh.

Theodyne led them to a small public garden. A statue of a fallen deity stood as a monument that time and ideas both passed into history, illustrating that even religion wasn't a stagnant concept. Oberon didn't like the portent of the statue. It sent a very bad message in a moment when they needed uplifting.

A hidden passageway opened onto a stairwell that went down into the belly of the city. The bolts lit the darkened stairs, illuminating the corridor in an eerie glow.

"You really should have let Jolen accompany us. He would have been able to track the necromancers easier than me." Theodyne hurried down the stairs, faster than safety allowed.

"And leave the stronghold that houses both the *demigoge* and Hierophant without an alchemist who is intimate with the layout of the villa? Not on your life."

"How did the world turn so upside down?"

Oberon held the bolt higher. "I suspect that it's been happening for quite a long time."

"When you can cheat death, you have all the time in the world."

"And more to manipulate those you wish to suppress."

Theodyne stepped off the stairs and started down the passage. "I respect the Hierophant, but I disagree with her on one point—killing an innocent child is something Hazrael will never forgive himself for, let alone reconcile it. Letting him see the incident, to remember it, is a mistake."

They started through the catacombs proper.

Cobwebs hung from the ceiling and clung to the walls, ghostly streamers stirred by the feel of life near them. One brushed against Oberon's cheek. It stung.

He slapped at his face. That wasn't right. Not on any day.

"Watch out for the cobwebs. They are laced with something painful."

His face continued to sting with the venom of a hundred angry bees. Looking down, he saw the projection of his cheek puffing outward as it swelled.

Theodyne stopped and turned to inspect Oberon's face. "Your eye is going to swell shut soon. The venom is advancing along your capillary bed."

"We don't have time to care for it now. Keep moving until we find Hazrael." Oberon motioned to the guards, some of whom had red welts puffing up on their faces and arms where they'd come into contact with the cobwebs. "A few of you move ahead of us and use your swords to clear the way of the cobwebs. I don't know how much of this venom is lethal to a human."

The one who had been designated the squad leader took up a position in front of the group, along with another guard. They drew their long daggers and began cutting through the webs.

Was it Oberon's imagination, or had they grown thicker the deeper they moved into the catacombs? "You were down here a few months ago. Did you encounter anything like this?"

Theodyne trekked beside Oberon. "We encountered much worse."

That was not encouraging news. If this was just a small dose of what the necromancers had to offer in the way of distractions or obstacles, they were very clever indeed. Nothing overt to start out with, but insidious enough to make lesser beings turn back. Not Oberon. He was determined to find Hazrael before the death dancers turned him again.

Hell, he'd just gotten him back. No way under the moon or stars he was going to let go so easily. He'd not make the same mistake he did last time. He tightened his hand into a fist before relaxing it again. Leave the rage and anger for dealing with the necromancers. Right now he needed to prepare for whatever else the bastards had to throw at them.

The corridor widened out and came to a bifurcation.

The lead guard stopped and turned to Theodyne. "Which way?"

"Right." Theodyne lifted his head and sniffed the air. "Yes, definitely right."

Oberon sniffed as well. Under the layers of mold, must, and dirt was the sickly sweet scent of decay. It was a scent common in mausoleums and mass graves. How it differed from the stink of the necromancers, he didn't know. He remembered nothing of his brief encounter with them on that horrible day. Not even the smell.

But he knew what they looked like on the astral, and he knew Hazrael's mind intimately. With those two tools, he could help speed the search. Instead of going fully into that place between worlds, Oberon unleashed only the smallest corner of his essence, staying connected to his body and able to move through the world as the other part of him searched the astral.

Not every alchemist had the ability to split their consciousness in such a way, but he had mastered the technique a long time ago. It wasn't something he did often, or even considered doing on most occasions, as it was not without inherent risks, but in this instance, the situation called for it.

It was a little disorienting at first. The only thing to compare the sensation to was having an extra eye looking down on the world as the other two gazed forward.

He narrowed the view of his third eye, trying to see in nothing but the color of Hazrael's essence. At the moment there was only darkness against endless obsidian. He'd have an easier time trying to find a white horse in a snowstorm.

He continued to monitor from the astral as they came around a corner and into a burial chamber. Bones were scattered, either by grave robbers or scavengers. Ribs crunched underfoot, skulls were kicked out of the way, and femurs rattled with a hollow wooden sound.

Disrespectful. The body was only the vessel for the living soul. Still, there was no reason to defile the final resting place of the former *demigoges*.

"Jolen was in a fight here. The necromancers reanimated the *demigoges* in some bastard skeletal army." Theodyne answered the unasked question.

"Nothing is sacred to a death dancer. Not even their own agents."

"We'll find him, Oberon."

"Perhaps, but I want to find him *before* they convert him. He's come so far since he was recovered."

"I don't think the real Hazrael was ever gone, just blocked."

Oberon took a few more steps, considering Theodyne's assessment. It fit with what they'd seen when they'd been inside Hazrael's mind. "I'm counting on that now. It might be the only way we can trace him."

The rattling sound increased. Not from the action of feet striking the scattered remains, but an eerie musical quality of percussion instruments.

Oberon gazed behind them but saw only the moving figures of the guards in the glow from the bolts.

Echoes of that same distant beat came from ahead. A breeze ruffled the hem of Oberon's gown. Objects, unidentifiable in shape or substance, brushed by his legs.

Oberon lifted his hand to the group. "Hold up. Let me see what's going on here."

He grabbed one of the bolts and held it down near ground level. Bones rolled along the floor of the catacombs. "This cannot end well."

Theodyne squatted next to him. "Not at all."

Chapter Nineteen

HAZRAEL FELT as if he were being split in two.

He lay strapped to the tomb of Akabar Kolhen, hands and feet spread to the four corners, a position that heralded pain and torture. A shroud-covered figure leaned over him. A terrible visage from the depths of a nightmare came closer. Fetid breath bathed his face, turning his stomach.

"You need reconditioning to remember your commitment to our cause." The words given with not one voice but many. The chorus repeated itself, a subtle echo that penetrated down into his skin.

The scars lit, acknowledging those who had placed their mark upon his flesh. Betrayed by his body, Hazrael closed his eyes.

"*Your* cause," he corrected. "It was never mine. You forced it on me."

Hazrael had tried several times to make the metal cuff around his right wrist expand to ease his hand out. No matter how much manipulation he sent to the restraint, it didn't budge from its current shape. The necromancers must have anticipated so basic a reaction from him and put measures in place to prevent it. If he could only make his hand smaller, he might be able to slide it through the opening. Once he had a hand free, he'd be able to use the blue energy to stun the necromancers.

He couldn't give up. Not now.

Where were the elementals? Why did they not come to his aid in this dark, desperate place? If they had been trying to protect him all this time, they'd failed. Once again, he was alone to face the necromancers.

He'd always been alone when dealing with them. Before, it had not been enough. This time, it had to be.

This time he knew what to expect.

Hazrael wiggled his hand back and forth in the cuff. Sharp metal sides began to cut into his flesh. Blood trickled down his hand. The skin burned where it was sliced open, but the blood managed to lubricate the area enough that he felt a bit of give. He wasn't free yet, but he was close.

As the necromancer leaned over him, Hazrael continued to work. He opened his eyes, trying to keep focused on what was before him, so his tormentor failed to discover the coming escape.

More of his scars lit with internal light. Instead of glowing in reds and oranges as normal, they were now pale blue. That was different, though whether good or bad, he had no idea.

A long, skeletal hand reached out from beneath the bell sleeves of the death dancer's robe. A bony finger traced along the path of the scars, never quite touching them. "What is this? Portal energy coming from the Kiss of Death?"

Hazrael didn't react. He couldn't afford to. If anything, he needed to remain stoic, unmoved by their taunts, threats, or curiosities. If he gave them any emotions, they might find a way into his mind. They might continue to have a connection to his body, but not to his mind. Not anymore. He wasn't going to allow it. There were ways to keep an invading presence from entering the subconscious. He'd just have to block the channels they'd used before—seal off the Kiss of Death.

The necromancer lowered his hand. An arc of violent power crackled outward, making him pull back in pain. His agonized cry filled the room. The edges of the necromancer's sleeve smoldered, sending the acrid scent of burned dust through the chamber. Hazrael turned his head into his shoulder, trying to block the stench from entering his lungs.

The necromancer glared with accusation. If he wanted to believe Hazrael did that on purpose, let him. It might make them think twice about touching him again. Yes, and that was more wishful thinking on his part. They were going to keep coming at him until they got what they wanted, which begged the question: what did they want?

If it was his power, they had used most of that up when they'd had him before—or not utilized it to its full advantage. If they had, they would have controlled the city-states by now.

Movement from the corner of Hazrael's eye captured his attention. This was bad. Very bad.

A solitary figure, dressed head to toe in the tattered robes of a burial shroud, floated over the ground, closer to the tomb where Hazrael lay. Strange gold sigils were stitched into his robes, symbols of death everlasting.

The *Necromon*.

There were entire chunks of Hazrael's memory missing, but the one of the *Necromon* was as vivid as the day he'd lived it. When pieces of his life among them had flooded back, it was his presence, his power that overshadowed them all.

Hazrael gritted his teeth and braced for the confrontation.

"We will incorporate you back into the fold. You will be legion."

Words were power, and if Hazrael used none, it was one less thing they had to use against him. Still, retorts battered at his teeth, ready to spill out into the space between them. Angry, vile words that the necromancers would soak up like the sweetest ambrosia. They took in hate, fear, and paranoia as if breathing air. It was what sustained them.

Hazrael twisted his wrists back and forth a little more, feeling it begin to slide through the cuff.

The *Necromon* lifted a thin hand and snapped his fingers in a sound resembling two dry sticks brushing together. One of the other robed figures moved forward and bowed in supplication.

"Bring me a bone blade."

Hazrael's stomach contracted. Fear bathed his insides before he checked it. They would feel that radiating out of his pores and into the chamber.

He watched in mute horror as a wickedly pointed white blade was handed over to the *Necromon*. The leader of the necromancers leaned forward, the tip of the dagger poised to cut into Hazrael's body anew.

Hazrael's hand slid from the cuff, and he threw it up, palm out, showering a string of crystals that covered him in a protective shield.

The blade crashed into the shield, shattering the bone on impact. Violent energy swirled around the chamber. A storm in a closed space. None of it penetrated the crystals to touch him.

With his one hand free, Hazrael turned and began to pull at his other restraint. Once both hands were free, he'd work on his ankles. He had time. At least he thought he did. Even as his breath hit the smooth boundary created by the crystal, there was no fog to indicate it was airtight. The temperature didn't seem to be rising inside the protective shell.

Outside, the necromancers unleashed everything in their arsenal to try and force open the crystals. Streams of lightning crackled against the surface, rocks bounced off the covering, fire licked at the wall, but nothing managed to penetrate.

His left hand slid free of the cuff. Hazrael sat up and started on his ankles. This was going to be harder to accomplish. He glanced over at the necromancers, who were busy trying to find ways to break through the barrier, then back down to his fingers. There was a violent reaction every time the necromancers came into contact with the portal energy, which didn't explain why they were so successful in using it to begin with—but it did give him an idea.

He need not break the cuff completely. Freeing himself only required he sever the links between the cuff and the chain anchoring it into the tomb. He rubbed his fingers together, generating energy. A speck of blue light crackled between his fingertips. If the necromancers had manipulated the metal on the cuffs in any way, shape, or form, then the blue light stream should break the bonds and crack the link apart.

It was a theory.

The only one he had to go on.

Hazrael sent a small jolt through the link. Sparks flew off, hitting his skin, burning him. It hurt, but nothing worse than a bee sting. As far as the pain he'd had to endure, it was nothing. The pulse also hadn't been enough to break the chain. A small divot was the only blemish on the otherwise pristine surface.

He hit it again, this time with a bit more force. Bits of metal broke away, spinning up to catch him in the face. Blood ran down his cheek where the shrapnel rent a small cut. He wiped the mess across his shoulder. One more hit should break it apart.

A stir of warning swam down his spine. The compulsion to look up to the actions going on around him rode him hard. He refused to answer that call. Whatever they did outside his protective cocoon was made to distract him. Distractions were a means to try and gain control over him. There wasn't a chance in all the wide caverns of hell he'd let that happen.

Hazrael kept his head down, even as the feeling of doom came closer. It breathed down his neck in chill breath. His stomach began to cramp. Sweat ran down his face, mixing with the blood.

He unleashed the last bolt of energy. The chain broke into pieces, freeing his right leg. He swung around to work on the next and came face-to-face with a horror so profound he was caught in the snare, unable to move, to breathe, to even blink the sight from his eyes.

Before him, on the other side of the crystal, stood a small boy. The skin around his eyes was sunken and black. As for the eyes themselves, empty sockets stared back at him in accusation. The neck was at an awkward angle, as if broken and never set to rights before burial.

A sick feeling of crawling flesh moved over Hazrael's skin.

He knew without being told, without the clear memory surfacing, that he bore witness to his greatest sin.

The mouth opened wide. Beetles crawled from the dark maw.

A thin, pale arm rose, finger outstretched, pointing to Hazrael. "You killed me."

Don't look. Don't listen. Don't hear. They want you to crack and break like the links in the chain. To gain control over you when you fall into despair. Don't give that to them now. Free yourself and deal with the emotions later.

By the elements, that was hard to do.

Even now, the memory tried to bubble and burp up through the cracks in his mind. Oh Gods! He could see the chamber—this chamber!—hear the sounds of battle raging around him. Smell the stench of fiendish constructs he'd help to create with the flesh of fallen warriors.

Gorge rose in his throat, burning it with acidic bile.

He was not the same man then. He had no consciousness, no thoughts that weren't given to him by the necromancers.

"It might have been my hands, but *they* were the ones who killed you!" Hazrael flung his hand out to illustrate the necromancers who moved around them. "They were the ones who used me like their own personal puppet. I had no more control over my actions than you do now."

The boy's mouth dropped down, the mandible unhinged. Gas floated out into the chamber. Poison? Chemicals released when the body decomposed, or a substance gained from the necromancers? The origin didn't matter so much as the fact the crystals began to dissolve under the onslaught.

This thing meant to persecute him was not the one who had died in the chamber, but one constructed for the sole purpose of torment. Hazrael took comfort in that fact and tried to reach for a way to save himself. To come up with some plan to get out of the chamber alive.

Putrid gas continued to hit what remained of the shield.

A steady drip began. Each drop that hit the tomb hissed with the burn of acid. One hit Hazrael's shoulder, sliding down his naked back. This time he couldn't escape the shout that begged for release. Tears filled his eyes. He channeled his agony to his fingers. The blue energy turned white-hot, melting the metal of the chain on contact.

He was free!

OBERON, THEODYNE, and the guards continued down the passageway, haunted by the sounds of rolling bones. The deeper they journeyed into the catacombs, the more bones joined the others. They turned a corner and came against a solid wall constructed entirely of the remains of dead *demigoges.*

Oberon lifted the bolt to see if there were any holes to exploit that might hint at a way to dismantle the forbidding construction. The bones fit together so tightly he couldn't even get his fingertip between them.

He held out his hand to one of the guards. "Lend me your dagger, please."

The guard pulled a long dagger from its holder and handed it to Oberon hilt first. "Are you going to cut our way through?"

"No. I want to see if I can slide anything between the layers in order to destabilize the entire structure."

Theodyne and the guard exchanged knowing glances.

"What? Am I missing something here?"

"Only that if the necromancers built this—and I have no reason to believe otherwise—we'll have to find a less conventional way of breaking through." Theodyne held up his hand. "And before you suggest finding another route to take, I can assure you, all these bones have not been going down the same passages. We're more than likely trapped here."

Not the news Oberon wanted to hear, though he'd come to the same conclusion. The necromancers weren't about to take any chances and let them out of the catacombs, not without a fight.

"Only until we find a way out." Oberon wiggled the dagger tip back and forth, trying to get it to pass between two of the bones. Normal contours and shapes suggested gaps where there were none. A bit of necromantic manipulation to make the bones fit as close as bricks.

Oberon turned his back on the group, pacing away as he lifted the crossbow. "I'd stand clear if I were you."

Theodyne and the guard moved back and lined up along the edges of the passage.

Oberon placed the bolt into the stock and eased the hammer back. If he hit the bone wall in the direct center, the impact might break the rest of the structure apart.

He lifted the crossbow and aimed. Light from the bolt aided in his direction. He squeezed the trigger. The bolt sang as it flew through the air. It struck the center, sending bones scattering outward in a fossilized shower.

When the fragments settled, there was a hole about the size of Oberon's fist. All that damage and a hand-sized opening was all he had to show for it. Progress of that sort was disheartening in the extreme.

Pieces shimmied up the bony tower, hurrying to repair the breach. Oberon rushed to the wall and used his hands to punch the loose sections out of the way. Jagged fragments cut his knuckles. Blood painted the bones, appearing black in the blue light. Theodyne pulled Oberon's arm away, keeping him from striking the wall again.

"Are you mad? Blood will only feed the spell and bind it to you."

Oberon stalled. His breath sawed in and out. Ragged. Desperate. Damn, he hadn't even stopped to think of the consequences, only the need to get to Hazrael.

The part of him monitoring the ethereal still found no light to indicate Hazrael occupied either plane. Had his life ended?

Oberon's breath caught on an exhale. "I... *we* have to find him."

Theodyne placed his hand on Oberon's shoulder and squeezed. "I know. You don't have to explain it to me. If that were Nico, I'd sail through that hole headfirst for a chance to save him. But no matter how tempting it is to risk body and soul, you cannot give the necromancers more material to construct their horrors. It takes very little for them to build an army."

Not if Oberon could help it. If the necromancers wanted to fight with blood magic, he would too. After all, what was blood but cells and substances, the same as rock, bone, water, or flesh? In the eyes of the Grand Matter, there was no difference.

He lifted his hand, knuckles busted and dripping blood. "As above, so below."

"Oberon?"

Oberon shook his head. "It must be this way."

"You may get caught up in their spell."

"And I may find the way out again." Concern for the outcome wasn't going to stop Oberon from pulling on the Grand Matter or using his own blood to bind the bones to him. Unlike the necromancers, Oberon had no intention of keeping the remains of the *demigoges* in his service for eternity, only until he freed Hazrael.

He twisted his hand to the right, pulling inward. The bones painted in the drops of his blood reacted, coming toward him. The hole expanded. He moved his arm in a pushing motion, taking the bones to the right, where they lined up in a military fashion.

In order to make all the remains act as the ones he'd already cleared from the wall, he'd have to drain his body of all blood. Since he had no intention of going that far, and they only required more space in order to fit through the opening, Oberon took the dagger he'd used before and sliced across the palm of his hand.

Theodyne turned his face away. Disappointment drew his mouth down.

Oberon refused to feel bad or even regret his decision. Life was full of choices. Hazrael had been denied his for so long, and Oberon had no intention of letting him fall into that pit of hopelessness again.

"You don't have to like this, Theodyne. I ask for neither your permission nor approval. If I become caught up in the spell, at least Hazrael will no longer be alone against the necromancers."

Theodyne glanced up sharply, his brows knit together. "He isn't alone. He has all of us with him."

A lump formed in Oberon's throat. "Yes."

He pressed his bloody hand against the bone wall and smeared. Streaks of dark red washed the surface. He worked from one side to the other, ensuring all the bones had at least a small portion of his offering.

When he finished, he turned on the guards. "Be ready to charge through. We don't know what is on the other side of this wall, and I fear my blood may have called the necromancers. For that I am sorry."

The lead guard studied Oberon with a resolute expression. "I don't pretend to understand the ways of the alchemists, but I trust you and your brothers to do what you must to eliminate the threat from Dominicál."

The statement from someone within the Medovin's service was humbling and uplifting. It was what he needed to hear at the moment, and he gave a nod in thanks.

This time he swept his hand out to the side. Bones swung outward, a gate composed of holy relics molested by a horrible power. It was another crime to add to the long list of those committed by the necromancers. Oberon intended to make them pay for each offense.

Nothing hid on the other side of the wall but a dark, endless forever. Blackness vibrated, sending waves outward to sweep over Oberon and the others. The effect was dizzying in the extreme.

Oberon went to his knees as the shock wave hit him. What in the hells had they done to manipulate the very absence of light? Was it real or illusion? He chanced a peek through slitted eyes and saw the guards were in an agony of their own.

Oberon touched the thread of his consciousness inside the ethereal. All was calm, steady. He grabbed hold of the thread, feeding more energy into the channel.

"Theodyne, place part of your consciousness into the ethereal if you can."

"What? Split it?"

"Yes."

Theodyne held his hands to the side of his head. His skin was pale. Sweat beaded his forehead. He opened one eye. "I don't think I can do that. One foot in this plane; one in the astral. It might make me even dizzier."

"You're strong enough to do it. Ask the elementals to guide you." Able to keep his good eye open now, Oberon clambered to his feet.

"Try. It's the only way to stabilize the illusion. I'll see if I can diffuse the effect to free the guards."

The poor men no doubt wished their little band had found real targets to attack rather than debilitating oscillations in the atmosphere. More than one of the men had to have a sensitivity to elemental forces in order for the spell to work on them. Perhaps that or their brush with the necromancers in the past gave them a susceptibility to necromantic influences. Either way, it didn't bode well for the untalented if they were vulnerable to the forces.

Oberon raised his hands, peering through the veil of illusion, trying to find that one specific cord to unravel the fabric. Lines of magic shimmered in the air, billowing linens caught in the wind. As a child, he got more than one spanking for snatching sheets from the line, thinking if he grabbed them while they rippled and snapped, they might carry him off into the sky. He followed the flow of the spell as he had that long-ago laundry, waiting for the precise moment he could rip it from the anchor.

There!

Oberon wound his fingers around one of the oscillating streamers and yanked. Much of the structure destabilized. The outer aspects kept up a steady stream, but those in the middle fluttered and faltered. He continued to pull the streams apart until there was nothing left but the tattered remains of the unspent magic.

Oberon reached over his head and pulled a bolt from the quiver. Using all his might, he plunged it into the heart of the rotted magic. Spikes of ungrounded energy shot off in all directions, hitting him in the chest, face, and hands. Pain raced throughout his body, but he held on, driving the bolt deeper into the core.

A sharp rise in oscillations preceded deafening quiet.

"Is it over?" one of the guards moaned. He still held his head on the sides. His knuckles blanched against his olive skin.

"No." Oberon placed the bolt back into the quiver. "That was only the second act."

Chapter Twenty

THE PASSAGES grew narrower as Oberon and the others plunged deeper into the catacombs. Along the way were visible reminders of the war that had raged below the holy city only a few months before.

At a cross section, Theodyne directed the band in the opposite way. "We don't want to use that tunnel. Believe me."

Oberon glanced down the darkened corridor. "Why not? It appears to be shorter."

"It might be shorter in distance, but longer in peril. Last time we encountered living vines down that way. We were rather hard-pressed to get ourselves out of the coil."

And that was reason enough for Oberon to follow Theodyne without further question. Bones rattled behind them, following them with all the obedience of trained dogs.

Oberon hadn't the slightest idea what he'd do with them, but he'd think of something when the time came to fight. They hadn't even begun to scratch the surface of everything the necromancers had in store for them, he was positive of that notion. Bone walls and oscillating spells were all petty annoyances used to slow them down. As diversions, both had worked very well. However, it wasn't the end.

Each step brought them closer to another danger. More time wasted when they needed to concentrate on saving Hazrael. What if they hadn't taken him to the catacombs? Would the necromancers have even bothered with traps if they were somewhere else, say the basilica? It seemed the miles of tunnels and turns below the city might keep them occupied for a long time, making diversions of any form superfluous.

Noise from up ahead filled the passageway. Angry shouts echoed along the walls. Theodyne made a motion for the guards to keep low.

Flickering light bounced off the walls, reflected from the flaming torches. These weren't sounds made by necromancers, but flesh-and-blood men.

A party rounded a corner, weapons drawn and ready for attack. At their head was a handsome and distinguished man, brought low in smears of soot and ash. Determination fired his green eyes.

"Juan-Carlo?" Theodyne blinked in surprise, as if not believing his eyes.

"Theodyne? What are you doing down here?"

"Searching for one of our brothers. Hazrael."

Juan-Carlo's shoulders sagged. "Bastards."

Theodyne's gaze scanned Juan-Carlo and the men with him. They were all dressed in guard uniforms, though with the dirt and grime, Oberon could not see the insignia on their leather tunics. He did remember hearing the name Juan-Carlo as tied to one of the *prolatial* families. If his estimation was correct, this was the DiCarni.

"Have you been fighting all day?"

"Most of it." Juan-Carlo gave a snort of derision. "The basilica guards burned my villa to the ground. It was retaliation for an earlier offense."

"What did you do?"

An evil yet satisfied look came into his eyes. "I killed their leader. He was highly infected with the stain of the necromancers."

Theodyne lowered his head. "You've only released him into their keeping. They'll use him more readily now than they have already."

"I'll kill him a hundred times over if it means getting rid of them from Dominicál." Juan-Carlo turned to Oberon. "You're the headmaster?"

"I am."

"We will follow you. Any place you're headed is sure to raise the necromancers' ire."

"Theodyne suggested we go this way. The tunnels back there are filled with living vines and walls constructed of bone. You'll not find safe passage."

Juan-Carlo looked back the way they had come. "There were a few tunnels we didn't try, but my alchemist had no sense that the necromancers were down there."

Oberon glanced through the crowd of men but saw no one he recognized. "Where is he?"

"Ellec!"

A young man pushed through the towering men. He was small and slim but wore the robes of an adept. "Yes, Your Grace."

The guards stayed close to the young master, protecting him as if he were a precious jewel.

"These are Masters Theodyne and Oberon of the Delaneux branch of the Gold School."

Ellec's eyes widened. He nodded in a quick show of respect. "An honor."

Oberon frowned. "Which school do you hail from?"

"Penegrin, under the direction of Headmaster Willis."

Oberon nodded. He knew the headmaster well. If Willis had advanced this young lad to the status of adept, he'd well deserved the honor. Still it was odd to encounter one of their members from another of their many schools in so unlikely a place as the catacombs.

"You've been well trained, then."

Theodyne caught Oberon's eyes over the top of Ellec's head. One eyebrow was raised.

A voice echoed down the thread of Oberon's consciousness stationed on the ether.

"Ellec is an extremely powerful etherealthant. *He is going to draw the necromancers like flies to a carcass. I suspect that is the real reason why the necromancers attacked the DiCarni villa."*

Oberon stared at Theodyne. *"Then we use him to draw the necromancers to us."*

Oberon placed his hand on Ellec's shoulder. "Your talents are going to be of great use to us."

"How so?" It was not Ellec who answered, but the DiCarni.

"I'm sorry, Your Grace, but your alchemist is a bit more than he appears."

Ellec's eyes widened. He shook his head. "I promise I'm not tainted by *them*, Your Grace. I would know it."

"I'm not talking about you being tainted in any way. I'm speaking of your ability to commune with spirit elementals." Oberon tightened his grip. "The necromancers are drawn to *etherealthants*."

A look of relief washed over the young master's face. "Then I wasn't imagining it. For weeks now—since coming to live with the DiCarni—I've felt hunted. I thought perhaps it was only living away from Penegrin for the first time since I was a baby that made me unsure."

Theodyne studied the lad's face. "The necromancers are very good at manipulating circumstances for their benefit. If they wanted you to believe you were homesick, that's what you'd feel and never question the emotion."

Ellec drew back from Theodyne, hand on his chest. "What if I am tainted?"

Oberon knew the exact moment Theodyne touched Ellec's consciousness. A flash of bright light lit up the astral. Blinding. Glorious. Powerful indeed.

Theodyne shook his head. "You're clean. I feel and see no taint."

Trust shone in Ellec's dark eyes. He might be a powerful *etherealthant* in master's robes, but he was still more boy than man. Having the approval of his elders was important to him. "How can I help?"

"We need to know the exact location Master Hazrael is being kept. I can't see anything on the astral that indicates him. There's a void."

Juan-Carlo gave a look of sympathy. "Could it be he's already dead?"

Everything inside Oberon seized up. He'd refused to think of that when it came into his own mind; he'd not hear it from another. Instead, he took a deep breath and tried for a center of calm. "When they took him seventeen years ago, we could not find him on the astral then either. It was one of the reasons we thought he'd been killed. We found no trace."

Juan-Carlo narrowed his eyes. "So they have ways of hiding their presence in the ethereal plane? The more I hear about them, the more I find to dislike."

Oberon was unsure if necromancers had any favorable qualities. There were none as far as he was concerned. He turned his attention back to Ellec. "Try to trace Hazrael through the spirit elementals. He was once the most powerful *etherealthant* in the Gold School. There should still be something left of the hallmarks in him."

Ellec frowned. "Why not ask the elementals to help?"

"Because they have refused him in the past. I have no reason to believe they will help him now." Despite the fact they professed to protect him, Oberon had no reason to trust their agenda. Not where Hazrael was concerned. If they had his best interests at heart, they'd have allowed him to be found all those years ago and not left him to rot.

Theodyne's expression changed. Hardened. He shot Oberon an annoyed glance but didn't refute the charges. "Can you at least try, Ellec?"

"Yes, of course. I serve the Gold School."

Ellec lowered his head, eyes closed. His hands came up in front of his face, fingers laced and locked together. "Join with me, Master Oberon, Master Theodyne. Let me show you where our brother is held."

Once again, bright light flooded into Oberon's inner vision. The initial contact startled, flared in awesome power. After a moment it settled to reveal a grid of the catacombs. Dots of glowing colors moved through the caverns. There were other parties traveling the catacombs, for what purpose, Oberon had no clue.

Off in a section apart from the rest of the tunnels sat a room, occupied by several duller shades. One pulsated in white-hot energy. Anger, fear, and confusion streamed from the essence. It brushed against Oberon, sending tingles all the way to his balls. Hazrael.

Oberon let out the breath he'd been holding. "You've found him."

Theodyne gave him a maniacal smile. "Let's go get him."

HAZRAEL DODGED the steady drips of acid raining down on him from the disintegrating crystal shell. He had to get out from under it, but move to where? The air was rancid with poison. Surely if those noxious fumes dissolved stone they would have an easy time dispensing with lungs. With nothing to tie over his nose and mouth, he had no protection against the vile air.

Did it even matter?

He was going to die in this chamber one way or another. Might as well take as many as possible down when he went.

The main section of the dome buckled. This was it. He'd run out of time.

He swept his legs out to the side and dropped down behind the tomb, using it as a shield. There had to be something with which to fashion a weapon.

Bones littered the floor of the chamber. Across the room, out of his reach, a femur lay in the dirt floor, partially hidden by years of neglect. If he managed to crawl over to it, he might be able to fashion a blade.

Before he could make it halfway there, the necromancers circled. This was really not a good position to be in—down on the ground. Naked. Without a weapon.

He grabbed a handful of dirt, said a few words, and threw it outward. Grains of dirt and sand, bits of bone, and a few lone teeth fused together as they shot out of his hand, forming a long, gleaming blade. Blue portal energy streamed along the length of the sides. The hilt was composed of protection crystals and fit his hand to perfection.

Hazrael pushed up from the ground.

He stood in the center as necromancers closed in on him. They didn't seem intimidated or even scared by his hastily fashioned sword. No matter. Once they tasted the cool kiss of the portal energy, they'd reassess their lack of caution.

Hazrael swung the sword in an underhanded hold, cutting through the bodies of several necromancers. Surprised shrieks filled the chamber. Lightning danced around the room, ricocheting off the walls and ceiling.

Bodies exploded, sending a wave of blood and gore showering over him, turning to ash as it landed.

The *Necromon* moved away from the circle, dropping back behind the others.

Hazrael danced closer, taunting the *Necromon* with the tip of the blade. "Not so brave after all? Using your minions for cover? Not even I ever sunk so low as to do that." Not since he regained his faculties.

The sharp words fell on deaf ears. Hazrael doubted anything he said would make an impact on the *Necromon*. He might as well have been speaking in tongues or moving his mouth without benefit of sound.

Hazrael moved a few steps closer, inching across the space separating him from the necromancers. Then he was in motion. He danced and spun, slicing through the tattered robes and fleshless bodies. Animated bones were all that stood between Hazrael and his quarry. They had no more intellect or ambition than a bag of rocks. Their only wishes were those imposed on them by the *Necromon*'s will.

Still, he was damned glad to send them back to the dust from whence they sprang. With each strike, more of the death dancers fell, spreading their horrible ash to settle over the chamber. The air became thick, clogging. Hazrael lost the ability to see his enemies, and it became uneasy to draw breath. A strange lethargy blanketed him in a need for immediate and endless sleep.

No!

To lie down now was to succumb to the *Necromon*'s wishes.

When he slept, it would be the final one for him. For now, he had to fight on.

A small body folded out of the falling ash. Its eyes glowed with unholy light. It reached out its child-sized hand. "Give me the sword, Hazrael. You do not know the power you wield."

"I know exactly what I wield."

He cut through the terrifying construct. Blue energy arced out in all directions. The head rolled to hit the wall with a dull thud. It was the only part of the body that failed to combust on impact.

"Your men have all perished under my blade. Stand now and meet your fate, *Necromon*."

The only answer came in the echo of his own words.

He was alone.

Chapter Twenty-One

HAZRAEL SLIPPED down the corridors without a sense of direction. He dared not cross into the ether to find his way, positive if he did the *Necromon* would follow. Time had passed since he'd fled the chamber—enough that the *Necromon* might have spun some new followers from bits of bone and dirt.

Any use of his talent might call the death dancers to him. If they didn't already know.

It might be years before he crawled his way out of the catacombs.

And it was dark. So unbearably dark.

Stones, bones, and other unimaginable things battered his feet as he made his way through the gloom. The light from his fingers was not bright enough to do more than keep him from running into a wall.

Panic rose and fell with every breath, becoming a constant, uncomfortable companion. Despair washed over him with each step. He came down hard on something sharp, puncturing his foot. He bit his lips together to block the cry of pain.

Whatever he'd stepped on remained in his foot. Hazrael leaned his bare buttocks against the rough wall. He bent his knees, then lifted his left leg to look at the bottom of his foot. An arrowhead stuck into the ball, in the bend right before the arch. It was a painful place for an injury. Though he had nothing to bind the wound, the fact remained the foreign body had to come out.

He gritted his teeth and gripped the arrowhead. It was embedded deep under the layers of skin, muscle, and tendons. The damn thing refused to give way, and he was losing his strength. The obsidian shard wasn't the easiest thing to get a hold of either. His fingers slid on the exposed edge, and it cut his fingertips. Blood leaked across the site, making it even slipperier.

All right, maybe he should send a bit of energy through the arrowhead and try and pry it out that way. Fact of the matter was, he couldn't walk on or leave this place until it was out. It was too painful.

Noises—voices—echoed down the passageway. Hazrael failed to make out the words, but from the tone and timbre, they were human, not necromancers. It didn't follow that they were untainted.

He doused the light from his hand and hobbled over to the far wall, using the sword he'd fashioned as a walking stick to help balance him. Once to the other side of the tunnel, he hugged the stones and tried to put the feel of bugs crawling over his hair and back out of his mind. It wasn't easy. He'd wait here only as long as it took for the party to pass by, and then he'd move in the opposite direction, away from them.

There wasn't enough energy left in his body to fight another army. He needed to conserve in case he met up with the *Necromon* again.

The voice grew louder.

"He should be right around here. Close." It was a voice he didn't recognize. Youthful, with an odd accent. One from a different region of the city-states, though Hazrael couldn't pinpoint where.

Lights from lanterns and the faint blue glow of portal energy filled the passageway. Shadowed figures grew out of the darkness.

Hazrael raised his sword.

A familiar set of shoulders and silhouette of hair came into view.

Oberon!

Did Hazrael dare believe he'd been found? He sagged against the wall, dropping the point of his sword into the dirt as Oberon, Theodyne, and a retinue of the Medovin's guards, along with others he didn't recognize, gathered around him.

"Dearest elements!" Oberon hurried forward and caught Hazrael around the waist as his legs finally gave out on him. Whether from relief or failure, he didn't know or care at the moment. All he knew was Oberon nestled him close, kissed his forehead, and mumbled words of thankfulness.

After a few moments, Oberon held him away, his green gaze searching Hazrael for injuries. "Are you hurt?"

"My foot. I stepped on an arrowhead. I can't pull it out."

Theodyne stepped closer. "Let me see. Lift your foot."

Hazrael did as instructed, embarrassed to see his leg shake as he held it up.

"You've driven it in quite far." Theodyne looked up at the guards. "I need a dagger from one of you."

Hazrael swallowed and tried not to get sick. Not that he had anything to come up but the burning taste of bile. There had already been so much pain, physical and emotional, enough to last him the rest of his life. He looked up at Theodyne, whom he'd trust with his very soul, and grimaced. "You'd think by now I'd be used to pain, immune to its effects. I fear I'm not that hardened."

"And may you never be so, my friend." Theodyne held out his hand as one of the guards handed him a dagger. "I'm not going to cut you. I only want to lay the dagger down this way." He placed the flat of the dagger against Hazrael's skin, then pressed hard. It hurt, but only from the way the action shifted the arrowhead. The motion exposed more of the arrowhead, allowing Theodyne to get a better grip on it.

Theodyne pulled. Stars appeared behind Hazrael's closed lids. It hurt worse coming out than going in. He took a deep breath and tried to work through the agony the best he could.

Theodyne gave a grunt of sound. The shard came loose, and relief washed through Hazrael's body.

Oberon moved away and stripped off his robe, revealing a plain homespun shirt and hose underneath. "Here. You can't go topside without something to cover you."

"Wait!" Theodyne took the robe from Hazrael before he managed to get it over his head. Once it was in his hands, Theodyne ripped one of the sleeves off. He glanced up apologetically to Oberon. "I'll pay for a new one, but I need the sleeve to make a dressing for his foot."

Oberon didn't seem to mind and took the destruction of his clothing in stride.

Theodyne wrapped the sleeve around Hazrael's foot to make a pressure dressing. It wasn't the best one ever, but it was better than dripping blood all over the catacomb floor.

"Where did an obsidian arrowhead come from?" Oberon took the artifact from Theodyne and held it up to the lantern light.

"There were a lot of odd things down here a few months ago." Theodyne tied off the ends of the sleeve, then helped Hazrael to a standing position. "Can you bear weight on it?"

Hazrael tested his foot and winced. "Not well, but enough to get me out of here."

"Good enough." Theodyne held out the robe and helped Hazrael into the garment. "Let's go."

Oberon motioned to a young man who wore adepts' robes. "Find us the quickest route out of here."

A tall man who walked beside the young master looked familiar to Hazrael. He knew him from somewhere, but not the where and when. An odd sense of self-consciousness swam through his veins. He averted his eyes when they caught and held the stranger's gaze.

The man frowned. "You are among friends, Master Hazrael. No need to feel ashamed. It is understood within the order of the *prolates* you had no choice in what your captors made you do."

And just like that the memory triggered.

Hazrael fell down into the blackest pit.

A CELEBRATION was underway. Everyone who was in the holy city for the election of the new demigoge *was present, including the Rinni's magus, Hazrael. The air was sweet with worry, envy, and greed. All the emotions that made a necromancer hunger for more.*

Fear, that was the most potent banquet. Hazrael lifted his nose, sniffing the crowd for the latent emotion and found only a trace of it, muted with a hint of concern.

His masters told him who to target, the one they called Master Jolen. The aerothant. *Hazrael opened his hand, spread his fingers, and stirred the atmosphere, trying to bring the scents closer to him. There was elemental blood on the wind, but it was touched by the decaying hand of a necromancer.*

Hazrael's lips curled back from his teeth in what might resemble a smile. He didn't know, since he'd lost the ability to feel anything but the need to commit atrocities at the bequest of his masters.

A small voice, buried deep beneath the layers of depravity, scorned his mission and called him a fool, told him he'd be better off sticking a knife through his heart than living this way. Hazrael gave a brief frown and started across the garden, ignoring the internal struggle as it grew louder.

The crowd parted, revealing the handsome young man who had shunned his alchemists' robes for those of a wealthy merchant. The Medovin dressed his lover well.

Hazrael moved through the celebrants, brushing ever so gently against Master Jolen. As he did, Hazrael gave a quick turn of his wrist, imitating the motion of driving a blade through the man's side to reopen his healing wound. Shock registered in Master Jolen's eyes, and he grabbed the wound.

It was done.

The best part was, Master Jolen hadn't seen a thing.

MISTS SWIRLED and time passed, though Hazrael knew not how long, only that the next memories came from after the ill-fated party.

HIS FEET hurt, and his back burned from the lashes he'd received. His masters were not pleased that he'd failed to kill the new demigoge. *Master Theodyne had seen to that by administering to the* demigoge-*elect in short order. Hazrael had tried to save himself and the mission by taking the back passages to the Medovin's villa. That was where the last piece of the* Elementica *had been traced. Without that final artifact, the necromancers had no hope of enslaving the elementals.*

His masters had caught him in an alley and punished him in the most severe of ways.

The inner voice returned, urging him to run, to free himself, but he pushed that aside as well, falling into the pain as the whip hit his back. He deserved the beating. Every last stroke of the whip. Every last drop of blood and rent of flesh.

Now he led an army of necromantic guards down into the bowels of the catacombs, to the tomb of Akabar Kolhen, where the other pieces were hidden. What did the man need with his tomb? He wasn't even in there. A body lay in the final resting place, preserved for all time, but it wasn't that of the statesman, only an opportune vessel used when Akabar Kolhen effected his transformation.

Hazrael pulled the child, Wendro, along. The spell that compelled the boy to steal the last piece of the Elementica *had rendered him too compliant. He was barely able to move under his own direction. It had been foolish to bring him along, but Hazrael was under strict instructions to deliver the child, along with the missing section, into the* Necromon's *hands.*

From what Hazrael could tell, the boy reeked with the scent of an etherealthant. *Was Hazrael about to be replaced in the masters' affections? Had he made one mistake too many?*

The voice urged him to get to the tomb, unite the pieces of the ruby tablet, and flee, return home. But where was home? He knew none but the brutal lash of the necromancers' punishments.

Corridors turned and twisted under the city, going on for miles. The tomb chamber opened up into a rotunda with the sarcophagus as the central focus.

Someone had been here and put a crude construction over the glass-worked casket. No matter. He was a master of all the elements, and he could push and pull through the thick stone casing and never leave a mark of his passing.

Hazrael rounded the tomb, trying to decide the best place to insert the final ruby piece. Dried blood fused his shirt to his back, sending fresh pain shooting through his skin every time he moved. Pesky nuisances and minor irritations jeopardized his mission. They pecked at his focus like a flock of angry birds.

There, on the very edge of the structure, was a spot where the stone was not quite as thick. Hazrael dug into his pocket and pulled out the ruby fragment. Holding it firmly in his palm, he concentrated on delving through the layers into the casket.

Sand sifted through his fingers. A triumph. The pieces of the Elementica *were united after being apart for a thousand years.*

Millions of voices cried out in despair, the elementals enchained by their new death-dancing masters.

"You have betrayed us, Hazrael. We will never forgive you for this."

He didn't want or need their forgiveness.

No! *The voice inside screamed.* You are a part of them, and they are a part of you.

The conflicting thoughts tore at his brain. Pain, overwhelming and excruciating, brought his hands to the sides of his head. Sand from the crust over the casket smeared along his cheek.

A figure appeared at the top of the stairs leading to the basilica proper. Light spread throughout the chamber, dull, thick. It was like looking at the world through a black veil. The Necromon.

Dizziness swept over Hazrael. He was being sucked down into a vortex he'd not soon climb out of.

All noise from the elementals cut off without warning. Balance returned. The image of the Necromon *disappeared. Had it ever really been there?*

A CHILL swept through Hazrael. His body quaked and his teeth chattered. Unsure if that had really happened outside the grip of the memory or if it was residual from the past battle, he tried to wrap his arms around himself, but they were as heavy as if they'd been infused with lead. There was no warmth moving within. He'd become corpse-like.

Voices moved around him—not the same ones that spoke in his head, but pleading, insistent ones. Hands tapped his cheeks and chafed at his arms. He tried to wake from the pull of the past, but he was caught firmly in its grasp.

ALL AROUND him a battle raged. Masters Theodyne and Jolen killed guards. Blood spilled, painting the floor in a crimson river. Hazrael became apart from himself, knitting the ragged pieces of humanity, dirt, and debris together to form more soldiers. Even as his mind rebelled, his hands worked in intricate patterns to construct reinforcements.

Where was the Necromon?

He'd promised to relieve him of the burden of command when the Elementica *had been joined. Yet he was in this desolate place alone, save a small boy and guards who only knew to kill their enemies.*

The tide of the battle turned. Master Jolen and the Medovin were at the tomb. The protective casing broke away and pieces of the Elementica *could be seen pushing their way to the top.*

How had that happened?

A rush of sound, emotions, and scent hit Hazrael with all the force of a tsunami. The elementals were free, and they were looking for the one who imprisoned them for their revenge.

Master Jolen advanced on Hazrael, a terrifying sight of rage.

HAZRAEL TRIED to hide from the next moments of the battle. There was no reason to look at them; he knew what came next. Saw his arm reach for the boy.

NO! STOP! Don't do it!

The words failed to penetrate the part of his body controlled by the necromancers. Rage he didn't feel twisted his face into an ugly mask of defiance. He threw the boy against the stone wall. The neck snapped, placing it at an unnatural angle to the body.

White light, searing hot, hit Hazrael square in the chest. All his senses overloaded, sending him into the murky depths of a half life.

OBERON TAPPED Hazrael's cheeks. No matter how vigorously he shook or tried to wake Hazrael, there was nothing there. Even his body had begun to grow cold.

He was dying, and there was nothing Oberon could do.

"Help him, Theodyne. Please."

The skin on Hazrael's exposed arm began to crack open. Rivulets of blood seeped from the carvings. Shiny wet spots began to spread across the front of the borrowed robe. "The Kiss of Death is bleeding again."

Theodyne moved around Hazrael. "I can see that."

In the dim light, a dark puddle began to form behind Hazrael.

Oberon's hand shook as he touched Hazrael's face. "We need to get him topside."

"I agree, but I fear we don't have time."

The DiCarni looked down at the scene. Horror put deep grooves around his mouth and lifted his brow. "Did I cause this? My apologies."

Theodyne glanced up at the DiCarni before looking back down at Hazrael. "Rest assured, Juan-Carlo, it's nothing you did. He's been battling this since his memory began to resurface. Certain words and phrases trigger them no matter how hard his mind tried to hide from the horrors he was forced to endure."

"The poor, wretched soul." The DiCarni turned to Ellec. "Find us a way out of here."

"Yes, Your Grace."

Theodyne shook his head as he checked Hazrael's carotid pulse. "He's fading fast. The only way I know to stop the flow of blood is to sever the tie binding him to the necromancers, to stop the flow of power to the Kiss of Death."

The necromancers had already found them; there was no longer a need to keep the channel open. Oberon gave a decisive nod. "Do it."

Theodyne closed his eyes, touching his fingers to the middle of Hazrael's forehead. Oberon let his mind unwind and follow the path Theodyne took down into the deepest levels of Hazrael's consciousness and beyond.

Where it was once a raging ocean of sludge, now it appeared scoured by huge claws. The wounds belched out a purulent pus that had infected Hazrael's thoughts for way too long.

Noises began as a soft rumble, echoing down the corridors. Stamps of heavy feet and the crash of armor. Oberon disconnected from Theodyne and Hazrael, turning his attention to the DiCarni, who stood with his guards, sword in one hand, pistol in the other.

Ellec pulled a small, brightly lit disk from his pocket. His gaze connected and held Oberon's. "Basilica guards. Infected by the necromancers."

The sounds grew closer. There was nowhere to go at the moment. They'd have to stand and fight in place.

Oberon grabbed the sword Hazrael had crafted. Sensation tingled along his fingers, sending a sense of final desperation and raw courage up his arm to bury in his heart. Hazrael had believed when he crafted the blade that it was his last moment: he'd done so not really believing it would work.

Oberon vowed if his lover survived this ordeal, Hazrael would never know another moment of doubt in his life. There would be nothing taken from them again, only the future spread out before them bright with promise.

The basilica guards rounded the corner. Oberon turned his back on Theodyne and Hazrael, and stood in front of them in a great wall of protection.

The DiCarni's guards engaged those of the basilica as the first wave of attack began. Swords clashed and firearms cracked, deafening in the small space. Unlike their previous encounters with tainted men, this time they left none alive to salvage. There wasn't time or opportunity to drive out the influence—not and get Hazrael back to the surface. This moment in time it was kill or be killed. Every last one of the basilica guards had come to end the fight here in the catacombs. It was evident in the way they charged and hacked, slashing at their opponents with a single-minded intensity that chilled the bone.

Oberon wielded Hazrael's blade. A guard came at him, a hellish gleam in his dark eyes. Oberon raised his arm to block the blow coming at him. Blue light sang along the bone sword, rippling outward. Instead of two swords clashing, the bone blade cut through the steel, breaking it off to a nub near the enemy's pommel, and kept moving. It sliced through the man, igniting him in a tower of blue flame.

Surprised, Oberon almost dropped the sword into the dirt.

The unusual manner of death did not seem to faze the other basilica guards. They continued to come at the small band of alchemists and *prolatial* guards without thought to consequence or knowledge of bodily harm.

It was little better than murdering men in their sleep, and yet there was no escape from the act. Spare these men and lose the war against the necromancers. There was no choice.

Oberon threw himself into the fight, ripe with the knowledge that he was helping to save all of humanity from this perilous fate. He towered over some of the basilica guards, using his height to his advantage to end the fight in a few short, powerful strokes.

Lights swirled, metal clashed, and guns fired. More than once a man yelled in pain, signaling that one of either the DiCarni or the Medovin's men had been hurt. Burn-off from the guns' reports covered the area in a heavy blanket of acrid smoke.

Shadows and silhouettes danced through the smoke-filled space, making it hard to see. A hulking figure advanced on Oberon, sword raised. Oberon answered him in a counterattack, only to realize it was the DiCarni. He let his arm drop at the last moment and stepped back from the blow the DiCarni couldn't stop in time.

"Heavens above!" the DiCarni cursed. "I might have killed you, Master Oberon."

Oberon glanced around. "I think we've managed to subdue this round of guards, but we have to move quickly. There is no time to waste."

Oberon turned to the bones he'd brought into his service as he pulled the pack with the lead boxes from his back. "Scoop up the remains of those who are ash and place them in the casks, if you would be so kind."

The bones complied.

The DiCarni shook his head. "I don't even want to know."

On the ground, Theodyne struggled to lift Hazrael. "We have to take him to the healing pool. The threads of the connection refuse to let go without Hazrael's permission. I can't sever them without his cooperation."

Oberon's heart sank. "What about the bleeding?"

"I've managed to stem that for now. The sites are weeping, but not badly."

That might be a comfort if Oberon didn't know how many of the scars Hazrael carried. He moved Theodyne out of the way. "Let me carry him. I can move faster with a greater load than you can."

"Ellec? Show us the way." The DiCarni had his guards in formation. Those who weren't injured helped to support the ones who were. None of the men would be left behind down here.

Ellec's robe was torn. There was a cut above his eye that bled in a steady drip down his face. He tried to wipe the flow away to see, but only succeeded in smearing that and dirt across his forehead. He didn't look too steady on his feet, but the determined set of his shoulders and the hardness around his mouth proved he was tougher than he appeared.

The young adept took point and led the group out of the area where they'd been ambushed and through the twisting, turning tunnels again. His direction proved infallible as they climbed a set of stairs that came up on the other side of the Divine Causeway.

Explosions rocked the square. Debris rained down on those unfortunate enough to be outdoors. Sounds of war kept the night alive, undermining the confidence that morning would come.

Their band turned down the main promenade to find the catapults were aligned and pointed at the basilica. Crates containing the globes were stacked next to the siege machines, ready to take down the very walls of religion.

Nico stood at the front of the line, shouting orders to the men behind the catapults. When he spotted Theodyne, he turned and strode to him, hand on a weapon at his hip. "I'd despaired of seeing you again tonight."

"And you almost didn't. Are you planning to fire on the basilica?"

Nico nodded. "With the *demigoge's* permission. The *Necromon* has taken up residence there and uses it as his stronghold."

Jolen came from behind one of the catapults. "The *demigoge* believes the only way to oust the infection is to splinter the walls and bring it crashing down. Then it is to be taken to the ocean where it will be protected by the water elementals for a thousand years."

Oberon stood there in amazement. All the treasures inside would be buried beneath the rubble. Lost to time and history. He hefted his burden and started walking again. "I have to get Hazrael to the healing pool."

Each breath Hazrael took was slower, fainter than the one before it.

Nico finally looked at someone other than his lover. His eyes widened. "Dearest elementals!"

Oberon didn't stop to explain the events in the catacombs. The DiCarni led him to the gates of the Medovin villa, where guards were readying more armaments, preparing for a full-out war.

"You've found him." The Hierophant and her entourage met them at the gate. "Come, he is in more desperate need of the pool now than ever he was."

Oberon didn't slow his stride; if anything he picked up speed now they were so close to their goal.

Steam rose from the pool, fragrant and inviting.

"Put him in up to his neck. Do not bother with removing his clothes." The Hierophant directed her servants with graceful hand gestures. They brought over blocks to prop him up against the side of the tub so he wouldn't slip and drown.

"His mind is a complete disaster," the Hierophant tsked. "Poor man, his trial is almost at an end."

Oberon cared not a bit for those words. There was a gentle finality to them that was most unfair. No one had tasted more death in his short life than Hazrael.

After all he'd been through, he deserved to live.

Chapter Twenty-Two

HAZRAEL FLOATED along on a vast ocean with nothing more than a plank of wood to keep him from drowning. Soft voices called to him from the heavens. At least he assumed it was the heavens, since he was the only one around for as far as the eye could see.

There were no bodies of land on which to take refuge or tall ships to rescue him. He was alone.

The voices urged him to keep going, but his reserves were fading. Weary in both body and spirit, it would be so easy to let go of the wooden plank keeping him afloat and fall into the abyss.

How had he come to be so far from shore? Had he been shipwrecked in a storm and woken up when a wave washed over him? That didn't feel right. There were no memories of being on board or even the sea spray as it hit his face.

The robe he wore was saturated, dragging him down as his legs dangled in the water. He tried to shake it off, but it wouldn't go. Every time he peeled one side of the soggy fabric off his shoulder, it would reappear before he got the other side down.

Was this his purgatory or the very essence of hell? Drifting over a world filled with nothing but water and no contact with other souls for the rest of eternity? Crimes were plentiful in his past. So many littered the road he'd traveled he had no chance of expunging them all, even if he lived to be a thousand. The necromancers were only responsible for a fraction of what he'd done. They might have been the ones to pull the strings, but he'd not fought hard enough against them. His crimes were those of complacency. He'd tried for a bit of redemption to touch his soul—to live in a manner that might *see all his bad deeds erased, but now he understood it had not been enough—would never be enough.*

The current pulled him along. He bobbed on the small waves as the seas grew rougher once he entered a pass where two large bodies of water converged.

He smacked his lips together, trying to draw moisture as he baked in the blaring sun. Blue, pristine skies mocked him with a lack of clouds. There would be no rain today. Drinking saltwater meant a slow, agonizing death.

A rumble of thunder came from the horizon.

Hazrael tried to shade his eyes from the sun's glare as he peered into the distance. Perhaps there were clouds below the line where sky met ocean, but he could not see them.

Hope, that was all he had left. There was nothing more. Not out here on a vast and desolate sea.

He was lost.

OBERON RAN his hand across Hazrael's forehead, moving the long hair from his brow. Tenderness swept through him, along with a large dose of concern.

Hazrael's color had gone very pale. His breathing was slow and shallow. Even the warm water of the healing pool failed to bring his temperature up to anywhere near normal. It wasn't working.

Oberon looked up at the milky eyes of the Hierophant. "We're losing him. Isn't there something more we can do to bring him back to us?"

The Hierophant shook her head. "No. He must make the journey alone. If he decides to return to his mortal coil, he will, but not until he's ready to do so."

"That's more a riddle than an answer." Oberon unleashed the flare of his temper. "You stand there, knowing the outcome of this war, and yet you hold back, saying things of little value or comfort to those of us on the front."

One of the acolytes started forward, probably to defend her mistress. Oberon wasn't afraid of a mere slip of a girl, no matter how many elemental powers she might possess. He was beyond caring about such trivial things at the moment.

The Hierophant held her acolyte's arm to keep her from going to the pool. "I understand why you feel that way, but I can only see possible futures or read the information in the parables of the past. It is my position to steer the outcomes in the directions that are beneficial to the city-states as a whole, not to the individual."

Oberon tried to swallow down his anger but failed. "He's bled for the necromancers, and now he bleeds for *you*. When is it going to be enough?"

Nico chose that moment to enter the room. His timing couldn't have been worse.

Oberon gave him a dismissive glance, then turned back to Hazrael. "Aren't you supposed to be bringing down the basilica?"

"Our spheres haven't had quite the impact I'd anticipated. I need you to come with me to the line and help to build more spheres."

Oberon had been trying to ignore the sounds of the besieged city that raged outside the villa's gates. He gave a rueful laugh. There was more pain than mirth behind the gesture. "I suppose it was too much to ask to be allowed to sit with Hazrael while he endures yet another brush with death."

"I am sorry, Oberon, but I wouldn't ask you this if I didn't think it was important."

Or come to ask for his help in person when he could have easily sent a guard with a message. He suspected the reason was because Nico knew how hard it would be to refuse a personal request.

Oberon ran his hand through Hazrael's hair again. He leaned closer to the unconscious man. "I have to go now, but I promise I will return to you as soon as I am able. Never forget how much I love you. We will make this right and heal you, by witness of the elements."

He placed gentle kisses on Hazrael's head, cheek, and mouth.

With a heavy heart and anger roiling too near the surface to hide it, Oberon stood and left the room, following Nico. As they walked through the antechamber, Oberon stopped to retrieve the quiver and crossbow.

Nico frowned. "Those won't have the reach we need."

"Maybe not, but when the walls begin to tumble down, the rats will all look for safe quarter. These bolts of Hazrael's have proved very useful in destroying the necromancers. No sense in leaving them behind when he went to great trouble to make them." Oberon hoisted the quiver higher on his shoulder. "Let's go so I can return here before they send me word of Hazrael's passing."

Nico stalled. He reached out for Oberon's arm. "Is he that serious?"

"The Hierophant says his survival is up to him. It could go either way at this point." Oberon looked Nico directly in the eyes as he choked on his next words. "If he dies alone, when I should have been there for him, I'm not sure *our* friendship will survive."

Nico's jaw clamped tightly for a moment before he gave a swift nod. "I see. I'll be sorry to note that, but I do need you with me."

"Very well. As long as you are aware."

Oberon said nothing more as they hurried through the garden. He stopped once more at one of the wagons. "The metal boxes? Did you bring them to the line?"

Nico nodded. "All the ones you left before heading out to the catacombs."

Oberon stopped his frantic search and stalked to the gate, then out into the street.

Chaos had intensified as the fighting escalated. Many of the stately villas along the promenade were damaged by cannon blasts, their walls breached and looters taking off with valuable treasures.

This small corner of the world had gone mad, and there was no calling it back or putting bandages over the abscess of contaminant.

Storms raged around the basilica, small and ineffectual. Nico was right; the globes had not done what they'd been intended to do.

Oberon took up a position behind one of the catapults. "I suspect the reason they aren't working is because the necromancers anticipated you'd use that method at some point. It was a predictable action. They've erected shields around the outer wall."

Nico placed his hands on his hips and stared at the spires rising above the great dome as if the structure mocked them by remaining intact despite the siege. "What do you suggest?"

Oberon took one of the bolts from the quiver and held it between his hands as he'd done back in the school. This time he'd prepared for the cold burn of energy as it leached into his hand. When he'd absorbed a sufficient amount, he took some of the sand nearby and made a cannonball-sized sphere. The depth of the orb swirled with the crackling of blue energy.

"I'll be damned," Nico said in awe.

Oberon gave him a knowing smile. "I think this will do the job quite sufficiently."

Nico hurried away, going down the line and speaking with the catapult crews. They looked to Oberon before some of the men broke away from their stations. They found other protectors who carried the energized bolts.

From this distance and through the dimness of the night, it was hard to tell who worked to make the spheres as Oberon did, but he knew it had to be those men who had been touched by the necromancers in some way. It seemed only those tainted by the touch could work the blue energy.

Finished with the first sphere, he loaded it into the catapult and gave a nod to the crew. "Whenever you're ready."

The operator wound the tension on the spring and released the lever. The sphere shot into the night, leaving a tail eerily similar to a comet in its wake.

The sphere hit the outer wall, exploding on contact. Splinters of brick and mortar shot out in all directions. A hole appeared, big enough for a man to pass through.

Cheers erupted along the line. For Oberon it was too early to celebrate. They had a lot more than just a single wall to bring down before the night was a success.

Oberon sat on the ground, spinning spheres as fast as his talent allowed. Each subsequent one had less of the portal energy as the transfer moved from flesh to glass. He'd need to stop and reenergize to keep going.

A barrage of spheres streaked across the square, heading to the basilica. Bright blue-white lights lit up as the alchemical incendiary devices found their marks. The outer wall collapsed, sending up a cloud of dust billowing out to the street.

"Advance the line!" Nico called to the catapult crews.

Crews pulled the great machines forward, moving closer to the basilica proper. The necromancers had nowhere to hide. The last bastion of safety was being pulled down around them. Bands made of *prolatial* guards and alchemists wandered the catacombs, sealing those exits against any necromancers wishing to flee.

Oberon finished the sphere he worked and hurried to catch up as the line advanced. The walls of the basilica shone stark white against the fires. They glowed with an unnatural light.

Jolen came up beside him, holding his hand up to call a halt to their progress. "The earth elementals within the stones beg you to stop the siege. You're killing them."

"Have they turned to serve the death dancers and deceive you?" Oberon thought it only fair to ask what most of those who heard Jolen's request were thinking. He knew that much by the unsure expressions on their faces.

Jolen closed his eyes and held out his hand. "No. They are pure of intent."

"Nico!" Oberon was in no position to make this call.

Nico strode with purpose through the ranks, stopping to talk to a few of the soldiers as he did. When he reached Oberon and Jolen, he raised a brow and waited patiently for the reason he was summoned.

"Jolen says the elementals within the basilica beg us not to destroy them with the catapults. It is killing them."

Nico wiped a hand down his face. "Have they a plan?"

Jolen nodded. "They do. They said they will collapse the structure from within, starting with the dome."

Nico mumbled something under his breath that sounded of invented curses. "About time they decided to assist."

He turned to the catapult crews. "Hold your fire!"

Jolen bid a hasty thank you and closed his eyes.

A great rumble started under their feet. Oberon looked down and noticed the ground shook from the efforts of the earth elementals.

Cracks began to appear in the brickwork between the heavy support beams that kept the dome aloft. The spire sank down, going through the ceiling to crash into the floor below. Viewed from the street, it appeared as if the spike simply vanished or retracted.

One by one the columns began to crumble inward. Dust rose in a white cloud, blanketing the sky.

Shrieks filled the night, with anger and betrayal.

Storms rolled in, covering the city in rain. As with the necromancers, it wasn't plain rain, but a thick, viscous liquid that came down in heavy drops that burned the paving stones with acid.

"Take cover!" Oberon shouted to the troops. Flesh had no resistance against a substance that bubbled up stone and made it run in a murky river.

Abandoning the catapults, the men ran for the nearest shelter.

For every advance the alchemists and elementals made, the necromancers had an answer that made a hasty retreat necessary. Fighting a war in such a manner slowed things down, and whatever else Oberon wanted at the moment, a conclusion was his greatest wish.

The sting of acid rain hit his hair, face, and arms. A drop landed on his cheek, close to where the venom still had his eye swollen. Skin bubbled and sent up a stink that made him cough.

He hated the necromancers for marking him, but he hated them even worse for the marks they'd placed on Hazrael, keeping him leashed like a trained monkey. No man had a right to hold dominion over another—not even if one of the parties were dead. Especially then.

They crowded into the space between the gates of the Medovin villa, all hurrying to get out of the killing rain. Those caught in the street screamed in pain. Hair burned away from exposed heads. Skin slid down their faces, melting as wax falls from a candle. Clothes smoldered, leaving gaping holes in the fabric, giving the wearer little protection from the caustic element.

Guards and alchemists shoved their way through the garden and into the main house. Oberon was caught on the tide of pressing humanity. He broke away and ran to find a window where he could watch the street without fear of being hit by the rain.

Theodyne and Jolen followed fast on his heels. When Oberon turned left, Jolen stopped him. "No. This way. There is an observation balcony that faces the basilica."

Oberon changed direction and let Jolen lead the way.

Nico met them there, as did the Medovin. Jolen closed his eyes and opened his arms.

Wind blew through the room and into the street. Angry clouds swirled above, churning to reveal a horrible face. The *Necromon*.

Jolen pushed at the air, moving the clouds away with a force of will that staggered the imagination. A secondary front of clouds moved against the first. These were elementals who did not take orders from the necromancers.

Figures formed in the sky, warriors made of water droplets and temperature fluctuations. A bolt of lightning zigzagged across the heavens, the first strike in a war between the elements. Those who had betrayed their kind to the necromancers against those who were loyal to the earth and mankind.

Theodyne folded his arms over his chest, his gaze riveted by the awesome display of power. "They will hold nothing back. I'm afraid this fight is one we have to leave for them to handle."

Oberon raised a brow. "I have no intention of becoming involved between a host of elementals fighting it out among themselves. We have no way to assist them." He turned with a weary sigh. "I am going back to the healing pool. If anything happens of interest, let me know."

"We will." Nico patted Oberon on the back a few times. "You do the same."

Knowing the elementals had the attack in hand made it easier to walk away. If only they had come to the alchemists' and *prolates'* aid earlier, a great deal of sorrow might have been avoided.

Odd how elementals did not concern themselves with the plights of men unless it affected them in some way. They hadn't offered to take down the basilica until man found a way to smash the outer wall. Then it was more about self-preservation than actual help.

Chapter Twenty-Three

HAZRAEL WOKE to the sway of the plank. The sea had turned violent while he slept. Waves crested, splashing him in the face. His hair was plastered to his head with saltwater. It covered his face and filled his mouth. He tried to spit it out, not wanting to ingest even a mouthful for fear he'd not make his way back from this landscape except through painful death.

Death he embraced, but he'd had enough pain to endure without adding to the amount.

The sky was painted gray. Not the shade expressed from normal clouds, but flat, deep, and sinister. Still no rain fell.

His eyes burned, vision turned blurry. A tall object on the horizon grew ever closer. Was that a ship with black sails to catch the errant wind?

Hazrael pushed his wet hair back from his eyes and stared at the shape. Waves rolled him up and down, making it harder to see. His only vantage point was when he came to the top of the wave before it broke. He held one arm clamped around the plank; the other he lifted high as he could, stretching for all his might.

The position caused him to cough and sputter. His lungs hurt as if he breathed in fire.

His pleading to the elementals fell on deaf ears and stone hearts. They didn't appreciate or care about his peril. Hadn't for a very long time.

What an end.

The situation brought a rueful smile to his lips. Of all the ways he had expected to die, stuck out in the middle of the ocean on a plank of wood wasn't one of them.

As he crested the next wave, a great ship was before him.

Hazrael looked up at the vast structure. He'd never seen a ship so large—massive. The tower of decks seemed to go on forever. Each one was fitted with cannons to blast an enemy out of the water and into the next realm of existence.

The exact center of the Kiss of Death patterned on his chest began to itch and fester. Hazrael looked down at what appeared to be the ends of ragged threads poking out of his skin. Without warning, a rope shot from his chest and headed for the prow of the ship.

Frantically he tried to pull the rope from his body, but it grew directly from his skin—was a part of him. Horrified, he watched as he was pulled through the water toward the great ship.

Each tug of the rope brought him closer, until he was directly under the masthead, looking upward. The horrible visage gazed down on the water. Its image carved from a single block of wood into the shape of a necromancer with his cowl pulled back and arms outspread, hands bent into claws. The mouth hung open on a scream, forever silenced by the simple fact it was formed from an inanimate object.

Hazrael had the feeling, however, that at any given moment that might be subject to change.

Not until he was directly under the hull did the rope pull taut with Hazrael's weight as unseen hands wrenched him up in a vertical ascent toward the top deck.

His skin stretched away from muscles and bones. For once he wished for blood, to see it running down his chest in a sure sign that the rope was giving way and he'd be freed.

His luck had always been bad.

He was yanked over the side and onto the deck. No one was there but the wind.

The rope disintegrated into dust, blowing away. Specks became lodged in the wooden planks.

A distinct sound of footsteps on wood echoed across the abandoned vessel. Hazrael stood there in his wet robe, shivering with both cold and fear.

Out of nothing an image formed, a man as he'd looked in corporeal form, not the rotted flesh he'd become when he'd expanded his life past its natural boundaries.

Akabar Kolhen—the Necromon—*studied Hazrael as a man of science might study an interesting specimen.*

Kolhen's memory as a great statesman and lover of peace was revered among the citizens of Dominicál. Hazrael doubted there were many among even the prolates *who would believe the man responsible for setting down the laws of the land was the same being who wanted to wrest it away from them again.*

And therein lay the answer to why the necromancers hungered for etherealthants*: they needed them to power the spells that kept Kolhen alive—such as his life was now.*

Kolhen took another step forward. His eyes swirled with a kaleidoscope of colors. In this realm, his power took on the color one might associate with angels. Bright white and golden sun. It was all illusion.

If this was the place Kolhen chose for a final confrontation, he'd chosen poorly.

"You have no power over me here, Akabar Kolhen."

"By the scars on your body, I do. They answer to me."

"But I do not."

Hazrael centered his mind, imagining his body as it had been before being set upon by the necromancers' knives.

Kolhen let out a hearty laugh. "Your attempts to erase my mark will fail. I am part of you now and always will be."

Despite Kolhen's assurance, Hazrael continued to try and remove the stain. The marks remained because he let them. He glanced down at his body, only now noticing the thin cord connecting him to Kolhen.

If he severed that tie, he'd be free.

The wispy thread was as elusive as the cord that bound the soul to the body, but even that delicate connection could be severed if cut in the right place. Hazrael glanced around, looking for a tool sharp enough to complete the task. Kolhen struck out with his hand, causing the boards beneath Hazrael's feet to wobble. He pitched to and fro, requiring a firm hand on the rail in order to keep his feet.

But no, that was what would be expected if he were of flesh and blood. On this plane he had the freedom to choose form—or change landscape. Hazrael put out his arms, using the robe as wings, and launched himself off the unstable deck, straight into the sky. When he came down again, he'd changed the landscape to the frozen wasteland of his despair, though this time it was fully intentioned and not a product of his emotions.

Before Kolhen could account for the change in location, Hazrael grabbed an icicle honed with the sharp edge of a blade. He sliced through the connection, severing the pieces.

"No!"

Kolhen lurched forward in a vain attempt to knit the ends together. As he twisted and turned, frantic in his dance, Hazrael noticed hundreds of other strings coming from Kolhen's body, shining in the winter sun. There were others like him, laboring under a connection they didn't wish or want. The time had come to set them free.

Hazrael rose up once again and this time flew toward Kolhen, arm outstretched, ice blade in hand. At the last moment, he swung the blade in an arc and cut clean through the bonds that powered Kolhen's resurrection.

A backlash of power exploded across Hazrael's senses, throwing him across the snow-covered field. He landed on his back as air rushed from his lungs. Then Kolhen was there, hands around Hazrael's throat, choking him. Skin began to flake and fall off the dried bones beneath. Without the magic of the etherealthants, *the spell no longer held Kolhen together. Even as the strength of his anger continued to coil around Hazrael's neck in sharp fingers, the transformation deteriorated.*

Darkness bled in from the sides, taking Hazrael's consciousness with it.

No. He'd not die this way. He might have believed he'd give all for the cause, but knowing the source of his torment, looking him in the eyes, Hazrael was determined to not only survive but live to ensure nothing like this ever happened again.

He gripped the ice blade in his fist and drove it up through the center of Kolhen's chest. Kolhen's eyes grew wide, and he looked down at the entrance wound.

"How could you? I made you into something greater, something more powerful than your alchemists ever conceived."

"The alchemists never once made a man into a puppet, but gave men freedom of will and conscience. What good is having unlimited power if you use it to destroy the things you profess to love?" Hazrael twisted the blade, only then realizing it was not cold to the touch, did

not melt in his hand. Crystals dripped with black blood from the heart of the Necromon.

The sky behind him lit up as explosions rocked the fabricated world. Hazrael lost his hold on the ethereal at the same time the Necromon *returned to the dust from which he sprang, leaving nothing behind but a tattered shroud.*

OBERON TIGHTENED his fingers on Hazrael's hand. Slowly the color began to come back into Hazrael's face. His breathing evened out.

The doors at the end of the chamber burst open.

"Oberon! Come quickly. You have to see this," Jolen called.

He didn't want to leave Hazrael's side, not when he seemed so close to waking. "What is it?"

"The end of the war."

All right, that phrase had the power to move him when lesser ones might have kept him in place.

He stood and went to the window to look out over the square. Light rose from the direct center of the rubble that used to be the basilica. The beam raced toward the heavens, lighting the sky in near-daylight brightness.

Below, on the promenade, people stopped to gawk at the sight.

"What does this mean?" The words were low, so much so that Oberon thought Jolen hadn't heard him.

After a beat or two of silence, a voice came from the back of the chamber. "It means I've defeated the *Necromon*."

Oberon and Jolen exchanged glances and hurried to the healing pool.

Hazrael's eyes were open but didn't stay that way for long. He seemed to try and force them open as he struggled to rise up a bit higher in the pool. "Someone get me out of here. No more water. Please."

"Take his other arm, Jolen, and help me lift him."

They stood on opposite sides of the pool, counting to three before they pulled Hazrael from the herb-scented bath. His gown was soaked through, and his teeth started to chatter as the cool air hit his skin.

"Help me get him to a room where he can get out of these wet clothes and lie down."

A broken smile lifted the corner of Hazrael's mouth. "A good rest without the threat of the necromancers rising up will do me proud for a long time."

Jolen placed his arm around Hazrael's waist. "Nico will want to know how you managed to defeat the *Necromon*."

"Once I understood what he used to compose his shell, it was easy. I had only to sever the power he used to generate the spells on the astral plane to destroy him." Hazrael shook his head. "It was foolish of him to think to attack me there—a place where he was at his most vulnerable."

"Shush now, Hazrael. You can tell us all about it once you've rested." Oberon had heard enough to turn the rest of his hair white. The thought of Hazrael facing the *Necromon* alone on the field of battle in the astral plane hurt on a soul-deep level.

"You should all know the identity of the *Necromon*. At least let me give you that before I fall into sweet slumber."

They had managed to get Hazrael into a small bedchamber off the main hall that led to the healing pool. Oberon guided Hazrael to sit on the edge of the bed, then began to remove the tattered robe. For his part, Hazrael made no protests.

"Well, do you want to know?" Hazrael had one eye peeked open slightly.

Oberon glanced up from where he attempted to disentangle the robe from Hazrael's legs. "I suppose, since you feel so obliged to tell us after I instructed you to rest."

Hazrael reached up a limp hand and gave Oberon a weak pat on the cheek. "That's one of the reasons I love you so much—the gruffness you use to hide your tenderness."

Oberon's heart was near to bursting. He covered his welling emotions with a cough. "I'm not that gruff."

Jolen went to the wardrobe, pulled out a simple nightshirt, and handed it to Oberon. "Quit interrupting him. Go on, Hazrael. Who was the *Necromon*?"

"Akabar Kolhen."

Oberon and Jolen exchanged confused glances.

"I can see by your expressions that you think my mind played tricks on me, but I assure you this accusation stems as much from my returned memory from the time I was under the necromancers' influence as from the fantastic journey I've just experienced." His light eyes shone with a note of pleading. "I'll explain more when I wake. For now, trust that I know his essence well."

HAZRAEL WOKE to the sounds of jubilation ringing through the streets of Gusan. He slid from the bed, his head slightly dizzy and legs weak, and walked to the small balcony situated in an alcove of the room.

Wagonloads of rubble were being carted up and pulled away from the site where the basilica once stood. Where marble and gold had once showered the city in opulence, the space was now reduced to only a stone-filled crater. Looters rifled through the remains, looking for priceless treasures. Guards wearing the house colors of the *prolates* patrolled the area, sending the treasure-seekers on their ways and confiscating the haul.

The artifacts under the cracked marble and twisted metal still belonged to Mother Church and as such were subject to seizure by the guards. Hazrael wondered how long it would take for some of the priceless baubles to show up on the black market.

He watched the scene for some time before he noted that something differed in the air. Not with the city in particular, but within himself. For the first time in years, he had woken feeling truly like himself again.

The skin along his chest and arms itched. He lifted a sleeve of the nightshirt and studied the scars. Where once white lines bled with angry intent, new pink healing skin emerged. The scars had not faded, but they were on their way to healing.

A knock sounded on the door a second before it swung open. Oberon stuck his head in and frowned when he noticed the empty bed. "Hazrael?"

"Over here on the balcony."

Oberon came fully into the room and headed to where Hazrael stood observing the scene below. "You should get back into bed."

"No. I've had enough of bed. I'm well rested now and extremely bored."

Oberon ran a hand down Hazrael's matted hair. "I'll make it worth your while."

Momentarily startled by the offer, Hazrael hesitated only a second before he leaned in close to Oberon. He needed this connection, wanted it in order to heal the parts of his soul that mere elemental magic hadn't touched—his heart.

"Come, let me care for you."

Hazrael allowed Oberon to pull him along, back to the bedroom. A dressing table with vanity sat against one wall. Oberon picked up a comb and directed Hazrael to sit on the bed in front of him. Getting his hair combed wasn't exactly what Hazrael had thought Oberon meant, but it might make him feel at least a bit more human.

"Your hair is so beautiful when it's combed and shining like reams of pale moonlight."

Hazrael sat and gazed at Oberon over his shoulder. "You don't think it makes me look like an old man?"

"I think it makes you look as if you've been touched by great power." Very gently, Oberon began to pull the wide teeth through Hazrael's hair, shaking out the knots.

His scalp was tender from all the trials he'd had of late. There had been more than one instance where his hair had felt as if he'd been snatched bald or his scalp set afire. All that was passed now. The Dominicál city-states were free from the necromancers and able to heal.

"The necromancers might have never returned to the city-states had Akabar Kolhen not found the secret of harnessing energy from the *etherealthants* to power his longevity." The observation came as Hazrael glanced down at the pink skin on the back of his arm. "I wasn't the only one he had tied to him with the Kiss of Death. There were others out there who I've freed. I only hope they are within the loving confines of ones who care for them."

Oberon's hands stalled. "I'm sure they will find a way. At least now they are free to use their own minds and are not working at the behest of a madman."

"He wanted to control the country he believed he built. That was his main goal. I just don't understand why he'd return as a conqueror when he'd left it as a benevolent creator." That part bothered Hazrael more than knowing Kolhen had decided to study the necromantic arts. One thing it proved was that the heart of man was capable of many emotions, and some terribly unexpected.

"We shall rise above this as we always have. The elementals will provide and cleanse the land. It might take time, but things will settle down, and then only our own petty problems and strife will remain." Oberon's tone was ironic, but he had a point.

Hazrael turned, taking the comb from Oberon's fingers. "Let us not worry about strife today. Only love."

Oberon's green eyes went heavy lidded. "I know that look."

"Does it make you nervous?"

Oberon let out a breath. "No. But I wonder if we should wait until you are fully healed from your ordeal before we take the next step."

Hazrael canted his head. "I once asked if you still loved me, but you declined to answer. Have your feelings changed?"

"Only insofar as loving you more than I did before." Oberon took Hazrael's hand. "You've shown amazing strength and courage. I fear I'd not have held up as well as you under the circumstances. There is much to admire in you, Hazrael, and much more than that to love."

Hazrael's heart beat hard, each strike like the gong of a bell. Joy exploded through his veins, unable to contain his emotions. He threw himself into Oberon's arms. Their mouths fused, tongues dueled. Before he knew which way was up or down, they were rolling across the bed, trying to undress each other in a frantic, eager ripping of fabric.

Oberon ran his lips down Hazrael's throat. "I think we better slow down a bit."

"No. I want this. I want you. As you are now. Filled with passion and need. With a hunger for me that will only be quenched when we're joined." Hazrael ran a hand down Oberon's body and cupped the tight sac of his balls.

Oberon's eyes closed, and his breath sighed out. "I've missed your touch."

"I've missed every part of you." Hazrael moved lower and took Oberon into his mouth.

"You shouldn't do that, my love. I'll have no resistance to you. Not after so long apart." Oberon cupped Hazrael's head in his large hands. Tenderness swept over Hazrael, coming from Oberon. So many memories of making love with this man—his heart—came to the surface, sweet, poignant, and full of promise. Life could be like that again. They'd make it happen.

With a gentle tug, Oberon pulled Hazrael up to meet his mouth, then rolled them over onto their sides, facing each other. "Let me make love to you. Let me show you how much I've missed you."

Hazrael was more than ready for that healing touch. The specter of his time with the necromancers hid in a dark corner of his mind and probably always would, but he refused to let it spoil this reunion. He wanted Oberon to reclaim him and wash away the past, make him feel whole again.

Hazrael gave himself over to the lovemaking, allowing Oberon to love him as only he could—to make Hazrael feel things only Oberon could bring out.

Oberon moved Hazrael into a prone position. "You've always had the most amazing skin. Smooth, but muscular and taut. Do you know I used to sit next to you in class and daydream about you?"

Hazrael smiled into the bedcovers. Oberon had told him that when they'd first become lovers. "You always did like the men lean."

Oberon ran a hand up Hazrael's leg, over calf and thigh, along the curve of his buttocks. "Only *this* man. You are the most beautiful person I've ever seen—and always have been."

"Even now?"

"Ethereally so."

Hazrael chuckled. "I look like one of those ice elves of the legends."

"Yes, but you aren't cold like they were reported to be, but warm." Oberon skimmed his lips over Hazrael's bottom, then placed a kiss on the small of his back. Hazrael's hard cock ground into the soft bed linens, creating an incredibly erotic friction.

Oberon continued to kiss his way up Hazrael's spine. "Your shoulders and arms are well-defined."

Oberon spread Hazrael's arms out away from his body. He ran his hands down Hazrael's sides, sending chills out and down the length of his spine.

Hazrael scooted back a bit, lifting his bottom to rub against Oberon's groin. The thick jut of Oberon's erection slid along his cheeks. "I want to feel you inside me, Oberon. I don't know how much I can take."

Oberon moaned. "Let me learn you all over again. I've waited so long, dreamed of having you back with me. I don't want to waste a moment of this time with you."

By the time he'd prepared Hazrael to receive him, Hazrael was out of his head with desire. Tears leaked from the corners of his eyes onto the sheets as Oberon pushed inside him.

Love welled up fair to bursting in him. He curled his fingers into the linens, trying to hold on to the world and the feeling of being reunited in both body and spirit with the one man who had always had his heart. Had it even before he knew what it meant to give it away.

"I love you, Oberon!" The cry came as Hazrael lost his fight to hold on. Then he was there, falling into an orgasm that turned his vision into a blinding white, cleansing his soul as Oberon followed him down into bliss.

THE AFTERGLOW faded, leaving Hazrael wrapped in a warm light. Loving Oberon was just as he'd remembered. He smiled, resting his head on his hand and looking down into Oberon's face.

Oberon's eyes were closed. His arm lay across his face, but he wasn't asleep. Hazrael would have known.

"There is to be a party in your honor."

The words startled Hazrael. He lifted Oberon's arm away to get a better look at him. "What do you mean *in my honor*?"

"What does that phrase usually mean? You are to be honored at a celebration, your full rights into the order restored, and your adepts' robes awarded." Oberon opened his eyes and turned to face Hazrael. "Nico has already ordered the robes cut. Refusal to accept is bad form."

"I have no intention of refusing admission back into the order, but a celebration? Now, that, I will not allow." In light of all the death and destruction he'd caused—whether wittingly or not—no commemoration of the events was necessary. To do that was bad form.

Oberon pushed up into a sitting position and then moved a pillow behind his back to rest against the headboard. "The idea of the party came from the servants. They wanted to do something to show their appreciation to you for all you've done."

"They are honoring the wrong man."

"If not for you, we would have never gotten here in time to save the city." Oberon ran his hand along Hazrael's side.

"I only helped power the portal. You figured out how to construct one," Hazrael pointed out.

"After all that's happened, can't you simply enjoy life?"

Good question, and one Hazrael had no way to answer. He desperately wanted to be that idealistic youth who had fallen in love with alchemy, Oberon, and the elementals. Not even a miracle from above would make that happen.

Finally Hazrael nodded. "I will attend the celebration but as one who honors the simple heroes who survived day in and out living in Gusan. To honor those who have given their life in a crusade to rid the world of the necromancers. Not for my own glory."

Oberon leaned forward and brushed his lips against Hazrael's. "So humble an answer."

Perhaps it was, but it was the only one Oberon would get. It was the correct one. No matter how the world might turn or where future history might take the Dominicál city-states, the one undeniable fact remained that they had come together in this place and time and defeated the necromancers because their order held together. Because they had counted on one another to see it through. Because the *prolates* and clerics banded with them to restore the balance. Not due to one man's courage, but many men's fortitude.

So should it forever be.

As above, so below.

Glossary

adept—highest level obtained by an alchemical master.

Adepts' Council—body of ruling alchemical adepts who preside over matters pertaining to the Gold School.

aerothant—product of union between human and air elemental.

Agia, Ignatius—*prolate* of city-state of Calabris. Head of the House of Agia; also referred to as the Agia.

alchemy—the search for enlightenment through the study of science, theology, and the esoteric, and how it relates to the natural world.

Anjufer—full fire elemental who resides in the Gold School in service to the alchemists.

aquathant—product of union between human and water elemental.

Asgarian, Rodderick—former cleric assigned to the Agia. Imprisoned for trying to warn his *desan* of the impending threats of the necromancers.

Basilica of the Heavenly Throne—capital/seat of the chief church of Dominicál.

Bertolini, Oberon—adept-level alchemist; Headmaster of the Gold School.

cardgran—highest level of cleric in the Dominicál city-states. Make up the council who elect a new *demigoge*.

Celsi, Master—first-level master. Chief assistant of Headmaster Oberon.

city-states—provinces/principalities in country of Dominicál. They are as follows: Auflaven, Bellor, Bonsuret, Brixton, Calabris, Devani,

Dharakhan, Flurian, Nequan, Pliern, Romanta, Sadonia, and Trumolo.

Delaneux—largest town in city-state of Calabris. Seat of the Agia family.

damsk—silver coin.

Dante, Mercurian—founder of the Gold School; ancestor of Count Nicodemus de Valencia.

demigoge—(pronounced: de mí gōche) derived from the word demagogue; supreme religious head of the Dominicál city-states.

deRosa of Bonsuret, Phillipe—*demigoge*. Now uses official title of Demigoge Alexander.

desan—A Holy See—highest cleric of a city-state; however, is one step below a *cardgran* in the clerical order.

DiCarni, Juan-Carlo—*prolate* from island of Nequan.

Dominicál—the country that comprises the whole of the city-states.

Donando, Headmaster—deceased headmaster of Gold School; murdered by Agia's guards.

Duard—first assistant to the Medovin Magus.

Elementica—stone tablet made of solid ruby, inscribed with the principles and laws of the elementals. Broken and scattered during the Great Purge.

Ellec, Master—alchemist assigned to the House of DiCarni. *Etherealthant*.

Eye of Truth—sacred text of the alchemists, a book of immense power. Contains codex of laws, spells, and incantations, and rubbings from the original Emerald Tablet—the basis of all alchemical study.

etherealthant—product of union between human and spirit elemental.

Fessen, Captain—head of Estobán Medovin's house guards in the Gusan villa.

gint—brass coin.

Grand Matter—also called Prime Matter; universal substance of which everything springs; origins of life.

Gregori, Silvanus—Master of alchemy. Scholar whose experiments are the basis for many of the workings used by the alchemists.

guitern—instrument, cross between harp, guitar, and mandolin.

Gusan—city where seat of the Basilica of the Heavenly Throne is located.

Hazrael, Master—former necromancer and in the employ of the House of Rinni as Magus. Most promising and powerful *etherealthant* of his generation. Abducted and held for seventeen years by necromancers as focus for *Necromon*. Bearer of the Kiss of Death.

Heavenly Throne—actual throne where the *demigoge* holds religious court.

Hierophant—religious appointment. *Demigoge's* female counterpart within church hierarchy. Offspring of an oracle and spirit elemental. Reads prophecies and portents in ancient writings.

Holy See—see *desan*. Highest clerical authority in a city-state. Terms Holy See and *desan* are used interchangeably.

Karis, Desan—head of local archdiocese in city-state of Sadonia.

Kiss of Death—necromantic spell carved into flesh for purpose of tracking and controlling *etherealthant*; also may be used as record of memories and to garner power from the life force of the bearer.

Krutarch, Master—adept who wrote keyed primer.

Lancor—largest town in city-state of Sadonia; seat of the Medovin family.

Lorelli, Journeyman—slight *etherealthant* talent. Is assigned to assist Master Hazrael.

magus—chief advisor for a *prolate* or *prolatial* house wholly unconnected to the family by blood.

Magus Gaius—magus/chief advisor to Estobán Medovin and House of Medovin. Viola Medovin's lover.

Medovin, Cesare—Estobán's cousin.

Medovin, Estobán—*prolate* of Sadonia; head of Medovin family, also referred to as the Medovin. Theodyne Thespacian's ex-lover. Current lover of Master Jolen Meripen.

Medovin, Viola—Estobán Medovin's sister; named heir to the House of Medovin.

Meripen, Jolen—master alchemist of the Gold School.

necromancers—also called death dancers; can raise or speak with the dead. Greatest foes of the alchemists.

Necromon—title of esteem and respect given to head necromancer. Also the primogenitor of all necromancers.

Olig, Desan—Holy See from town of Delaneux under the auspices of the Agia.

plazo—small garden or gathering place within the confines of an estate, usually decorated with colorful stones.

prolate—ruler of a city-state, also head of his family.

prolatial courts—courts where *prolates* decide matters of state and preside over local civic and criminal matters.

pyrothant—product of union between human and fire elemental.

Renvic—young guard in the employ of Estobán Medovin, who distinguishes himself in service to his *prolate.*

Rinni, Claudio—*prolate* of city-state of Bonsuret; held in thrall by the necromancers.

seal of Devani—seal worn by officials of that city-state to denote them as dignitaries; seal used in all official city-state correspondences.

slew—copper coin.

spagyrics—alchemical term; act of breaking down a substance, then putting it back together in its highest form.

Sulith—guards that protected the elementals who worked to carve the principles of the *Elementica* onto the ruby tablet. The elite guard who protects the *demigoge.*

terrathant—product of union between human and earth elemental.

The Great Purge—war between necromancers and the elementals one thousand years before *Alchemists and Elementals* takes place. The Great Purge saw the ousting of the necromancers from Dominicál and elementals taking a lesser role in the affairs of man.

Thespacian, Theodyne—former thief; Adept-level Master and chief healer for the alchemists.

tonza—gold coin.

Valencia, Count Nicodemus de—alchemist adept. Direct descendant of Mercurian Dante, head of Gold School.

Wendro—deceased servant boy once employed at Medovin's Gusan villa. *Etherealthant.*

Don't miss how the story began!

Eye of Truth

Alchemists and Elementals: Book One

By Cassie Sweet

Theodyne Thespacian is a thief. Caught and imprisoned, he's done his time and vowed never to return to the life of pulse-racing excitement and easy money. But when one of his former associates tells him about the Eye of Truth—an artifact that will open worlds of untold wealth—it seems like the perfect crime. However, for Theodyne, with the brand of a thief on his face, to be caught again means death. So instead he goes to the Villa of Nicodemus Valencia, the Master Alchemist who owns the artifact… and applies for a job.

Nicodemus descends directly from the founder of the Gold School, and of all those in that bloodline, he possesses the strongest gift for alchemy. His formulas have made him wealthy, though they've failed to give him the one thing he's longed for most—love. When Theodyne appears at his Villa, he recognizes potential for alchemy and offers him apprenticeship. But then an ancient foe purged from the lands long ago reappears and threatens the Gold School, the Eye of Truth, and all the Dominical city-states. Nicodemus and Theodyne must now band together in courage to battle evil and can only hope they will not lose all they've come to hold dear.

Taste of Air

Alchemists and Elementals:
Book Two

By Cassie Sweet

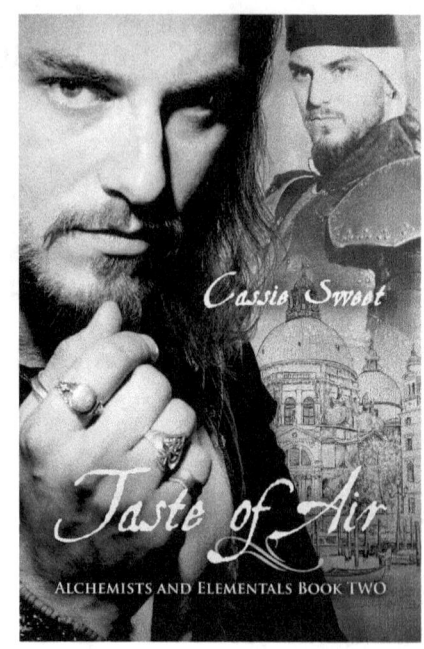

The reappearance of necromancers to the Dominincál city-states worries Sadonia prolate Estobán Medovin. Ever since Masters Nico and Theodyne drove the necromancers from his mind three years before, he's suffered an odd affliction—painting while asleep. It is a secret that, if discovered by his enemies, could bring his rule to an untimely and violent end. On the eve of the demigogal elections in the holy city of Gusan, fearing the new candidate might be under the necromancers' direct influence, Estobán requests an alchemist well-versed in ferreting out death dancers to join his mission to seek out conspirators.

Evil floods the streets of the holy city, and the elementals are anxious. Master alchemist Jolen Meripen should know; as an aerothant—hybrid of a human and air elemental—he can hear their voices in his head, telling him of the corruption festering under the pristine edifices.

When Jolen discovers a piece of the ruby tablet known as the Elementica in Estobán's possession and the necromancers bid to collect them all and thus rule over the elements, he knows he must do everything he can—including sacrificing his life to bring peace to Dominicál and save the man he has come to love.

http://www.dreamspinnerpress.com

CASSIE SWEET lives and works from her home office in the New Jersey Highlands, where she shares space with her over-affectionate Golden Retriever and artist husband. Her writing takes her to many destinations, both real and imagined.

http://www.mystickat.com/
https://www.facebook.com/MKMancosKScott

Hot Water

By Cassie Sweet

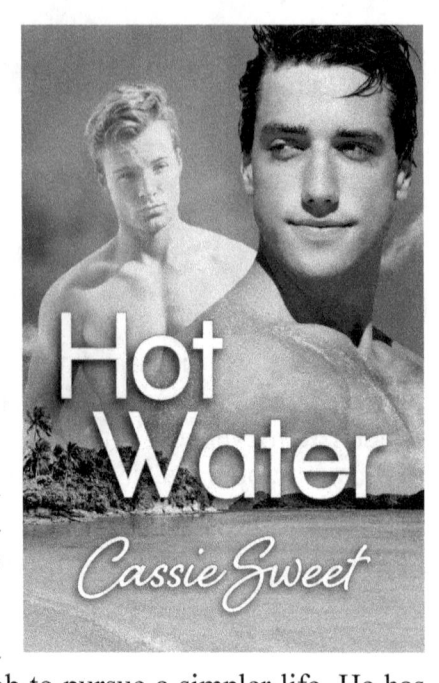

Summer never ends on the tiny South American island of Santa Juanita where the people are beautiful and the water is always—hot!

Dive master Clive Ducaine left a disastrous affair and corporate day job to pursue a simpler life. He has no regrets about his decision to move to Santa Juanita to teach tourists the fine art of spelunking. With the unlimited banquet of hot bodies and casual sex to fill his days and nights, he has truly found paradise on earth.

Eight years ago Trevor Donohue's lover was gunned down on a New York street and died in Trevor's arms. Life changed that day, and not for the better. Now, working as a VP for a medical manufacturing company leaves Trevor no time or desire for another relationship. But then, during his first vacation in years, he meets the resort's sexy dive instructor, Clive. Suddenly abandoning his tight schedules and video-meetings for a little vacation romance looks a lot more promising.

http://www.dreamspinnerpress.com

K.C. WELLS

A BOND OF THREE

http://www.dreamspinnerpress.com

FAMILY OF LIES
SEBASTIAN

SAM ARGENT

http://www.dreamspinnerpress.com

SUI LYNN

ADEL'S PURR

http://www.dreamspinnerpress.com

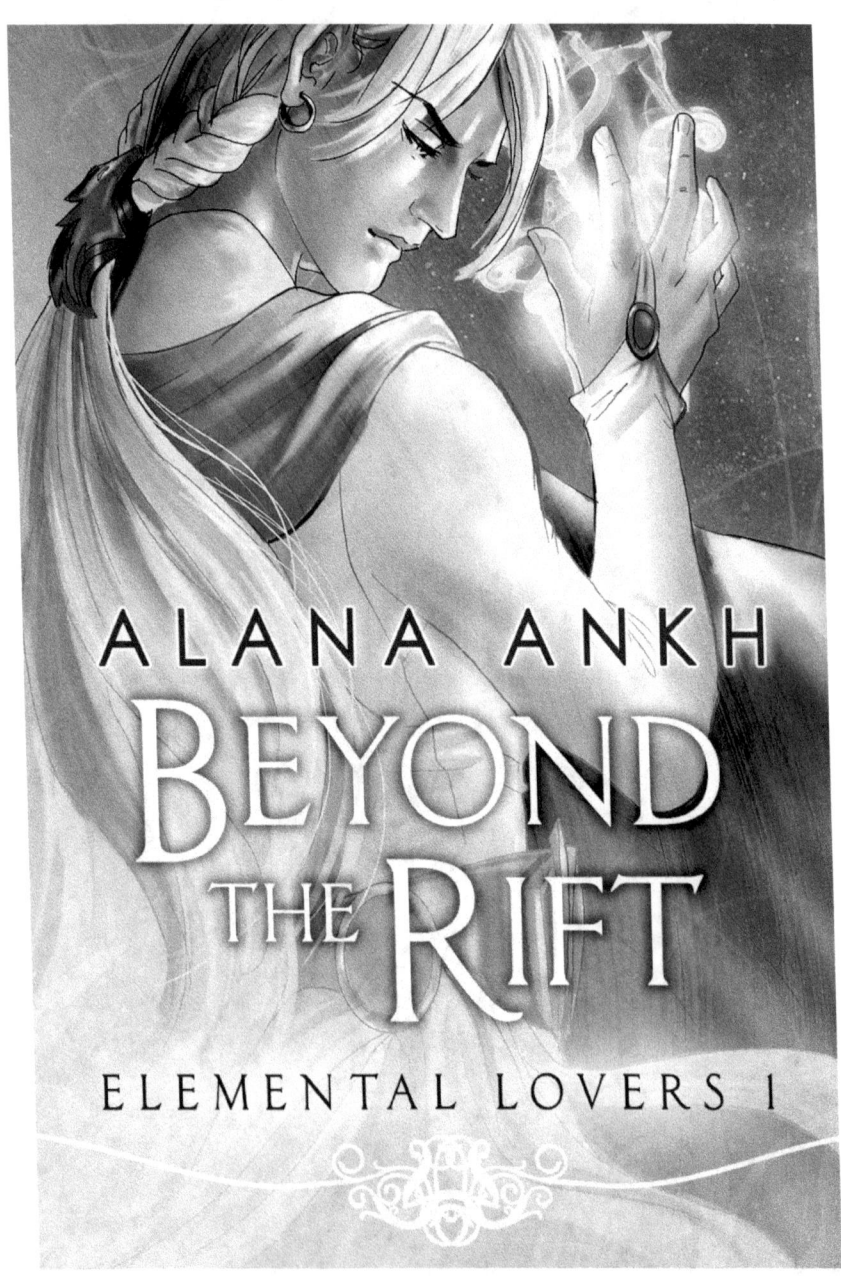

ALANA ANKH

BEYOND THE RIFT

ELEMENTAL LOVERS 1

http://www.dreamspinnerpress.com

CANES
and
SCALES
the novel

S.A. GARCIA

http://www.dreamspinnerpress.com

http://www.dreamspinnerpress.com

http://www.dreamspinnerpress.com

www.ingramcontent.com/pod-product-compliance
Lightning Source LLC
Chambersburg PA
CBHW051632260626
47170CB00004B/1140